Praise for *Smothered*

"In this whimsical confection from up-and-comer Autumn Chiklis, a boomerang kid who just graduated from Columbia makes the perilous decision to move back in with her loving pa and indefatigable ma. I wasn't sure which was more fun—the endlessly chipper directives from Mama Shell to daughter Lou on how to eat/sleep/exercise/live her best life, or figuring out which anecdote actually happened in Chiklis's real-life household—the one she shares with Vic Mackey, er, the Emmy-winning Michael Chiklis, and her fabulously chic mom, Michelle."   —Lynette Rice, editor at large for *Entertainment Weekly*

"Autumn Chiklis is a bright new voice in fiction, a hilarious and astute observer of all things fun and female. There isn't a mother or daughter on earth who won't fall in love with Autumn Chiklis and *Smothered*."

—Randi Mayem Singer, screenwriter of *Mrs. Doubtfire*

"Autumn Chiklis brilliantly captures the absurdity of truth in her first novel, *Smothered*. Treat yourself to a book that will have you crying with laughter as Autumn highlights the hilarious relationship between mother and daughter in a uniquely twenty-first-century way."

—Michelle MacLaren, director of *Modern Family* and *The Nightingale* and executive producer of *Breaking Bad*

"Hilarious [and] adorable, readers will be smiling from beginning to end. Mama Shell is a character who will stay with me for a long time! Author Autumn Chiklis uses an engaging combination of journal entries, Facebook and text-message exchanges, and shopping receipts to create a fun and well-paced novel that will keep readers smiling from start to finish."

—Susan Mullen, coauthor of *We Are Still Tornadoes*

SMOTHERED

Autumn Chiklis

WEDNESDAY BOOKS
NEW YORK

SMOTHERED. Copyright © 2018 by Autumn Chiklis. All rights reserved. Printed in the United States of America. For information, address St. Martin's Press, 175 Fifth Avenue, New York, N.Y. 10010.

www.wednesdaybooks.com
www.stmartins.com

Designed by Patrice Sheridan
Vector illustrations courtesy of Shutterstock.com/eveleen; chawaliit si waborwornwattana; aratehortua; Nikolaeva; Denis Gorelkin; snegok13

LIBRARY OF CONGRESS CATALOGING-IN-PUBLICATION DATA

Names: Chiklis, Autumn, 1993– author.
Title: Smothered / Autumn Chiklis.
Description: First edition. | New York : Wednesday Books, 2018.
Identifiers: LCCN 2018001591 | ISBN 978-1-250-30678-4 (trade paperback) | ISBN 978-1-250-30775-0 (hardcover) | ISBN 978-1-250-15050-9 (ebook)
Subjects: | CYAC: Mothers and daughters—Fiction. | Family life—California—Fiction. | Jews—Fiction. | California—Fiction. | Humorous stories.
Classification: LCC PZ7.1.C498 Sm 2018 | DDC [Fic]—dc23
LC record available at https://lccn.loc.gov/2018001591

Our books may be purchased in bulk for promotional, educational, or business use. Please contact your local bookseller or the Macmillan Corporate and Premium Sales Department at 1-800-221-7945, extension 5442, or by email at MacmillanSpecialMarkets@macmillan.com.

First Edition: August 2018

10 9 8 7 6 5 4 3 2 1

To Mom, for a lifetime of inspiration

SMOTHERED

Month One

The Real World

TO THE FAMILY OF
ELOISE LAURENT HANSEN

The Faculty and Administration
of
Columbia University
invite you to join us in celebrating the
Graduating Senior Class
at this year's
Commencement Ceremony

Location: Outdoors on the Morningside Campus
Date / Time: May 13th at 11:00 a.m.
There will be a reception following the ceremony.
Please purchase tickets on the Columbia website.

Two traits I've inherited from Mother that invalidate any "secret adoption" claims I may have made in the past:

1. My horrible fear of public speaking and
2. Her original nose.

Neither were easy growing up with, mind you . . . but at least the former was avoidable, since it wasn't the focal point of my face. I hate, hate, HATE public speaking. Ever since my then-crush Ezra Steinbeck walked out on my bat mitzvah speech to smoke weed in the back parking lot, talking to crowds has made me nauseous. The only reason I agreed to give this stupid salutatorian speech at all is because representing your class is "*such* an honor" . . . even though technically the speaker should have been my roommate, Natasha. *She's* the one with the second-highest GPA. But naturally she turned down the invitation, since she's protesting the graduation ceremony's wasteful use of printed programs by refusing to accept her diploma in person.

. . . And also by handcuffing herself to the administration building.

This is probably for the best, however, since her version of a graduation speech would have likely been some sort of beat poem with bongos and a steel drum. Disastrous.

But I digress from my total agony, which has taken place in three stages. Stage one of my descent into postgraduate madness (officially coining as an academic term: PGM) began yesterday, as I started packing up my dorm room. Call me crazy, but somehow reducing my entire life to a small stack of isolated boxes in less than twenty-four hours made my whole existence feel dreadfully insignificant. All my textbooks, all my records, all my minimalist movie posters: tightly and precisely smashed into 18 × 16 cubes of cardboard to be flown cross-country, where they'll soon reside in my childhood bedroom . . . exactly twenty-one steps down the hall from my mother's room.

Oh dear god, my MOTHER. Somehow, against all physical odds, Mom managed to overpack her luggage by twenty pounds for a two-day trip to New York. TWENTY. That's *ten pounds* extra per day. It's remarkable. Though I'll never understand what compels her to pack like a nomadic Grace Kelly, even THAT nonsense feels only moderately absurd in comparison to Dad and his rental car. He insisted on renting a minivan for the weekend because Mom refuses to take the subway. Logically, I suggested an Uber or a cab, but apparently he read somewhere that it's cheaper to just rent a car and pay up-front. This is definitely not true and I suspect he's making it up, but Dad hates relinquishing the wheel to anyone, and anyway, his Uber account is still suspended for aggressive backseat driving.

Stage two of my catastrophic PGM spiral took place tonight at the Plaza. Despite living in Los Angeles, the Hansens have been regular Plaza patrons for more than twenty-five years, making us C-list celebrities among the staff. In fact, the Plaza is the only place where people still call me Eloise, which would be fine if it weren't a painful reminder of my somewhat legendary conception.*

My walking pace was quicker today than usual (probably due to excess energy manifested from anxiety), so I arrived at the hotel fifteen minutes early, instead of my usual ten. I decided against going inside and facing the front desk ("*GASP!* Is that Eloise Laurent?? MY GOODNESS, have you grown up! What's the plan, college grad? We all expect BIG THINGS from you, young lady!!"), so I waited on the famous velvet steps facing Fifth Avenue in the muggy East Coast heat, contemplating how many passing New Yorkers were survivors of PGM

---

*Will NEVER name child after designer, car brand, or place of conception. Cruel and unusual for poor, innocent child.

or similar disorders. Half an hour later, Dad's bright-red pearl-coated minivan screeched up to the valet, Mom's bulging designer suitcase strapped to the top like a Christmas tree. Three attendants immediately descended on the vehicle, as though it belonged to the Kennedys or Windsors or Baldwins instead of just the Hansens.

Before the car stopped moving, Val slid the door open, leapt out of the backseat, and ran up the steps, looking like a goddamn siren. Maybe it's because she's missing a few days of high school to be here, but my sister was positively glowing: her bronze hair in climate-defying, frizz-free beach waves, skin golden as the hotel's awning, arms lean from hours in the selfie position. I threw my own less-defined arms around her while she gushed non sequiturs: "Oh my god, the flight was crazy. I can't believe it, you're so old!!!"

Behind her, Dad was helping the three bellmen unhook the sofa-sized suitcase from the hood of the van, shouting orders like the captain of a sinking ship. Val kept gabbing until we both saw a single Manolo Blahnik appear in the passenger doorway, followed by a freshly manicured hand and bejeweled wrist. I instinctively adjusted my oversize T-shirt as an attendant received the free hand and pulled forth Mama Shell: all five foot five inches of fabulous.

Mom was thinner than usual (how, HOW is this possible??), in a navy Gucci blazer with white trim, over a silk camisole and light-wash jeans. Her reddish-brown Dior sunglasses covered her narrow face, her Prada purse dangled from a bent arm, and her gloss-covered lips pouted into a smile. I suddenly regretted my choice of ripped jeans, awkwardly crossing one leg over the other to hide the overtorn hole at my knee.

Before I could lift a hand to wave, Mom was up the stairs and on me (impressive, considering her stilettos), kissing my head, fixing my hair, subtly checking out my outfit. From the second she left the car in her devastatingly perfect ensemble, Mom was talking, and she did not stop talking until we were all seated for dinner an hour later.

". . . Okay, so I have our whole postgrad life planned out. I'm thinking yoga, hiking, and cycling classes. Once-a-week facials and mani-pedis . . . maybe a biweekly massage? Oh! Monday nights are still *Bachelorette* viewing parties with the Red Hot Ladies, of course. This season's so intense, you're going to *die*. Oh, excuse me, Jonathan? Yes, Jonathan, I'll have a Shell-tini,* please . . . bring four. Yes, of course she's of age, she just left her ID in the car. Thank you! Where was I? Oh! Lulu, we play mah-jongg once a month now at Susan's. You'll love it, because it's a game of strategy. Oh my gosh! Wait 'til you see the pugs! Muffin's gotten so big, he's twice Baguette's size. I don't mind, though—pugs can pull off a bit of chub. Oh, and I just bought them the most *adorable* collars . . . they're so chic!"

Jonathan handed me a Shell-tini and I instantly started chugging. Bless the sacred mix of cucumber and gin. I ordered a second. And a third. Because somewhere around the talk of chic dog collars, I was overcome by the third and final stage of my PGM, rendering me virtually mute for the rest of the evening. Whatever else Mom said at dinner was completely drowned out by my existential inner monologue:

It's happening. Tomorrow. No more classes. No more papers. No more freshly printed textbook smell. OH GOD. I no longer get student-discount tickets at theaters or museums. As of tomorrow, I stop getting aggravating emails from random university organizations that I have no interest in joining.

Tomorrow, I am receiving a summa cum laude degree from one of the most venerated and esteemed academic establishments on the planet . . . and I am both job- and apartment-less.

---

*The bar created the Shell-tini for Mom's fortieth birthday, in honor of her signature order. Naturally, it's become their top seller and frequently appears on their Instagram page. Ingredients include: cucumber for hydration; ginger and lime juice for digestion; dry vermouth, gin, agave, and basil to "combat stress."

After my fourth Shell-tini, I finally kissed my family good night, pledging to text Mom when I got home, and began stumbling uptown. I found my way to the subway, then quickly stopped by the Columbia administration building to give a protesting Natasha my leftover veggies before heading to my dorm. (You know, for someone who'd been handcuffed to a doorknob for three days straight, she seemed far more relaxed than I am.)

Shoot. I'm still a bit buzzed from the Shell-tinis. I need water stat, or I risk delivering a dehydrated graduation speech tomorrow, and the *last* thing I need is dry mouth. Ugh. All right, all right, *focus!* What else do I have left to accomplish? My boxes are packed. Speech is printed out. Cap and gown are pressed and ironed . . . everything seems to be in order, except for me.

Okay, Lou Hansen: you've got this. You are a warrior. You are a champion. You are an intellectual and academic badass. The next time you write in this journal, you will have gone from an exemplary undergraduate student to an overqualified bum.

. . . On second thought: bottoms up.

GRADUATION GOALS
Short Term
- *Establish new living-at-home rules/expectations with parents.*
- *Rid closet of all unnecessary and unprofessional outfits.*
- *Email Professor Richmanson about job opportunity!!*
- *Buy more ink for label maker.*
- *Start waking up at 7:30 A.M.*
- *Tell Mom about Theo.*

Medium Term
- *Move out of parents' house within 9 months.*
- *Secure a job in a field that I can commit to for the rest of my life.*
- *Learn how to cook something that isn't cereal.*
- *Lose 5 to 7 pounds.*
- *Find a one-bedroom apartment that's reasonably priced.*
- *^That Mother will approve of.*

Long Term
- *Forbes 30 Under 30 article (could actually be considered medium-term . . . feeling very, very old).*
- *Modern-style house in Pacific Palisades*
- *My very own NPR segment (nonnegotiable).*
- *Have kids: one boy, one girl.*
- *. . . ?*

MAY 13

10:40 A.M.—MISSED CALLS: (5) Mama Shell

Mama Shell

10:43 A.M.

MS Lulu, where do we park??

MS Your father is getting road rage. Just yelled at an old lady turning left.

10:45 A.M.

MS Oh, I brought you a belt! Wear it over your robe—always good to cinch the waist whenever possible!!

MS Call me.

10:50 A.M.

MS Did you get your hair done??

MS   You better have gotten your hair done.

MS   Also, if your nails are chipped, take the polish off completely. Right now.

11:01 A.M.

MS   Found parking!! A few blocks away and I'm in heels. 😵
At least I'm burning calories! 💪

11:06 A.M.

HI I'm so sorry Mom, I was getting ready! Yes, I got my hair done, yes, my nail polish is off, and no, I can't wear the belt.   Lou

MS   Fine—then be sure to pose with your hand on your waist. So proud of you!!! 🤍

Shelly Hansen
@ShellyHansen

Can't believe @LouHansen is a college graduate!!! So smart, so chic. When you take over the world, you better buy Mama a #Birkin. #girlboss

---

Mama Shell

1:15 P.M.

Mom, are you telling everyone that I'm your stepdaughter?   Lou

MS   No, of course not! Why?

Because both the president and the dean of my school definitely just called you my stepmom . . .   Lou

MS   Ok, I did it just this once, but you'll never see these people again and I'm too young to have a college graduate for a daughter.

MOTHER   Lou

MS   *Stepmother

It's a good thing I'm leaving the state tomorrow, because showing my face here is no longer an option.

I spent the first half hour of the ceremony just trying not to vomit from anxiety/the tiniest of Shell-tini hangovers. Strongly considered running offstage and deferring my degree. Honestly, who wants to take advice from a person who spent half an hour last night in the fetal position, drunkenly weeping beside a stack of overstuffed boxes with her face smashed into the filthy dorm-room carpet?

All of that said, my sacrifice was not in vain, since I somehow managed to make it through my speech without tripping on the way to the podium and/or passing out. I remember almost none of it, since I was mostly focused on keeping my voice at a human-sounding pitch, but from what I've been able to piece together through Snapchat, it looks like I did a fine job!

It wasn't until after the ceremony, however, that things took a turn for the absolutely miserable.

I now understand why Mom packed a sixty-pound suitcase: the shoes alone must have weighed ten. She was dressed in all white, with the exception of a summer scarf that was thirty different shades of pink, and a series of jangly bracelets made of various metals and stones. It looked like someone had spray-painted two bricks silver and strapped them to her feet with Grecian silk, and her floppy sun hat was on par with the best of the Kentucky Derby.

She looked fantastic. People were staring. It was horrifying.

The minute I walked offstage, Mom ripped the rhinestone-covered sunglasses from her face and all but threw her silver clutch at Val, who was taking selfies with a copy of the program. (Natasha would be outraged on my behalf.)

"MY BABYYYYYY!!!" she bellowed, tiny arms outstretched as she strutted toward me, her silver brick-shoes flattening the grass beneath her. "You . . . were . . . absolutely AMAAAAZING!!!" As she pulled me in for a hug, I could feel her adjusting my hair.

"I am completely OBSESSED with your speech! You are so brilliant. I just loved every second of it."

Dad and Val followed suit with the hugging, praising my poise and grace and good posture and other things I'm positive I don't have. They were in such high spirits I actually considered bringing up my still secret boyfriend . . . until Mom waved over a discount Ralph Lauren model from this season's commencement catalog.

"Lulu, this is Travis. I sat next to his mother during the ceremony . . . she is such a doll. Anyway, he was the captain of the rowing team, and he says you've never met!"

I gaped at her, dumbfounded, before looking up at Travis. He was watching me expectantly, a self-assured grin on his stupid smug preppy athlete face. I bet he was wearing khakis under that robe. Ugh. I opened my mouth to say something, but all that came out was a sort of choking noise and probably a bit of spit.

The two of them laughed, as though this were *so* typical Lulu, and Travis whipped out his phone to "hit me up on Facebook."

A moment later he popped up as "Travis Winston Yates Jr." Ew.

Anyway, we're finally back at the hotel, and our luggage is all packed up. Mom is at the sauna, "sweating out her martini bloat," so I have a few minutes to think. Our flight tomorrow leaves at eight A.M., so we ABSOLUTELY MUST check out of the hotel and be in the car by five. Alberto* has arranged for a driver to pick us up at the airport, and the pugs are being dropped off at noon. As long as everything goes according to plan, we should be all set!

---

*Note: Recently discovered that Mom (being the stay-at-home parent) was once in charge of managing our finances. However, after a few years of hiding her shopping expenses, she was fired as the family accountant. Thankfully Dad found Alberto, who deserves a much better title than business manager. He's more like business manager/ accountant/generalized life coach/saint. Changing contact in phone to "head executive of life predicaments," or HELP.

Rules and Expectations for Parents now that I am moving back home as a fully realized and capable adult:

- *Where I go, who I see, and why I am seeing them are no longer subject to inquisition-style examination. No judgey comments or faces will be tolerated.*
- *I, and I alone, choose what I wear in the morning. Suggestions are fine, but nothing more.*
- *Comments about the state of my hair, skin, nails, eyebrows, armpits, posture, upper lip, jawline, toe hair, breast placement, and bikini region should be kept to a maximum of <u>three</u> per day. TOTAL. This is nonnegotiable.*
- *Mom <u>has</u> to delete the Find-My-Friends app from her phone.*
- *And finally: If at any point I decide to bring a male home—<u>if</u> being the operative word—the family will do their best to trust my instincts, be kind, and not make any comments about his buckteeth and/or skinny legs.*

MAY 14
10:25 A.M.

So we missed our flight this morning.

Mom's Cartier bracelet kept setting off the metal detector, which would usually just result in a pat-down, but Mom got so nervous that she started giggling uncontrollably . . . so much so that it was deemed "unusual and suspicious behavior" by security. This would have also been fine, if Dad hadn't started yelling at the TSA officer about the absurdity of detaining a woman on the grounds of hysterical laughter. Though he made a fair point, apparently TSA officers do not like being reprimanded at six thirty in the morning, so we were sent to see the head of security for questioning.

Meanwhile, Dad still thinks that bracelet's a knock-off.

It's all okay now. Thankfully the head of JFK security had better things to do with his time than question an overdressed blond woman about her inappropriate giggling. Plus, I was able to pin Dad's behavior on emotional instability due to his eldest daughter's college graduation. Somehow, I figured "he's just a total loudmouth" wouldn't go over as well.

Unfortunately, there isn't another flight today with four available seats, so we are going to have to split up: Dad and I are taking the first flight, and Mom and Val are going on the second. This is exciting news, seeing as I won't have to deal with Mom's horrific fear of flying. Score.

Added bonus: This gives me an unprecedented six captive hours alone with Dad. This should be the perfect opportunity to discuss graduation and life and my expectations list, but breaching the subject of adulthood with Charlie Hansen is nothing short of terrifying. As the textbook definition of a self-made workaholic,* he's probably not taking my unemployed state particularly well. Hopefully the proximity of 200-plus strangers will keep him from being too harsh.

Well, this is it. In T-minus seven hours, I'll be back in my childhood bedroom. Can't wait!

---

*The *Los Angeles Times* once wrote a piece on Dad called "The Baron of the Boulevard," hailing him as the best real estate agent in the San Fernando Valley. To my horror, they featured a picture of his family, in which I had braces and was partially blinking. Most of his properties are residential, but more and more he's been working with office buildings, restaurants, and, to my mom's delight, shopping centers.

Mama Shell

3:30 P.M.

> Mom, what happened to my room?!? Lou

MS SURPRISE! Susan helped me with the decor.
Isn't it so posh?

> It looks like a poacher set up a trading camp in Beverly Hills. Lou

MS Fur is so in! And of course it's all faux. I'm completely obsessed with white and
silver . . . it's just so sophisticated.

MS Don't you LOVE the Moroccan poufs??

Val

3:33 P.M.

> Why didn't you tell me about my room?! Lou

3:50 P.M.

Val SHOOT, I was going to tell you on the plane, but then we were split up!! 🙈
Mom didn't tell us until it was already over. Dad JUST got the bill. 🙏

Val Also, I didn't want to ruin you getting Sunni Cum Laude.

> *Summa Lou

> Sunni is a denomination of Islam. Lou

Val Wait, really??

Val Shit.

4,372 likes
socal_soval So proud of the
#graduate #sister #queen 💎 🎓 🎉

MAY 15

7:50 A.M.

The one positive effect of jet lag: it helped kick-start my 7:30 wake-up goal! I was out of bed by 6:45, made coffee in the kitchen, and then let the pugs out back for a walk. I've lived in this house for over twenty years, and I'm still overwhelmed by the excess of color every time I step outside. There must be over thirty different beds of flowers of the brightest variety painting the perimeter of our property, which I imagine is single-handedly causing the California drought. As both an environmentalist and a minimalist, I find this completely maddening, but Mom maintains that the flowers are uplifting for our pets (despite the fact that dogs are color-blind). So I watched as Muffin and Baguette ran around the yard, sniffed some of the "uplifting" bushes, then walked inside and peed right on the carpet. So much for "positive potty training."

Dad was in the living room by the time I came back in, drinking coffee and watching the news. It's crazy how much my dad watches the news. Equally impressive is how little my mom retains of it. My parents sit in bed and watch the news *every single night,* and yet Mom recently asked if the Arab Spring was a salon in Burbank. Clearly, I inherit my intellectual curiosity from his side of the family.

Speaking of genetics: Dad also made a list of rules/expectations in anticipation of my move-in, once again proving that we share the same brain. Astonishingly, he had zero objections or concerns during our big flight conversation, and promised to relay all my requests to Mom . . . though he's not entirely confident in her ability to meet the criteria.

Dad's Rules/Expectations are as follows:

1. There will be no *technical* curfew, but if I come home after midnight, the pugs will bark like crazy, so my unofficial curfew is midnight.
2. The first person awake makes the coffee.
3. If I ever tell Mom about his late-night snacking, he's cutting me off.

The conversation only became nerve-racking after I mentioned my nine-month move-out goal. I rambled on for what felt like an hour before he finally stopped me:

"Lou, I'm not worried. You're my kid. When I was your age, I had two small businesses working out of my garage and a day job at Bobby's Mechanics, where I had to scrub car grease out of the bumpers of old beaten-up Chevy Camaros."

"Wait—I thought at my age you were already working in real estate?"

"Doesn't matter. The point is, you're a Hansen. Hard work runs in your blood. You're clearly not afraid of it, and I'm so proud of you for pursuing a high level of education. You'll figure it out just like I did—only you won't have to break any car windshields to get there."*

I realize he was trying to be supportive, but somehow his self-owned businesses and potential mafia engagement only added more unexpected pressure. Maybe this was a backwards, *Inception*-esque mind trick that was *disguised* as reassurance, but was really meant to scare me into motivation and productivity? Huh. Interesting thought.

With this bizarre idea, I snapped myself back to the reality of my kitchen, poured myself another cup of coffee, and joined Dad in the living room for his morning news marathon.

"Where's Mom?" I asked, noticing the unusual lack of chitchat as I plopped myself down on the couch. Dad took a swig of his coffee, eyes fixed on the TV at what appeared to be some sort of coup d'état.

"At a new juice bar across the street. She's bringing home algae shots."

I spit out a bit of my coffee.

"Algae, like . . . from the sea?"

He gave a single solemn nod, still focused on the foreign rebels overthrowing their ruthless dictator. What country was this? Were they also being forced to take algae shots?

"According to your mother, it rejuvenates the skin. We have them once a week. Welcome home."

Ugh. Can't stop imagining the taste of vile blue-green sea moss that was probably scraped off the bottom of a rock somewhere in the West Indies and bottled at an overpriced smoothie shack for fifteen dollars a shot. Considering a family coup.

I should probably start unpacking my boxes today (especially

---

*I've learned to never ask Dad about these kinds of offhanded comments. In most cases, I imagine I'd rather not know.

since I'm not busy working at Bobby's Mechanics or for the mob), but I really, *really* do not want to. Partly because I no longer know where anything belongs (thanks to Mother's unsolicited bedroom purge), but also because . . . well . . . because I just don't want to. Despite my usual desperation to feel productive, I'm making today a rest-and-relaxation day—a time to reboot before I run headfirst into the metaphorical fire. For once in my life, I'm going to unwind. I just graduated from college! I deserve to read a book, take a bath . . . maybe even a nap?? The possibilities are thrilling and endless!

The Han Fam

8:00 A.M.

MS RISE AND SHINE, FAM!!!

MS I signed us up for a 10:00 am cycling class. We got so lucky . . . There were FOUR OPEN SEATS! It was a sign. 🙏

> Wait, you mean for today?? Lo

Val Welcome back, babe.

> That sounds really great, Mom, but is there any way you can ask one of the Red Hots to go? I just closed the education chapter of my life . . . plus I'm super jet-lagged. I was hoping I could maybe take the day off? Lo

MS You were in New York, not Australia.

MS Get your Lulus on, Lulu.

MS Now, do you guys want lemon juice or ginger with your algae?

10:20 P.M.

So my day of "rest and relaxation" turned into a day of "sweat and aggravation."

Dad opted out of cycling on the grounds of "I paid for this class and also for everything else," so Mom decided to bring her BFF Stacey from the Red Hot Ladies instead.* The class itself was pretty alarming. It mostly felt like my lungs were being poked from the inside with a hot spike, which can't be a good sign for my overall health. Stacey Hoffman—the sepia-toned version of my mother, with her spray tan and dark hair extensions—was on the bike next to me. She and Mom kept perfect time with the instructor, bouncing in their saddles like two petite middle-aged fitness cheerleaders in their matching cycle sweaters.** At one point, Mom took her sweater off and started twirling it over her head, eliciting cheers from the other cyclers. Ugh again.

Val had made plans with friends for noon, so she was able to escape immediately after class. I, on the other hand, was stuck with Mom and Stacey, who insisted on stopping by a little boutique across the street where, of course, they knew the general manager.

"Daaaaarlings!!! It has been much much MUCH too looonnggg!! I haven't seen you ladies in a month. You simply have have HAVE to see our newest summer collection!! Soooooo stunning."

Naturally, their newest summer collection was "LA-life inspired," which in reality has nothing to do with LA life. Most people in Los Angeles wear *actual* clothing, not beaded strips of fabric and flip-flops. I imagine if you live anywhere other than Los Angeles, you think we've all descended from some blue-eyed, fat-lipped Native American tribe and worship the gods of cold-brew coffee and froyo.

But clearly my shitty performance in spin class is reflected in my midsection, since I've gone up a full size since last year. As I hopelessly searched for the head hole in a fringe-covered lace-up contraption that was supposedly a dress, Stacey poked her little bronze face through the curtains, her voice three pitches higher than her usual soprano.

---

*Been thinking of new ways to describe the Red Hot Ladies to my friends. Came up with *Sex and the City* meets *The Golden Girls,* with some *Mean Girls* undertones. Spot-on.
**If I EVER used the term *middle-aged* to my mother, I expect she'd write me out of the will.

"Oh my goodness, Lulu, I almost forgot! Guess who's coming to town in August?"

I froze, arms stuck above my head, tangled up in the bullshit lace labyrinth that couldn't possibly be meant for a human body. *Please no,* I thought. *Please, God, don't let it be . . .*

"MEGAN!!!" she squealed, slipping past the curtain and into the dressing room, gingerly adjusting the fringe folds that were consuming me whole.

"She's graduating from Vandy next week! I can't believe it. Where did the time go? It feels like just yesterday you two were running around naked in Neiman's."

I tried not to cringe at the memory. Even then, Megan was obsessed with her prepubescent thigh gap. Clearly not sensing my overwhelming dread at the mention of her precious niece, Stacey barreled on:

"First she's going on a Euro trip with some of her Kappa friends, but then, get this . . . she's finally MOVING TO LA! How amazing is that?!"

She gave a gentle tug and the dress magically slid over my head and down to my hips, where it stopped, unable to stretch further. I stared in horror at the glorified Pocahontas costume and grunted.

"Wait. She's . . . moving here?" I asked, panic rising. I turned back and forth in front of the mirror, still trying to comprehend the physics of the tiny hippie outfit. I cleared my throat and tried sounding as casual as possible: "You don't mean, like, *indefinitely,* right? I mean that would be *great,* of course, it's just . . . I thought she was moving back to the Bay Area? With her parents??"

My voice broke a little toward the end. Stacey laughed, tossing her head back, her bun still perfect, even post–spin class. "Why would she move back to the Bay Area when she's dying to break into fashion? I'm so proud of her, really—right out of college, and she's already working for a stylist as iconic as Elyse Wok. Not that it's too surprising, since Meg's always had *such* great taste . . . Anyway, she just can't *wait* to see you! She's been talking about it for weeks. Expect a call from her soon."

"Hold on—did I hear that Megan is moving to LA?!" Now Mom's head appeared through the dressing room curtains, her eyes quickly scanning my suffocating body.

"Lulu, isn't that fantastic?! Megan is *such* a great friend for you. And she's going to be working for *Elyse Wok*! That's so exciting! You have to take Meg to lunch."

Before I could even feign excitement, Mom waved over the manager and pulled the curtain back, exposing my reverse muffin top to the entire store.

"This is so cute, but do you have it in one size up? Lulu, baby, I'm going back across the street to buy us a cycling package. I'm so proud of you for taking the semester to focus on your thesis . . . but now it's time to put that same focus into toning up your thighs!"

. . . Adding, "work out thrice a week" to my list of short-term goals, as well as "Murder Megan Mitchell."*

MAY 16

Theo 🖤

9:45 A.M.

Just a reminder that I changed flights, so I'll be landing at 3:30 p.m. instead of noon.

> It's already in the calendar! Which airline again?   Lou

Delta. Flight 3657: JFK to LAX.

> Perfect! 🙂 I'll be there.   Lou

---

*In the unlikely event that Megan Mitchell somehow mysteriously dies in a freak accident and I become a prime suspect, I would like to take this opportunity to clarify to the police that this is entirely hyperbolized and that I'm much too anxious to commit premeditated murder. Please do not use this in court.

Th Woohoo! Awesome sauce. Only 2 more days!! 🖤

9:47 A.M.

Th By the way, please send me the video of your graduation speech when you get the chance. I tried to livestream it, but the Wi-Fi at my parents' house is spotty.

Oh right, I forgot! I'll ask Mom to send me the video and I'll forward it your way. Lou

Th Great! Speaking of which . . .

Th I don't mean to be a nuisance, but have you said anything to your mom yet?

No I haven't yet. 😔 I'm so sorry. I was going to once I got home, but then Mom and I got into this whole argument about Moroccan poufs and I didn't think it was a good time. Lou

Th Moroccan poufs?

I'll tell you later. Lou

11:35 A.M.

Theo moves to LA in just two days, and I still haven't told my family he exists. I think this qualifies me as the world's worst girlfriend. Or at least in the bottom five.

Theo has been working part-time at Farmhouse Catering since his sophomore year in college, so when he told me that he was transferring to the West Coast branch after graduation, I burst into tears. Mostly because it meant we could stay together, but also because I was terrified of telling my parents I had a serious boyfriend—especially one whose jean size is smaller than mine.* I had only two notable romantic encounters in high school: the first was Carl Rosen, whom Mom referred to as Cardboard Carl for the whole five months we were dating. And then there was Jeremy Lockman, with whom I went to my

---

*We discussed the option of moving in together, but ultimately vetoed the idea. I want at least one year of emotional/financial independence before I can commit to a shared rent. I wouldn't ask my parents to supplement that money, and I *refuse* to have Theo as my sugar daddy.

senior prom. Mom Photoshopped every one of our pictures to cover his acne and stretched his image to make him six inches taller, which he found incredibly insulting, and consequently he dumped me the next day.

When I told Mom what had transpired, she waved a hand at me. "I was doing him a favor! If he can't see that, he's not smart enough for you."

Sigh. Mom has somehow managed to sabotage every single one of my relationships—even the imaginary ones with celebrities. ("Eddie Redmayne? Really? Why not Ryan Gosling or Zac Efron??") So when I started dating Theo, with his lanky limbs and strong nose . . . well, let's just say I was protecting the innocent. I know I shouldn't care so much, but Mom is relentless in her opinions, with all her judgey comments and passive-aggressive asides. And with the uncertainty of graduation upon us, I didn't think telling her would be worth all the meshuggaas. Theo is my slightly awkward but endlessly charming prince, and I didn't want Mom twisting him into some weirdo hipster pauper.

Oh, *come on,* Lou! This has gone much too far! You're officially staying together postgrad, he's moving fifteen minutes away . . . it's time to break the ice. Anyway, she might LOVE him! So what if he's a bit geeky? For the first time in your life, you're with someone who really gets you—he's smart, he's funny, he's inquisitive, he's driven, he doesn't mind watching endless *Buffy* reruns . . . and dammit, he makes you happy! Doesn't that count for something??

You know what? It's time. I'm going to do it!

 Travis Winston Yates Jr. Poked You!
Poke him back?

No. I can't do it. At least not yet. I'm not ready to risk ruining a fulfilling relationship over Mother's approval . . . not when her approval is guaranteed to the kinds of guys who probably beat Theo up in grade school.

UGHHHH, WHYYY couldn't I have a normal mother?? Any other mom on earth would see that Theo is an absolute gem! Sure, he's questionably thin for a chef, but he's kind and talented and knows what he wants to do. Hell, that's more than I can say! He's been on a career path since age four, when he made his first PB and J with cinnamon and sliced banana (for texture).* The guy's a total prodigy. It's only a matter of time before he's a proper, honest-to-goodness head chef with his own farm-to-table restaurant . . . and at this rate, if I'm lucky, I'll get to be the hostess wearing a recycled apron and name tag. Ugh.

It's not that I don't have interests. I have plenty of interests! It just so happens that most of these interests don't translate into a stable career . . . or at least not one that I'm in love with. And why shouldn't I be in love with my job? I don't want to wake up years from now, full of regret that I never pursued my dreams! Oh god, what if I end up a fifty-year-old divorcée stuck at a dead-end job, typing numbers into a computer that's smarter than I am, staring out of the corporate window at the gray-tinted world outside, contemplating how I can get my hands on more of my mother's leftover Xanax?!

I refuse to resign myself to that fate. All I want is a career that I am passionate about and will never get tired of, which provides a stable income for me and my future family, is important to the human race, and will one day get me an NPR segment or *60 Minutes* special. Is that too much to ask??

---

*At age ten, I told my parents I wanted to be a Western philosopher, which Mom interpreted as "homeless bum" and rushed me to a therapist.

I should probably go on a run. Or take a long walk. Or at the very least get out of bed.

MAY 18

Theo 🩶

3:45 P.M.

> I'm parked by the curb at Terminal 3   Lou

> Let me know when you're coming outside!   Lou

Th   Yay! So excited to see you!! 😊 Just waiting for my bag . . . it shouldn't take too long.

> Okay! As long as I'm back by 5 . . . we don't want to get stuck in rush-hour traffic, and Mom is having the Red Hots over for Bachelorette Night.   Lou

> My presence is required.   Lou

Th   Oh dear god.

> I know.   Lou

Th   I'm on my way out. See you in a sec. 🩶

Mama Shell

3:47 P.M.

MS   Why are you at the airport??

> ???   Lou

MS

> MOM, I thought you said you deleted that app! Lo

MS I'm sorry, but it relaxes me! I just like to see that you're safe. You could be filming a porno for all I care, just as long as you're not dead on the freeway!

Lo

MS So why are you at the airport?

> I'm at the airport because Lo

> Natasha asked last minute if I could pick her up. Lo

MS Natasha is here?

> Yeah . . . she's visiting her cousins in Silver Lake! Isn't that great?? Lo

MS Oh. Okay. That's fine.

MS But you know how I feel about Natasha. She's just so dark.

> She's not dark, she's profound. Lo

MS I've stalked that girl's Instagram. Her filters are so gloomy, and she wears too much black.

MS And why didn't her cousins pick her up?

They had work today. She needed my help. I'm just dropping her off and coming straight home. Lou

MS Okay, fine. As long as you're home for the first Bachelorette Night!! 😘

10:30 P.M.

The Red Hot Ladies came over tonight, and though I have an extreme moral objection to the Bachelor series (I'm convinced that it is negatively influencing the way young people view and participate in love/dating culture), it was hilarious watching the ladies in action. Stacey and Susan cried when one of the men snapped his rose in half . . . apparently that was a huge deal. Like Twitter-trending huge.

Mom's friend Lisa cooked a gluten-free, dairy-free kale dip that was completely inedible, though the pugs seemed to think it was great. Dad was forced to watch for a bit before mumbling something about "too much estrogen" and escaping to his home office. Val regaled the ladies with drama about her high school friends before somehow taking an incredible picture of the taste-free asshole kale dip and picking up another three hundred followers on Instagram in the process.* It's been a long time since I've seen the whole gang together, and for a minute I was rather emotional.

But then Susan asked about my love life and Mom went into her whole fantasy about me finding a six-foot-five real man with a Harvard degree in frat life and steak grilling. Needless to say, I did not

---

*Val has over 10,000 Instagram followers because she's a genius with photo-editing apps and has mastered the art of "flow," which apparently just means that all of your pictures look exactly the same. This talent might just land her in USC's communications program to study public relations. She's seventeen, and she's already on a more stable career path than me.

mention scrawny, earnest, Scrabble-loving Theo, who was probably in the middle of color-coordinating his graphic T-shirts.

Until Theo's proficient in a sport that isn't badminton, he'll stay undercover as Natasha.

Not that this excuse is much better . . . Mom is hardly Natasha's number one fan. Admittedly, she does wear a lot of black, but she's easily one of the most brilliant people I have ever met. Coincidently, she's also one of the least stable. She once went camping with her ex-boyfriend, during which she claimed to have an intense spiritual connection with a bunny, which promptly convinced her to go vegan. Now she has one of the most followed vegan lifestyle blogs on the Internet and a potential book deal on the way. Typical Tash. She graduated second in our class only to this guy Richard Chung, who literally no one knew existed until he was announced as our valedictorian. I came in third.

I should probably ask the real Natasha not to post any Instagram pictures for the next week or so—at least until I sort this situation out. But it might take some convincing. Real Tash is currently on her way to India to write a journalistic profile about its cultural violence against women . . . all things considered, "visiting cousins in Silver Lake" might not be the most realistic cover.

Going to bed early tonight. If I wake up at 7:30 tomorrow, I'll at least feel accomplished enough to continue checking goals off of my list. Remember: productivity breeds more productivity!

MAY 19

9:25 P.M.

I'm going to qualify today as the least productive day of my life.

I pressed my snooze button a record-breaking twelve times this morning, which completely destroyed my motivation for the day as well as my ego. Instead of working out, emailing Dr. Richmanson, or even leaving my house, I moped back and forth from my room to the pantry, where I'd occasionally sneak handfuls of chocolate-covered almonds and skinny popcorn. The only remotely constructive thing I've done today was to change my profile picture on Facebook. It has only ten likes so far.

Theo is furiously unpacking with his roommate/coworker, Jett, which has kept him totally swamped. Not that it'll be easy to visit, anyway. When I told Mom I was hanging out with Natasha, she rolled her eyes and said, "Fine. Just don't come back with a nose ring."

Considering changing my move-out deadline from nine months to six.

MAY 21

 Email

To: **Alberto Rodriguez (HELP)**
From: **Lou Hansen**
Subject: **I'm Back!**

Hi Alberto,

Good news: I'm officially a college graduate! Less-good news: I'm still unemployed! Even-less-good news: I've moved back in with my parents to save money on rent that I don't have the income to afford!! Hahahaha!!!!!

In my defense, I haven't really been applying for jobs, so it's not as though I'm being rejected. I was actually considering applying for a part-time job at your company, but as we learned last summer from my lovely internship at Time Warner, finance quite literally puts me to sleep. I probably shouldn't pursue anything that involves counting. Bless you and your affinity for numbers, Alberto.

Anyway, until I have a better sense of what I want to be when I grow up, I'm staying with my parents, which brings me to this email. Is there any way you can send me Mom's car insurance information? She scraped her bumper on a curb backing out of Bloomingdale's yesterday and doesn't want Dad to know. It's not bad, but this is the third time this year, so she "wants to keep it on the DL."

I have to end my correspondence here, because I've actually been waiting to pay for Mother's rosé in the longest checkout line Ralph's has ever seen. Some old lady is paying for her groceries exclusively with coins. Wish I were kidding.

Thanks for everything, and undoubtedly I'll be emailing you again soon.

Best,
Lou

Sent from my iPhone

MAY 22

Val

2:37 P.M.

Val: Babe, how many colleges did you apply to?

Lou: Thirteen. Why? What about you?

Val: Holy shit, really?? I was thinking, like, five.

Val: But USC is definitely my first choice.

Val: Tbh I just really, really wanna be in Kappa. 🐨

Lou: Don't worry . . . you're a Kappa legacy. Mom and I are both Kappas. Your chances go up exponentially.

Lou: Also, I'll write you a letter of rec.

Val: YESSSS ugh ur the goat.

Lou: I'm a goat?

Val: Lol omg ur the Greatest Of All Time

Lou: 🙂 You too, babe! But seriously, why am I a goat?

I finally went over to Theo's apartment to help him and Jett unpack. You have to trudge up five flights of stairs and wiggle the lock to get to unit 6: a two-bedroom, one-bathroom, charming shithole left in total shambles by the previous tenants. The paint is chipping, the floors are warped in places, and the whole apartment reeks of marijuana thanks to Jett's three-foot bong. (Apparently, he operates the bottom part of it with his toes. This is equally impressive and horrifying.)

That being said, I was happy to brave the smell just to spend the day with Theo, who was in such a good mood, he spoke in a bad German accent while he was putting together the furniture.

"Vhat do you zink, Fraulein Lou? Ze angels must be perfect, jawohl? Ah, ze engineering of zis Swedish Ikea cabinet is inferior to zat of our German cabinets, iz it not??"

After a full day of building and unpacking, the enclave began to resemble a real place of residence. By the end, I was even fond of it. Because the view consists entirely of tree branches, we've started calling it the Treehouse, which is thematically consistent with its exposed wood and lack of working utilities. Once we were satisfied that the Treehouse was well on its way to being presentable, Theo and I escaped to our first postgrad date at a local hole-in-the-wall Thai place called "Thai Restaurant #2." Once we were eating our fried rice and pad see ew, he hit me with the dreaded question:

"So, Louie, when do you plan on telling your parents about me?"

I bit down too hard on my noodles and caught the tip of my tongue. I groaned in pain, and Theo threw his hands up in surrender.

"All right, all right! Just thought I'd ask, since it's been six months."

He was more hurt than mad, which made me feel even worse. Ugh, why couldn't he just be mad at me?? I swallowed both my food and my pain, shaking my head furiously from side to side.

"No, no, no, I bit my tongue! I promise I'm going to tell them. I just wanted to wait a week . . . you know, to settle in!"

His annoyance faded into concern as he reached out and grabbed my hand. "Oh, shoot, tongue biting is the worst! Are you okay? Is it bleeding? Here, take some of my ice. It'll help."

He reached a hand into his Thai iced tea and retrieved a few rounded cubes. I plopped them into my mouth, careful not to swallow them whole, before delivering my sad excuses with a slight lisp.

"Pleesh don't shink shish ish about you. It'sh not. It'sh about my mosher. She'sh sho protective, and shuper jushmental, and I wanted to be shure we were shtaying togesher before I brought shish up!"

He smiled and shook his head, amused by my struggle, before bringing my hand up to his mouth for a kiss.

"I know; we've gone over this. And it makes sense that you wanted to wait until graduation. But the great news is: I'm here now! I've moved! There's no need to wait any longer!"

He reached into his glass and pulled out two more ice cubes, shoving them into his mouth.

"You shee? We're in shish togesher!"

I smiled as much as I could with a numbed mouth, chewed up the remaining ice, and stuffed my face with more rice noodles. As we finished our third order of egg rolls, I realized that Theo was right: there really is no need to wait any longer. The time has come to break/chew up the ice, and the sooner, the better. Hell, I should do it tonight! What's the worst that could happen?

. . . On second thought, I'll wait until Memorial Day. I'll tell them all about Theo at the Hansen Memorial Day Dinner, with the entire family seated together, surrounded by our amazing friends who will also serve as an emotional/physical buffer. Yes, that seems like the mature decision! Memorial Day it is!

.ıll AT&T 🤝   @ ✳ 80% ■

‹ Home   **Megan Mitchell**   📞 ▭))

9:45 P.M.

BABE HI!!! OMG I can't believe it it's been like FOREVER. How are you?? How are the pugs?? How's your gorgeous mama??? Send them ALL my kisses.

So I'm sure my auntie's told you, but I'M MOVING TO LA!!! AHHH!!! :D :D :D <3 <3 <3

9:46 P.M.

So, so stoked. You know I've always wanted to live there! It's been on my inspo-board since, like, five-ever. The Bay is nice, but UGH, so techie. No fun at all. Like, why even, you know?

Anyway you HAVE to come visit my apartment OMG. It's this beautiful brand-new place in West Hollywood with a view of, like, ALL of LA. Unreal. Like legit unreal.

9:47 P.M.

BUTTT I'm not going to move until August. 😊 I'm leaving for Europe this week for funsies, and then I have to stay in Paris to do some style research for Elyse . . . SO exhausting. Blegh.

It's just wayyyyyyyyyy too much bread and cheese, you know? I'm gonna be, like, SO done.

9:48 P.M.

ALSO Stacey tells me that you're funemployed! I'm so, SO jealous of you . . . Now THAT'S the life to live. You don't have to do anything but relax! Me? I'll be suffering Paris jet lag and macaron overload. Sigh. The things we do for money.

So anyway call me!! I can't wait to get coffee or lunch or maybe take a cycling class? Stacey told me you have a class package! LOVE YOUUUUU xoxo <333

9:50 P.M.

PS: LOVE your new prof pic. I wish I had a butt like yours . . . curves are SO in!

10:15 P.M.

If I had to excommunicate one person from the Church of My Life, it would absolutely be Megan Mitchell.

For my birthday last year, she sent me a tooth-whitening kit and a pair of "baby bump" pajamas from a company that specializes in maternity wear. When I asked for the gift receipt, she shrugged and said she was "just guesstimating my size based on recent pictures." She's shallow, she's catty, she completely lacks substance and possibly a soul.

And of course she's Mama Shell's favorite.

Mom and Stacey have been best friends since their sorority days at the University of Miami,* so Megan and I were basically brought up as cousins. And much like an annoying and undesired cousin, Megan has been a relevant nuisance in my life only once or twice a year. But of course she just HASSSS to move out to LA because she's DYYYY-INNNGGGG to work in fashion and her AUUUNNTTIEEEE is BESTIESSSS with ELYYSSEEE. UGH UGH UGH.

Project Murder Megan Mitchell is officially under way. Possible options include: poisoning her via juice cleanse or suffocation via Spanx.

MAY 24

Mama Shell

3:30 P.M.

MS Are you still home?

Yeah, I'm in my room. What's up? Lou

MS Muffin peed on my bed again. 🙈

---

*When I told Mom I had no interest in sorority life, she locked herself in her room for three days. It wasn't until Megan became social chair of Kappa that I felt compelled to rush, if only for my mother's sanity and favoritism. Thankfully, Columbia Kappa is NOTHING like Vanderbilt Kappa . . . Instead of tailgating or going to frat parties, we mostly dressed up in frontier garb and chanted a lot in Latin. Mom does not know this, and she never will.

MS I need help stripping the sheets. Will you come and help me?

Lou Mom, you really need to train your animals.

MS They are trained!! He must not be feeling well, is all.

MS It's been so fun having you home, sweetie. Why would you ever want to move out?? Now come help me strip these sheets before your father gets home 💜

9:50 P.M.

Another entirely useless day. I accomplished exactly zero of the tasks on my graduation goals list . . . I'm convinced I've taken steps backwards. Ugh.

I'm really missing Theo. He's been so busy since our date night, we've hardly had time to see each other at all. We went from basically living together in college to being virtually long distance in my hometown. At least it feels that way. It's like we're regressing. Oh god. My relationship can't crumble right before I tell my parents about it! What's happening to me?? I went from the president of three different academic clubs to a sad, soon-to-be-single cat lady living in her childhood room.

. . . To be fair, Theo hasn't even been here a full week, but that's beside the point!

The point is, *he's* super busy shopping for coffee tables and getting ready for his super awesome job. Valedictorian Richard Chung was offered a full-time position at Google, Tash is studying feminism in India, and I'm watching *The Bachelorette* with a group of fifty-year-old women who are arguably cooler than me. How is it that all of my friends are off pursuing careers and passions and flights of fancy? How am I supposed to stay sane if even Megan Bitchell has a job while I aimlessly scrub pug pee out of my bedroom drapes like a curvier twisted variation of a pre-1960's Disney Princess??

Officially moving my deadline to six months. I'm emailing Dr. Richmanson tomorrow, lest I find myself singing at Baguette and Muffin to put my hair into short pigtails with ribbons.

PS: Found out today that apparently GOAT means "greatest of all time"? I can't keep up with this shit.

‹ Home   **Natasha McPatterson**   📞 📹

10:25 P.M.

Hey, Tash! How has your summer been treating you? How's India? I can't wait to see all of your pictures!!

10:26 P.M.

Speaking of pictures, I would tremendously appreciate it if you didn't post any on Instagram for at least another week or so. It's rather difficult to explain the situation, but it involves my mother and my being a terrible liar.

I'm so, so, so sorry to do this to you . . . will clarify the specifics later. I owe you meatless meals for a week.

MAY 25

 Email

To: **Dr. Nathaniel Richmanson III, PhD**
From: **Lou Hansen**
Subject: **Job Opportunity**

Hello, Dr. Richmanson,

I hope you have been enjoying your summer vacation thus far! Anything exciting to report? I've mostly been taking time for myself before diving headfirst into the myriad exciting opportunities that lie ahead. Yes, sir, there are some really amazing prospects on my metaphorical horizon. I know exactly what I'm doing.

With that in mind, I wanted to follow up about that job opportunity you mentioned this past spring. I know you said it didn't seem exactly like my cup of tea, but I firmly believe in considering all of my options. After all, I did graduate summa cum laude with a double major in art history and philosophy—I imagine that qualifies me to do *something* practical.

Anyway, please send some information my way when you get the chance. Thanks again for everything those last two semesters. At the risk of sounding corny, I wanted you to know that you've always been an intellectual inspiration to me, and your classes were easily the most stimulating. "Time, Time Travel, and the Other Six Dimensions" completely changed the way I look at prisms. Truly, fascinating.

Best,
Lou Hansen

Theo 🖤

2:45 P.M.

Th FINALLY unpacked the last box!!

🙂 And it only took a week! Well done. **Lou**

Th Haha, yeah, Jett's been a drill sergeant. For a stoner, he's oddly tidy.

You have to come check this place out now. It looks unreal!
Th SO much better than before.

Th I even stocked the pantry with Puffins just for you. 🐦

!!! **Lou**

OH MY GOD CEREAL. Mom literally threw all of the processed food out of the house. Even the shitty gluten-free pretzels. I've been subsisting on celery and protein shakes. **Lou**

Th Is that a legal thing she can do?

Apparently. I have to escape Bachelorette night, so I'll be over in half an hour. Pour a bowl of Puffins for me? **Lou**

On it. I'm making a Bolognese for dinner . . . and mayybeeee a celebratory
Th coconut meringue for dessert. ☺️

You're my hero. 🖤 **Lou**

MAY 27
2:50 P.M.

As Facebook, Instagram, and Snapchat Story won't let me forget: Megan flies to Europe today on her BFF's private jet, starting in Italy and ending in Paris. For an entire month, these ladies will be traveling from city to city, "finding themselves" in all of the most Westernized foreign lands, eventually turning the experience into a twentysomething blog that will later be adapted into a bestselling Urban Outfitters coffee table book. Ugh.

Anyway, with the Memorial Day Dinner fast approaching, I've suddenly become aware of a glaring absence in the Hansen home: Rosa.

Wow, I can't believe it's taken me this long to notice! What is wrong with me? I suppose I've just been too caught up in my drastically changing universe to even acknowledge the disappearance of our longtime housekeeper. Ugh again.

Rosa has been working for us since I was six or so. I am pretty much 1,000 percent certain she is an illegal immigrant, and to this day she speaks only ten words of English, but she's also one of the most loving and hardworking human beings on the face of this earth. Since I'm the only Hansen who speaks any semblance of Spanish, I'm the designated translator por la familia. If you can even call it that.

"Hola, Rosa! Er . . . por favor, necessito . . . uh . . . tu lleva, no . . . llevas? Is it llevas? Tu llevas los . . . windows? Como se dice windows??"

It's pretty humiliating, but at least it's better than Mom's feeble attempts at communication. For some reason, Mom thinks that speaking louder somehow lowers the language barrier.

"HI, ROSA! YOU TAKE TWO WEEKS OFF! I STILL PAY! YES?"

Thankfully, Rosa shrugs off this mild racism with the patience only a woman with seven children could have. She is a part of our family, and even though she has never heard me speak a complete, grammatically correct sentence, I know she loves me dearly.

"Mom, where's Rosa? Why hasn't she been here?" I asked while Mom was on her way out to get a mani-pedi. She walked back into the living room, where I was sitting on the couch sandwiched between the pugs.

"Oh! She's visiting her family in Guatemala until July. Apparently there was a family emergency . . . Or at least I think that's what she said. I can never be too sure. Anyway, I can't wait for her to get back! The carpets are starting to smell like dog pee."

"Don't you scrub the pee out?"

"Of course! But I can do only so much. Remember: hard labor ruins a manicure!"

She wiggled her fingers at me and I snorted.

"So if Rosa is gone, who's going to help with the Memorial Day Dinner?"

"Oh, I didn't tell you? We're canceling the dinner this year!"

I let out a small gasp. "Wait, what? Why??"

Mom took a sneak peek at the blacked-out television, using its reflection as a mirror to check her lip gloss.

"I can't believe I didn't tell you! We were invited to a party at the Mattfelds' family ranch out in Topanga. You remember the Mattfelds, don't you? You went to preschool with the oldest son, Wolfgang. I did some Facebook stalking, and Wolfgang grew up to be drop . . . dead . . . gorgeous. You want to see?"

Mom thrust her hand into her purse, searching for her phone. I stopped petting the pugs so I could fiddle with my rings.

"Well, um, actually, Mom, there's something I—"

"Here we go!" She pulled the phone from her bag like a sword from a sheath. She flicked her prescription sunglasses from her head to her nose, rapidly scrolling through her photos for a screenshot. "Just give me a second to find it."

"Okay, Mom, but I really need to—"

"Oh my god, look, he is SO CUTE! Look at him, Lulu. Isn't he cute?"

She shoved the phone an inch from my face, so I had to lean back on the sofa to focus. There was Wolfgang, topless on a yacht, wearing coral-colored Chubbies and a baseball cap. I sighed and gently took the phone.

"Yes, he's very cute, Mom, but I should tell you that—"

"Oh shoot, you should probably know this before we visit them. His mother, Rita? The one who sells me all my jewelry? She's recovering from surgery."

My mouth froze open. "She . . . what?"

"I know. She just posted a picture of herself in bandages with the hashtag *bye-bye, boobies*. I think she may have had breast cancer? Life is so unpredictable—one day you're designing diamond-studded nipple rings for Rihanna, and the next you're taking hospital selfies in awful fluorescent lighting."

Baguette pawed longingly at my arm while Muffin started digging into the couch furiously, as though a forgotten bone was waiting on the inside. Mom ignored the destruction and kept on: "But anyway, they're having a huge party on Memorial Day, and both she and I would just LOVE it if you got to know Wolfie! Would you? Would you at least talk to him?"

I stared at her for a minute, speechless, before looking down at Wolfie Mattfeld and his six-pack of beer/abs. His mom just had surgery? How do I say no to a woman who's recovering from breast cancer surgery??

"Yeah, Mom, of course I'll get to know him. I just—"

She snatched her phone from my hand and beamed down at the picture.

"YES! Eloise Laurent Mattfeld. Rolls right off the tongue, doesn't it? Oh, I have to call Rita!"

And with that, she danced out of the room through the front door, off to call Rita and discuss the upcoming nuptials. Muffin finally tore a hole through the slipcover, letting loose a flurry of goose feathers, which Baguette started chasing.

Three more days, Lou. Three more.

MAY 30

9:20 P.M.

ARE. YOU. KIDDING. ME?!

We celebrated Memorial Day at the Mattfeld ranch—all seven sprawling acres of it. The ranch itself is tucked away deep in the heart of the Canyon and can be accessed only by a single bumpy, narrow dirt road . . . as though the Mattfelds didn't have enough money to pave it. The whole way there, Dad was cursing, reiterating his conviction that our hosts are the perpetrators of an elaborate pyramid scheme. "*Five* houses? A seven-acre ranch in the Canyon??"

"They're very successful, Charlie."

"She sells jewelry out of a goddamn trunk! How successful can she be??"

"She has celebrity clients, Charlie!"

"So do I! Only I sell them freaking houses, not goddamn bracelets!!"

"Well, he's also a filmmaker, Charlie."

"He made one film. Back in the seventies. And it tanked! I'm telling you, Shelly, these assholes steal their money. You're going to see Rita and Mark Mattfeld on the news one of these days in handcuffs, mark my words."

This debate raged on until we finally arrived at the parking area, where we were forced to abandon our vehicle and take a VIP shuttle, which brought us to the actual party. There we were greeted by the alleged criminals themselves—Rita's bandages visible under her translucent top.

"Rita, darling!" my mother cooed, tenderly wrapping her arms around her in a squeeze-less hug. "How are you feeling?"

"So lovely, Shelly dear!" Rita cooed back, her words slightly slurred and her eyes glossed over. "I feel like I'm soaking in Botox!"

Her husband, Mark, stood beside her with a hand on her back (and also part of her butt). "Sorry about her; she's a little loopy from the meds. I'm so glad you all could make it!" He leaned over and kissed my mother on both cheeks, then did the same to Val and me. He and Dad exchanged a firm handshake before we all walked toward the rest of the party. "Please, relax and enjoy! If you want to hang by the pool, you'll have to take one of the golf carts to the West Camp, but the food and booze is all here on the South Side."

Dad nodded, shooting Mom a quick glance before his attention landed back on Mark. A drugged-out Rita turned toward me with a goofy smile. Oh boy.

"Soooo, I hear someone's a college graduate now!"

I smiled with teeth, hoping that false confidence might keep her from asking any unwanted questions.

"Yes, I am! Out in the real world!" I offered, hoping she would move on to Val. She didn't.

"Ahhhh, of course! So what are you doing now? What's the plan??"

I felt my cheeks flush. "Well, at the moment I'm just getting settled—"

"She's living with me!" Mom chimed in, as though this were the pride of her life. I broadened my smile, trying to appear equally joyful.

Mark stepped in. "Rooming with the old folks, huh? I understand—in this economy, who can afford anything?"

Dad shot Mom another sharp look. "I was just saying the same thing to Shelly, Mark."

"Why don't you go find Wolfie?" my mom urged, eyes wide with expectation. "Val and I will stay here and chat with Rita."

Rita began pressing her fingers into her own face."Yes, go find Wolfgang! He should be near the pool with some friends. Honey, why does my skin feel like leather?"

I left Rita to discover the texture of her own body and headed toward the pool. This involved a ten-minute ride in the backseat of a golf cart next to a man who did not acknowledge my existence once. We just sat next to each other, inappropriately fascinated by our cell phones as the driver blasted a mix of white noise and classical music until we arrived at the West Camp. Wolfie was lounging by the pool with his buddies, a perimeter of discarded beer bottles clearly marking their territory. He was wearing another pair of Chubbies—these were lime green instead of coral—with flip-flops, no shirt, and a white Vineyard Vines sweater tied around his thick neck. As I got closer, I realized that all his friends were wearing a similar uniform; only the color of shorts and flip-flops varied.

It took between three to six minutes for anyone to actually notice me, and when they did, I suddenly became acutely aware of how awkward my hands felt. The boys' abrupt attention turned me back into a gangly twelve-year-old on her first day of middle school, and my palms got balmy at the memory.* I put on a big smile, shoved my sweaty hands deep in my pockets, and leaned a little too far on one hip. "Hey, Wolfgang!"

Wolfgang squinted a bit at me, like I was somehow out of focus, before lifting his chin up and nodding slightly. "Oh, right. Lou Hansen, yeah?"

The Preppy Boy Band all gave me the "'sup" nod, which I tried emulating, only it ended up looking more like a twitch.

---

*If it provides any context, I fainted my first day of middle school while eating lunch in the bathroom, and had to be rescued by a group of hot firefighters whom Mom took a picture with at the hospital.

"Your mom said I might find you here!" I kept on, as though this were a cool thing to say. Wolfgang snorted and gave another head nod to the side . . . I think meaning yes, but I'm not sure. I don't speak bro.

"She still high as tits?" he asked, his yuppie squad all chuckling at the idea. I nodded and tried chuckling myself. It sounded like a hiccup.

"Yeah, Rita's still pretty loopy. You know how drugs are!" This statement made it glaringly obvious that no, I do not. I cleared my throat. "Anyway, I'm glad she's making a speedy recovery! She looks great."

Wolfgang took a swig of his beer, squinting into the sky, as though in deep thought. Doubtful, though.

"Ha. Well. She better look great for all the money it cost."

My jaw dropped. The *money*?? How could he think of the money?! What an insensitive, intolerable, dopey-looking, beer-soaked little DOUCHE BAG!!!

"Haha, what do you mean?" I valiantly defied.

Wolfie stretched his arms overhead, accentuating his rack of abs. Damn. If nothing else, he was a phenomenal physical specimen. Well done, Mattfeld genes.

"I just mean if you're gonna have plastic surgery, and you pay good money for it, then you best be looking pretty dope, ammaright?"

The boys all gave an "AYO!" in support. I looked around the group, utterly confused.

"Wait . . . so your mom didn't have breast cancer?" I probably should have asked something subtler, but my instincts told me Wolfie wasn't great with nuance.

His face scrunched up into a tightly knit ball, air blowing out of his tanned nose. "What? Naw, she just got her implants taken out. Said they made her look too big up top."

One of his buds grabbed two handfuls of air in front of his pecs, and everyone laughed except for Wolfie, who smacked him across the back of the head.

"Cut it out, man, that's my mom!"

"Ow, sorry, bro!"

"Asshole!"

I was just about to turn around to drown myself in the pool when Wolfie turned his attention back to me.

"Yo, Lou . . . you're Valentina's sister, right?"

You've got to be kidding me. I gave him two thumbs-ups, dropping my convincing "cool" facade. All the yuppies started gushing.

"Whoa, wait, you mean So Cal So Val??" "No way! You're THAT Hansen?"

"My sister gets all her Instagram ideas from her!"

Within ten minutes, I had summoned Val to the West Camp to take pictures with the Preppy Pals—all of whom flexed their biceps for the camera.

The whole way home, I sulked in the backseat, unable to bear the embarrassment of being my sister's photographer. Dad was cursing again, only this time Mom joined in the profanity.

"How the hell is she fifty-six years old?? She doesn't look a day over forty!"

"I mean, seriously, twelve bedrooms?! There are only four people in the family!"

"And she *swears* she's never had a facelift. Not even an eyelift!"

"Maybe it's tax evasion? A Ponzi scheme? Maybe she sells her leftover Vicodin??"

"Charlie, this is serious! Ugh, maybe I *should* go soak in Botox!"

Month Two

June Gloom

Mom burst into my room at 7:15 this morning in curlers and a leopard-print robe.

Muffin and Baguette dutifully filed in behind her, jumping onto the bed and attacking my head before I could half open my eyes.

"Drink this." Mom thrust a steaming mug under my pug-clobbered face. I pushed the goons off and inhaled what I assumed was coffee, only to snort up a nose full of choke-inducing spices. My nose hairs started singeing.

"Oh god. Should I even ask?"

"It's hot water with lemon and cayenne. We're having one in the morning and one before bed."

"Can I humbly object?"

"Sure. If you want to have wrinkles at thirty."

Sigh. Mom has an incredible way of disguising demands as options. I halfheartedly pushed myself onto a forearm, fending off Muffin with the other arm while he chewed on my hair. I grabbed the mug and peeked over the edge at its contents—little red specks and lemon seeds floating in what looked like murky nitric acid. The fumes burned my eyes.

"Uh, Mom? Are you sure this is healthy?"

"Of course it is! They say it flushes out toxins."

"And who is 'they' again?"

"Oh, you know—everyone."

Starting to think the proverbial "they" Mom often refers to is *People* magazine. Or maybe Satan. Could be either.

I took a sip and almost coughed up a lung. "Ugh, this is worse than the algae."

"Hush, bubbe, and take your medicine. If Rita Mattfeld can look forty forever, so can I. And besides, it's a new month! Let's not waste it!"

As she turned on her heels to leave, the pugs chased after her, biting at the trail of her fluffy leopard robe.

It took a few minutes before I dared to take another sip, but I must admit, once my tongue was numbed by the cayenne concoction, it really wasn't half bad! I mean, I don't feel *that* different, but I'm certainly more awake. Maybe toxins are a real thing after all? Will research later.

I can't believe how New Age I'm about to sound, BUT Mom does make a good point about June. A new month IS a chance to start over, and since I haven't been particularly productive in my first three weeks postgrad, why not take the opportunity to grow? This could be a new me! And you know what? New me is going to be motivated. New me is going to make stuff happen. New me is going to be like Martha Stewart meets Steve Jobs, only *better*.

JUNE 2
7:30 A.M.

Woke up at 7:10 this morning (!!!), twenty minutes BEFORE my alarm went off, and spent my first five conscious minutes posing like Wonder Woman. (Shonda Rhimes wrote that posing like Wonder Woman in the morning helps empower her throughout the day. Would very much like to be a blonder version of Shonda Rhimes.)

As a sort of psychological rejuvenation, I am revising my list of short-term goals for the month of June. I am also going to switch from drinking coffee to the lemon-cayenne concoction. If I'm trying out this new hippie idealism, I'm committing 100%.

GRADUATION GOALS (REVISED)

Short Term

- Establish new living-at-home rules/expectations with parents. (Should probably reiterate these.)
- ~~Rid closet of all unnecessary and unprofessional outfits.~~ (Thanks to the Mama Shell Bedroom Purge of 2017.)
- ~~Email professor Richmanson about job opportunity!!~~
- Buy more ink for label maker. (Can't find label maker itself, <u>also</u> thanks to the Mama Shell Bedroom Purge of 2017.)
- Start waking up at 7:30 A.M. (Will be tough without coffee, but must stay strong.)
- TELL MOM ABOUT THEO!!!
- Work out ~~thrice~~ twice a week. (Realistic goals are key.)
- ~~Murder Megan Mitchell~~ (Holding grudges is immature and prison is not on my list of long-term goals.)
- Substitute coffee with lemon-cayenne water

Mama Shell

3:15 P.M.

MS   911

?? What's going on?   Lou

Dad's on his way home already. I need you to go to the front of the house and sneak the Barney's bags into your room. Hide them under your bed, please. Already in trouble for this month—forwarding you an email from Alberto.

Email
To: **Lou Hansen**
From: **Shelly Hansen**
Subject: **FWRD: BILLS—MAY 2017**

Hi, Shelly,

Attached are the bills/financial records for this past month, May of 2017. At your husband's request, I broke the information in the first two weeks down so you can see what you're spending money on. As you will note, I highlighted the most frequent offenders and made a few comments in the margins. If you have any questions regarding the charges or do not recognize any of these charges, feel free to email or call me.

Best,
Alberto Rodriguez

Business Manager, WG&S
ARodriguez@wgs.net
310-205-5163

MAY 2017

Nordstrom's	$362.57
Whole Foods	$277.34
Hair appointment with Tracey	$75
Lucy's Nail Bar	$55
Valet service	$8
Lunch @ Montage	$128
Lululemon	$212.22
Barney's NY	$472.85
Parking ticket	$68
Gas (full service)	$102.88
Moroccan Poufs	$125.89
Cycling	$35
Miraj Hair Coloring and Cut	$672.55
Valet service	$10
Doggie Day Spa	$190.99

This is a thing? ←

Dinner @ Bottega Louie................... $105.86
Hair appointment with Tracey $75
Barney's NY $319
Parking ticket $77
3-Day Soupure Soup Cleanse $275
Just Food for Dogs................................ $60
Bloomingdale's.................................. $319
Botox.. $200
Valet service...................................... $15
Drinks @ BHH $54
Cycling.. $35
Whole Foods...................................... $125
Hair appointment with Tracey $75
Saint Laurent $650.35
Jessica's Waxing Salon........................ $110
MindPower Yoga $30
Valet service...................................... $13
Dinner @ Mr Chow's $82
Barneys NY.................................. $6,254.89 ← *Is this a mistake??*
Valet service.. $8
Breakfast @ So Smoothie $15
Lucy's Nail Bar...................................... $45
Hair appointment with Tracey $75
Lunch @ Café Gratitude $66.34
Lululemon....................................... $160.00
MindPower Yoga $30
Valet service...................................... $45 ← *Where on earth was this??*
Dinner @ Iroha Sushi $110.57
Gas (full service)............................. $112.77

Mama Shell

3:19 P.M.

The deed is done. If Dad finds out, I'm an unwilling accomplice.

MS   I don't know what that means, but thank you!!! Taking you shopping for this. 🖤

Mom, that's part of the problem.

MS   Don't be so uptight. I'm sending you another email . . . can you check the
      spelling? xoxo

Email

> **To:**   **Lou Hansen**
> **From:**   **Shelly Hansen**
> **Subject:** **RE: FWD: BILLS—MAY 2017**

Darling Al,

You're so wonderful to do this for me!! Would be even more wonderful
if you kept the Barney's bill between us. It was for Lulu's graduation
outfit . . . that is, my outfit for Lulu's graduation. She was stuck wearing
that frumpy cap and gown with no waistline. Blegh.

Anyways, I'm turning over a new leaf this month. Already returned a few of
my Bloomie's purchases, which may only give me credit, but it's a good
start!

You haven't heard of Doggie Day Spa?? Changed my life. The pugs are
so lively when they've had a massage! Tell your wife about it.

Xoxo,
Shelly

10:45 P.M.

An *excellent* start to the month! My first two days of positivity are proving successful and encouraging. Posing like Wonder Woman has in
fact done wonders . . . whether those results are psychosomatic is
completely irrelevant.

Somehow managed to get lunch with Theo yesterday without raising any questions from Mom. I told her I was buying summer reading
books, and she asked if I could pick up the newest edition of *People*.

Previous "they" suspicions confirmed.

I ran for forty-five minutes on the treadmill today, and only briefly considered amputating my feet at the ankles. In fact, I think I experienced a bit of runner's high! Or dehydration. Regardless, a gentle tingling was experienced through my appendages, and it was goddamn glorious.

Might just add "run marathon" to list of long-term goals.

Mom was barely home today (presumably hiding from Papa Hansen and the monthly bill), but after my lunch yesterday, I am finally gathering the confidence to tell her about my boyfriend. There's zero reason she should dislike him. He's any parent's dream: he's kind, he's brilliant, he makes a killer organic pesto . . . what's not to love? Besides, when Mom met Dad, he was wearing a metallic panda shirt and already losing his hair. I'm hardly tarnishing the family bloodline.

I'll give myself one week. One week of cayenne and inner confidence is all I need to spill the boyfriend beans. Who knows? If all goes well, Theo might even get an invitation to mah-jongg!

. . . oh god, what is happening to me?

JUNE 3
4:15 P.M.

Over forty-eight hours without coffee and I'm still feeling great! Have experienced on-and-off headaches, but nothing wretched like most coffee addicts groan on about. In fact, that pain has been pleasant in comparison to the seething post-run lava that was pulsing through my legs this morning.

Instead of another run (unthinkable in current condition), I went with Mom and Susan to their noon yoga class. Turns out, it was Bikram Yoga, which is sort of like normal people yoga, only in 1,001-degree heat. I was immediately tempted to turn around and walk out, but caught a glimpse of an ancient relic in a sports bra doing crow pose and decided to swallow my pride.

The woman at the front desk could not have weighed more than ninety-eight pounds soaking wet—which she was, only with ~~sweat~~ "glimmer." She had five piercings on each ear and a shirt that said *Nama stay in bed*, which I regretted not doing. She looked up at me with her perfectly messy topknot and introduced herself as Harvest, because of course.

Though old, less-positive me would have hated tiny Harvest and her tiny, poreless yogi face, new me decided to breathe out all of my black energy or whatever and give the glimmering pixie a chance.

Shocking admission: I actually enjoyed the class. I'm not sure what it is. Something shifted once Harvest lowered the lights and turned on the electronic candles. The room smelled oddly similar to my college dorm (possible connection to living with Tash?), and the stretching made my lava-filled legs hurt so damn good. Mom and Susan hid in the back left corner, where I'd occasionally hear them exchanging giggles at a downward dog gone wrong.

"Set an intention for your practice," guided Yoga Pixie Harvest. "Forget everything going on outside of these doors. Just be here on your mat, with an intention, in the present, right here, right now."

And just like that: I did. It took ten minutes of arm quivering and belly twitching, but I completely forgot about my short-term, medium-term, and long-term goals. Suddenly all of the aching went away and was replaced with a sort of odd humming sensation. I sweat like a faucet. Possibly to the point of hallucination. Maybe I'm hallucinating that I like yoga? Can't be sure.

Work out twice a week: check. Look out, June! I'm on a roll.

Mama Shell

5:15 P.M.

MS Hey, I just made a hair appointment with Tracey tomorrow. Do you want her to do yours after?

Why? Is there an event going on? **Lou**

MS Why? Does there have to be?

MS Also, Tracey has lost SO much weight and I think it's because she's on Adderall.

MS Do you think she'll let us try a few?

MS I'll pay for it, of course.

Mother, that's drug dealing. **Lou**

MS No it's not, you were prescribed Adderall at seven!

MS If I knew back then it would help us stay in shape, I would have taken ADD more seriously.

 Lou

MS Fine, no hair appointment for you. Remember, the Dry Bar is an excellent resource. Tracey just knows how to frame my face.

JUNE 5

10:15 A.M.

Theo starts his new job today, which would normally send me into a tailspin of self-comparison and anxiety about my own future, but *new me* is going to focus on being productive! I'm going to unpack all the remaining boxes in my room and get rid of anything superfluous. I told Mom about this endeavor, and she asked if I wanted an Adderall. I told her thanks, but that I'm boycotting the illegal purchasing of drugs from our hairdresser.

She said that I'm no fun.

JUNE 6

 Email

> **To:** **Lou Hansen**
> **From:** **Dr. Nathaniel E. Richmanson III, PHD.**
> **Subject:** **RE: Job Opportunity**

Miss Eloise—

First and foremost, I must congratulate you on the most thrilling accomplishment of graduating summa cum laude last month! Very, very exciting. Few students at Columbia are able to achieve such a high honor, and even fewer are able to make any use of it. After all, undergraduate accomplishments are rarely acknowledged outside the world of academia. In fact, many question whether students' efforts would be better spent developing practical and social skills rather than relentlessly chasing a high GPA.

That was a joke. Ha-ha.

Of course, I am not concerned about you in the slightest. You were easily one of my finest pupils, and I—unlike millennial parents and the liberal media—am not one to dish out false or undeserved praise. How many students would stay up for seventy-two consecutive hours and consume sixteen Red Bulls, all to complete their senior thesis a week in advance? That is the mark of a winner. I hope that you've been enjoying a well-deserved break from the madness, and that most of your hair has grown back.

That being said, I'm pleased to hear you're not taking too much time off this summer. After all, you're trapped in a perpetual summer now.

Ha-ha-ha.

Now, in response to your inquiry. The job opportunity I spoke to you about this past spring is at a start-up in Manhattan. The concept is a monthly subscription to a line of stylish high-end puppy clothing.

Let me elaborate.

Once a month, Manhattan's elite can expect designer-quality outfits for their precious pooches via the post. Though I myself would never shame an animal in such a manner, I know many Manhattanites who would undoubtedly stoop so low. Forgive me for saying so, but anyone who puts an article of clothing on their dog is the same sort of coddling, bleeding-heart communists who would hand out participation trophies to children and drink bastardized milk made from cashews. However, an old student of mine founded the start-up and has been looking to hire fellow Columbia grads.

I'd be happy to send along a recommendation if you would like.

Sending my warmest regards,
Dr. Nathaniel E. Richmanson III, PhD

12:10 P.M.

Excuse me as I set my hard-earned degree on fire.

PUPPY CLOTHING?! This must be some sick, twisted joke. Don't get me wrong—it's a cute start-up idea, and I'm sure there are plenty of Oberlin graduates that would absolutely love working there part-time while pursuing a passion in motion-blur photography. That sounds great! Wonderful! Sell those tiny Chanel hats!!

But not me. Certainly not me. I just don't understand! Dr. Richmanson is a universally respected voice in the academic community . . . he can't seriously think I'm THAT desperate.

. . . am I that desperate?

I called Theo in a fury, storming to the kitchen while still in my pj's.

"Yeeello?" I could hear the clanking of plates behind him. Oh, right: he's at work.

"So I heard back from Dr. Richmanson." I ripped open the fridge, searching for some sort of solace. Why is there never anything in the fridge?

Theo gasped. "And?!?" Excitement bubbled in his voice. Damn

him and his encouragement. I slammed the fridge shut and made my way to the pantry.

"Well, for one thing, it's for a new start-up in Manhattan." I scanned the pantry, fingering a box of stale flaxseed crackers before sulking back to the fridge.

"Oh, shoot—that's not ideal. Okay, well, what's the start-up? Did he tell you?" I opened the fridge again with lowered standards and settled on some almond butter.

"Oh yes, he told me. It's a monthly subscription to—get this—high-end puppy clothing."

The phone went silent except for the clamor of kitchenware. A whole thirty seconds passed before I heard his hesitant voice. "Okay, well, um . . . so it's not *exactly* in your field of interest—"

"I won the John Pakozdi Undergraduate Award for Outstanding Academic Achievement, Theo!" It came out louder and more hysterical than I meant it to. I scooped up almond butter with my index finger and plunged it into my mouth. "I will not sell booties to millionaire Pomeranians."

He chuckled at my mania. "All right, take a breath. Of course you won't! You are so much more capable than puppy PR."

"But here's the scary thing, Theo. What if I'm not? What if I peaked? What if being a student was the only thing I'll ever be great at??"

"Well then, you'll go to grad school and then law school and med school and collect diplomas and PhDs and student debt. Plenty of people do it! Just ask Saint Richmanson himself."

I chortled. Bless Theo's humor—dry and ruthless and exactly what I needed.

"Excuse me, I do *not* think he is a saint. He's completely boorish, but he's brilliant."

"And so are you, my lady. Brilliant, only without the boorishness and with the beauty."

I smiled in spite of myself. He's so good to me. Why is he so good to me? I should start being this good to me. Also, extra points for alliteration.

He went on, "I'm sorry, Louie-love. I know you're disappointed. But hey, think of it this way: you're one stupid, terrible job choice closer to finding your dream one. And selfishly, I'm very, very happy you're not moving back to New York!"

Sigh. Darling Theo. The most positive cynic I know. Where can I get that kind of disposition? I have to go back to yoga.

Lucky for me, Theo got off of work a bit early, so we're meeting in half an hour at Froyolo to celebrate his new job and my disappointment. Hey, who knows? If I'm lucky, maybe they're looking to hire!*

Mama Shell

1:45 P.M.

MS   SPOTTED!!!

MS   Just passed you walking down Ventura Blvd!

MS   Is that an ice cream I see you eating?? 💀

     Wait, what?! **Lou**

     Where did you see me? Where are you?? **Lou**

S   Stacey and I went to Bloomies to use my newly earned credit! Picked out a few little things: a scarf, some bracelets, a few pairs of shoes.

S   She's driving me home right now . . . you're busted with the frozen fat!

S   (PS: who's the serial killer?? Stacey called him Charlie Manson!)

---

*Kill me.

DISASTER. Complete, abject disaster.

First of all, I would like to point out that Theo bears *no* physical resemblance to Charles Manson whatsoever. His hair is a bit on the longer side and his teeth are slightly bucked, but other than that, there is nothing about him that suggests sadistic mass murderer in the slightest. It must have been the Nirvana shirt. Or maybe the yellow skinny jeans.

But more important: the absolute worst is happening. How is this possible? Mom hasn't even met Theo yet, and she's already shattering my perfect union. How on earth was I supposed to respond??

What serial killer, Mother? Oh! You mean the one who I've been emotionally and physically committed to for the past six months of my life? The person who I've been trying to tell you about for six months? The man who feeds me delicious carbs while you're not looking??

"Who? What, you mean Theo??" I frantically typed, waiting as that little ". . ." sign showed up, then disappeared, then reappeared, then disappeared again. Finally the message came:

Mom: Theo? You've never mentioned him . . . Is he a friend of Natasha's? I'm telling you—that girl keeps weird company.

Panic. White-hot panic.

Me: NOOOO he's just a friend from school! We took physics together!!

Lie. Total lie. Theo went to New York University and majored in environmental science with a double minor in biology and visual arts. We met when he catered a Columbia event (at which I was presented with the Larry Widenbaum Honor for Academic Integrity, I might add). I chased him around all night in hot pursuit of those chipotle-infused mini quesadillas, and even gave him a shout-out in my speech as "the closest thing I have to a date tonight." I accidentally knocked over the mic on my way offstage. We've been together ever since.

Mom: What a creeper. Is he safe to drive you home? Do you want me to come pick you up??

Code Red. SOS. DEFCON 5. RIP.

Me: Noooo, he's totally great!! Such a sweet guy. Could never hurt a fly.

I mean he COULD, if it came to a physical confrontation in which someone felt threatened, but he would never INITIATE violence.

Also he loves football.

And steak.

This was when the laughter started.

One appallingly miserable trait that I picked up from my mother is her nervous laughter—the kind reserved for the worst conceivable moments, like funerals or serious injuries or public displays of rage. It's not that I find any of these circumstances funny. This is just how my body chooses to handle uncontrollable nerves—very, very inappropriately.

Theo stopped dead in his tracks.

"Oh no. What happened? Who's hurt? Who died??"

I shoved my phone so deep into my pocket that I think I tore a hole. What was I supposed to tell him? That my mother and her best friend were gossiping on Ventura Boulevard about the gangly murderer trying to kill me via artisanal sweets?

"No!" I lied again. "No, nothing's wrong at all! I'm just remembering something that Val told me . . . yesterday . . ." I petered out pathetically. Jesus, I'm such a bad liar.

He crossed his arms and raised a bushy eyebrow. Dammit, he's so cute when he's dubious.

"Lou, you're manic laughing. And you've started fiddling with your rings."

I looked down and sure enough: there I was, ring fiddling. My hands flew to my hips in protest.

"No I'm not! Everything's fine! It's just about . . . Natasha. She's not feeling too well."

Poor Natasha—she is so under the metaphorical bus.

"Natasha? What's going on? Is she all right?"

"She'll be fine, she's just . . . you know . . . caught something in India. A bug of sorts."

The bushy brows knit together.

"She's sick? Is she okay? Did she see a doctor?"

It took all of my mental strength to keep from ring fiddling. Why, oh why was this happening??

"Oh yeah, she did, and he said it's all fine. It's just a minor case of . . . er . . . parasites."

PARASITES. Somehow the one thing I maintained from my subconscious hours of constant news cycling at home is that parasites are a problem for white people in India. So that's what I chose to give Natasha in my moment of desperation: motherfucking parasites.

Now Theo seemed legitimately worried. "Parasites?" he asked. "How'd she pick up parasites? Was it something that she ate?"

"Oh, of course your mind goes right to the food!" I joked, hoping to change the subject. But I had just given Natasha parasites. The subject was not being changed.

"Seriously, is she going to be okay? Parasites are nasty . . . What else did she tell you?"

Rings. Fiddling. Must. STOP.

"Nothing—nothing at all. She just said that she wasn't feeling good, that she went to see a doctor, and that she had a minor case of parasites. She's fine, not to worry, she'll be better in a couple of days."

I held my breath for what felt like an eternity. Finally the brows unknit.

"Well, all right," he conceded. "I'm not sure parasites come in minor cases, but as long as she says she's okay . . ."

"She is!!" I all but screamed, larynx choking on frantic giggles.

"She's positively, absolutely fine. I'm sorry if I worried you—just keep it between us, if you could. Tash asked me not to tell anyone."

Theo shrugged, shoving his hands in his pockets—his physical equivalent of a white flag.

"Sure, I'll keep it a secret. Just keep me updated, will you?"

I nodded hysterically, spooning a giant bite of cookie-dough froyo into my face to shut it up. The hole I'd dug was deep enough, but regardless, I had done it. I'd somehow lied well enough to keep Theo from knowing the unbearable truth: that my mother had just called him a serial killer, and that I had claimed he liked physics.

For him, I'm not sure which is worse.

9:25 P.M.

Still spinning from the horror show that was my day. Tried having some cayenne water to calm myself down. The spice made me cry, so I pulled out chocolate-covered espresso beans instead, which are technically still not the same as having coffee, so I'm in the clear.

1:52 A.M.

Somehow forgot how much stronger espresso beans are than coffee. Caffeine is biting me in the ass. I can't fall asleep. Still panicking. Have been lying in bed thinking of ways to untangle the Natasha-Theo-Parasitic-Murderer mess that I've woven. Lack of sleep is not helping the anxiety and is clouding my brain. (On the bright side, heart rate acceleration might help with cardio?) Googling how to handle panic attack.

2:14 A.M.

Google told me I'm having brain aneurysm. Can't fall asleep for fear that I'll never wake up. No wonder I've been so anxious. Oh god. I hate Google. I hate my brain. I hate India. Going to try posing like Wonder Woman.

2:35 A.M.

Decidedly not feeling like Wonder Woman. Maybe Wonder Woman post-kryptonite. Wait, no, that's Superman. Superman's weakness is kryptonite. Holy shit, I'm losing it. I have to wake up in less than five hours. This is how I die.

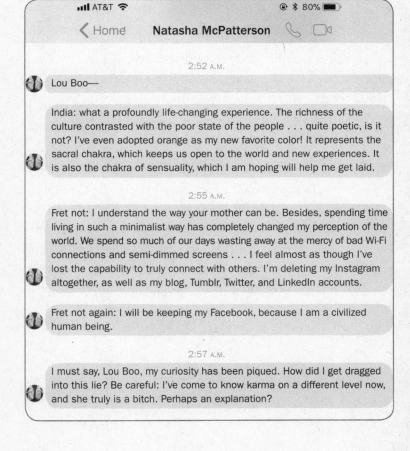

..ll AT&T 🛜   🔕 ✲ 80% 🔋

‹ Home   **Natasha McPatterson**   📞 📹

2:52 A.M.

Lou Boo—

India: what a profoundly life-changing experience. The richness of the culture contrasted with the poor state of the people . . . quite poetic, is it not? I've even adopted orange as my new favorite color! It represents the sacral chakra, which keeps us open to the world and new experiences. It is also the chakra of sensuality, which I am hoping will help me get laid.

2:55 A.M.

Fret not: I understand the way your mother can be. Besides, spending time living in such a minimalist way has completely changed my perception of the world. We spend so much of our days wasting away at the mercy of bad Wi-Fi connections and semi-dimmed screens . . . I feel almost as though I've lost the capability to truly connect with others. I'm deleting my Instagram altogether, as well as my blog, Tumblr, Twitter, and LinkedIn accounts.

Fret not again: I will be keeping my Facebook, because I am a civilized human being.

2:57 A.M.

I must say, Lou Boo, my curiosity has been piqued. How did I get dragged into this lie? Be careful: I've come to know karma on a different level now, and she truly is a bitch. Perhaps an explanation?

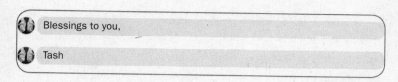

Blessings to you,

Tash

JUNE 7
10:45 A.M.

Waking up at 7:30 was simply not in the cards.

I finally fell asleep around 3:00 A.M., after Tash confirmed that she's boycotting most forms of social media. Since she's the only person I've ever met who's avoided becoming Facebook friends with my mother (suddenly grateful for Mom's lack of interest in Natasha's existence), at least one crisis has been averted for now. Not that it helps much. For the precious few hours I did sleep, I was haunted by visions of serial killer Theo, tormenting people with a paring knife and skillet.* Ugh ugh UGH. ☹

I can't tell Mom. Whatever hope I had for Theo's acceptance just died with the rest of Manson's victims. I suppose the only reasonable thing left to do is to start leading a double life, whereby I spend six months in LA and six in Italy or Spain or someplace where having hips is culturally accepted.**

10:48 A.M.

Oh boy. Mom just came in to check on me.

"Why are you still in bed?" she asked, arms already crossed, mug of sweet, sweet-smelling coffee in hand.

"Uh . . . I don't feel very well," I croaked, which was completely true. In fact, it was an understatement.

---

*This is ridiculous, since if Theo were a serial killer, I imagine he would use puzzles as his primary form of torment, a la the Riddler. Oh my god, how am I indulging this??
**Just so long as in one of these lives, I have a successful career.

"Oh no! What's wrong, sweetie?"

I shoved my face into a pillow and moaned. How could I possibly explain what was wrong?? I felt her hand snake under the cushion and land on my forehead—the all-knowing ther-MOM-eter.

"Well, you don't have a fever," she concluded, doubt rising in her voice.

"It's just a stomachache."

She nodded, suddenly understanding. "I'm telling you, it's that ice cream. Dairy gives you agita."

I sighed into the pillow before tossing it on the floor, just in time for Muffin to stroll in and pee on it.

"I'm okay, Mom. I just want to sleep in a little. Is that okay?"

She leaned over and kissed my forehead, both as a loving gesture and a secondary fever check. Once she seemed confident that I wasn't dying, she smiled and straightened back up.

"All right, well, let me know if you need anything. Oh! You know what will make you feel better? A nice cup of lemon-cayenne water!"

And with that, she ran out of the room—undoubtedly toward the kitchen spice rack.

I have to talk to Val. She's the only person who can conceivably help me through this mess. Who better to help me with Mom than Mini-Mom?

DRAT. I forget that she's back at school. Ugh, lucky bitch. I'd do anything for an essay to write. Or a history test to study for. Just anything to distract me from my actual life.

•   •   •

Val

12:15 P.M.

Hey, Val, when you get home from school, can I talk to you?   Lo

12:47 P.M.

 Val   Obvi. What's up?

> **Lou:** Ok . . . well, I really need your help with something. It's about Mom.

> **Val:** Omg. What did she do now? Did she drop ur glasses in the garbage disposal again?

> **Lou:** No, this is so much worse.

> **Lou:** I really messed up. In a big way, and I don't know how Mom's going to take it.

> **Lou:** You and Mom have a similar way of thinking. I need your advice. Can you help?

> **Val:** Girl, I'm on it. Be home around 3:30.

> **Lou:** THANK YOU!

> **Lou:** You're the GOAT!

> **Val:** . . . girl don't.

           ·   ·   ·

5:30 P.M.

Valentina Hansen started turning into Mini-Mama around age five, when she strutted into the living room wearing nothing but Christian Louboutins and pearls.* Val has since followed categorically in Mom's footsteps, making her both a perfect and an impossible child for Mom to raise. Watching them fight is like watching an aggravated cat scratch and hiss at a mirror for twenty minutes— amusing and terrifying all at once.

I heard the faint purr of Val's car roll up to the house at 3:20, and rushed outside to meet her. She'd barely opened the door before I grabbed her by the arm and started pulling.

"Let's go for a walk," I urged, all but dragging her out of the driveway. "We only have seven minutes before Mom gets suspicious and uses Find My Friends."

"Whoa, whoa, what's this about, babe? You've been acting totally weird . . . OW, you're hurting my selfie hand!"

---

*I once did a similar thing with Dad's boxers on my head.

I loosened my grip from her delicate wrist, and she rolled it around a few times.

"Sorry," I mumbled, looking over my shoulder to see if Mother Dearest was following.

"It's all good, just gotta take care of the moneymaker, you know? Now: what's up?"

I checked the street one last time before lowering my voice to a whisper. "Okay, so, I, um . . . all right, so this has to stay between us."

She rolled her eyes. "Lou, of course. What's going on? Did you, like, get a job stripping or something?"

That honestly felt like a better alternative. I waited until we rounded the corner before taking a deep breath. "No, I'm not stripping, I . . . well, I might, sort of, kind of . . . have a boyfriend?" I asked, as though it were a question.

Val's beautifully chiseled jaw hit the floor. "WHAT?!"

"SHHHHH."

"How long? Who is he? What's his name? Is he tall? Why didn't you tell me??"

The questions came faster than I could answer them. Wow, Val has NEVER been so interested in my life before. Huh . . . actually, it feels nice to finally be the center of intrigue. Maybe I should keep more secrets, and become a sexy mysterious free spirit type who hitchhikes to music festivals and sports an infinity tattoo.

"Okay, okay, calm down. His name is Theo, and—"

"Oh my god, *Theo*—that's a hot guy name. Theo. I like it. It's, like, quirky but fire at the same time."

I snorted.

"Well, emphasis is on the quirky."

She raised a sleek brow and crossed her arms, Mom-style.

"Hmmm . . . quirky, huh? What's his full name?"

"Theodore Greenberg."

With lightning-quick speed, Val whipped out her phone and typed his name into a search box. I gasped.

"WAIT, HOLD ON! He's not nearly as attractive in his pictures!!"

"Is this him? Theo underscore Green?"

She flipped her phone around, revealing Theo in a bright-green apron using two tongs as hands. That was it: we were exposed. I exhaled, preparing to fight for his honor.

"Yes, that's him, BUT I promise he's amazing and interesting and so clever and talented and absolutely adorable and—"

"Lou, what are you talking about? He's so cute!"

I froze midsentence, startled.

". . . wait, really?"

"Yes!! I mean, look at those eyes! DAMN, girl, those eyes! And he's a chef?? That's so sick!!"

She continued to scroll through Theo's Instagram as I gawked in bewilderment. Her eyes grew bigger as she continued her assessment: "Lou, this profile is on point. His food is, like, freaking artwork."

I nearly fainted.

"You think so?"

"Yes! I mean, look at these waffles! How did he do that? They're, like, melting off the plate."

I peeked over her shoulder and down at the phone screen.

"Oh, those were Salvador Dalí–inspired for my birthday."

Val covered her eyes with one hand. "Stop it. I'm shook."

". . . Is that a good thing?"

"DUH! Lou, he seems so cool! I totally approve."

SWEET, SWEET SISTER, VALENTINA BETH. If Val deems Theo cool, then it's a definitive truth. No argument can be made against it. It is law. Relief and something resembling pride flooded my entire body as I let my shoulders melt away from my ears. How could I have been so paranoid? He truly is so talented. And you know what? He really does have tremendous eyes. Like sapphires, or two shrunken versions of Neptune. Val put her phone back into her pocket and cocked her head in genuine confusion.

"Babe, what were you so nervous about?"

All at once, sheer embarrassment crept up into my face, turning my cheeks and ears bright red. I looked down at my feet and shoved my hands in my pockets.

"I don't know. I guess he wears a lot of plaid?"

"So? Come on, Lou, do you really think Mom is that shallow?"

I blinked a few times before realizing she was serious. I sighed again as we turned back toward the house and started walking. A full minute of contentment passed before I was reminded of the final and most treacherous obstacle.

"Um . . . Val? There is one more thing I haven't mentioned."

She rolled her eyes yet again and chuckled. "Um . . . yes?"

"Mom saw us getting froyo yesterday and called him a serial killer."

Val stopped walking and stared at me. It was her turn to decide if I was joking. The stoic look on my face made it clear that I wasn't.

". . . well, fuck."

JUNE 8

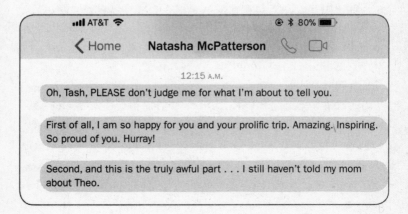

.ıll AT&T 🤏   ⊛ ⅄ 80% 🔋

‹ Home   **Natasha McPatterson**   📞 ▢

12:15 A.M.

Oh, Tash, PLEASE don't judge me for what I'm about to tell you.

First of all, I am so happy for you and your prolific trip. Amazing. Inspiring. So proud of you. Hurray!

Second, and this is the truly awful part . . . I still haven't told my mom about Theo.

I KNOW, I know: I'm the lowest human being to ever disgrace the species. I don't deserve progeny. I'm the actual worst.

But I swear, I was JUST ABOUT to tell her when she saw us walking on Ventura Boulevard eating froyo and she texted me that he was Charlie Manson and I panic-laughed and Theo asked about it, and then I told him you have parasites. PARASITES. I don't know why I did it. Oh god. WHAT IS WRONG WITH ME?!

12:20 A.M.

IF by some impossible chance Theo asks about your condition, PLEASE tell him that you are sick. I looked up some potential symptoms for parasites online, as to make your story more convincing. As someone infected with parasites, you would be experiencing the following:

Abdominal pain, nausea or vomiting, diarrhea, fatigue, stomach pain or tenderness, gas, or dysentery.

Much love from the States, Liar Lulu Hansen

8:45 P.M.

FINALLY! Some positive news to report!

After a day and a half of nonstop worrying, I get to spend a glorious night at Theo's apartment, away from the mounting pressures of living a total lie.* The Treehouse has started to take on a whimsical, rustic aesthetic, which is a giant improvement from the junkyard theme it was sporting earlier. There's a tiny succulent garden in the kitchen, as well as a sustainable herb pot (my touch). The mismatched pieces of furniture give it an eclectic, cultured vibe, and Theo's room could easily be the set of a Wes Anderson film.** Basically, it's a

---

*Mom thinks I'm sleeping over at Natasha's place for a girls' night, which is ridiculous, since Natasha will participate only in nongendered events.
**Big fan of the symmetry, as well as the bright color scheme and the small collection of vintage cameras.

Pinterest dream . . . even if the stovetop burners can only be lit with a match.

Anyway, it's positively wonderful being out of the house and with my boyfriend again. I feel like a real-life adult! I swear, for reasons unknown to psychologists, staying in one's childhood home causes a person to revert into an incompetent teenager, as though everything one learned in college and beyond about functioning has gone completely out the window, and one is somehow inhabited by the whiny ghost of one's inept, angst-ridden, sixteen-year-old self, unable to recall any of the life skills or good habits so carefully developed while one was living happily on one's own. Ugh.

BUT I refuse to focus on that. Tonight, I've been completely stress free, and I wish to keep it that way. Theo cooked us salmon with jasmine rice and some sort of honey mustard reduction, while Jett whipped up a quick chocolate-and-peanut-butter mouse, as though that were normal behavior. The two of them gossiped about their fellow caterers and "who's who" in the kitchen (Axl Blain should not be working hot food, while Kara Mayer is queen of the salad line) before Jett went to go smoke in his bedroom. Theo and I watched the History Channel, discussed the crisis in the Middle East, and will soon be solving crossword puzzles in bed . . . honestly, a perfect evening. I haven't felt this relaxed in ages! And I didn't even mind the marijuana smell radiating from Jett's bedroom. It smelled a little something like freedom.

I can't give up on Mom. As long as Val is on my side, I stand a chance against her judgment. Besides, it could be worse! At least Mom called him a serial killer, and not a librarian or a flamenco dancer or something. At least *killer* implies a certain level of manliness, right? Right??

JUNE 10

Mama Shell

2:15 P.M.

Hey, Mom, where are you? Lou

MS That depends. Are you with Dad?

No . . . ? Lou

MS Barney's.

3:45 P.M.

Today was the very best day! Why? you may ask. I'll tell you why! Today was the best day because today Val and Theo met for the first time, and not once did the earth open up and engulf me in raging red flames!

The whole operation was very covert: while Mom was out shopping at Barney's, Val and I requested Theo on FaceTime, using the pugs as a makeshift alarm system. I even opened Find My Friends as a backup and tracked Mom's coordinates to determine when she was on her way home. Hahaha! It works both ways, Mother!!

Theo was at work and wearing his hairnet, which makes him look a bit like a balding horse, but Val seemed to think it was interesting and, "like, so profesh." They discussed her social media presence, and how all restaurants need an Instagram-able item on the menu. The one *tiny* snafu happened halfway through the conversation, when Val took it upon herself to add yet another lie to the equation.

"Oh, *obvi* we've heard all about you, Theo!"

His pointy ears perked up. "Really? You have?"

Val gave out a slightly exaggerated "HA!" before going on. "Of course we have! Lou never stops talking. We'd love to have you over for dinner sometime . . . We hear you're, like, the best cook in town."

Theo couldn't contain his excitement. A giant lopsided grin stretched across his face, revealing his front bucked teeth.

"Hells yes, I would *love* to come over for dinner! What kind of dessert would your family like? Something dairy-free, I'm guessing? Oh, maybe a berry dish! I have so many ideas. I'll get to work ASAP!"

He was so earnest and happy that for a moment, I almost forgot that it was all a fabrication. I imagine him showing up at the door in a tweed vest and bow tie, berry dish in hand, with that goofy grin planted on his face.

"Hiya, Mr. and Mrs. Hansen! Thank you so much for having me over! I'm Theodore, the serial killer your daughter's in love with! Tell me, do you like locally sourced berries?"

At the end of the call, Val turned to me with a raised eyebrow and the tiniest smirk.

"Well??" I begged, desperate for some sort of validation. Finally the smirk turned into a full-on smile—hers a little more balanced than Theo's.

"Girl, he rocks. You have nothing to worry about. This will be, like, a piece of cake."

I threw my arms around her and hoisted her into the air, just in time for the pug alarm to start sounding. Mom poked her head into the living room, did a quick visual sweep for Dad, then ran swiftly into her bedroom with three stuffed shopping bags in each hand.

One Hansen down, two more to go.

JUNE 11

Mama Shell

6:15 P.M.

 MS   Honey, I want to talk to you about something.

Sure . . . what is it?   Lou

 MS   It's all okay, but I've been a little worried about you recently.

MS	You've let your roots grow out, you haven't been wearing any makeup, your nails are chipped
MS	And you've been snacking a lot after 9 p.m.
MS	I know you're going to start looking for jobs, but I just want to make sure you're not turning into a hippie.
MS	Maybe it's time to take a break from Natasha?

9:10 P.M.

Living under my mom's regime is starting to feel like some sort of parental GTMO. Everywhere I go, everything I do, Mom has something to say about it. I can't even walk out of my room without some sort of judgment being cast upon my very existence. Literally, no split end goes unnoticed.

"Did you brush your hair today?" "Are you going to wear those socks with those shoes?" "Did you see that Megan and her friends are in Europe?" "Didn't you already have two snacks today?" "Who are you meeting for lunch?" "What do their parents do?" "What's their social security number?" "Why isn't your Find My Friends tracker working??"

I recently reiterated my requests for (a) fewer parental remarks and (b) the removal of Find My Friends. However, Mom seems physically incapable of controlling her constant nagging and apparently needs to keep the tracker on me, "in case I'm abducted."

Ugh, I really have to get back on track if I want to move out within nine months. I went to yoga today in the hopes of clearing my mind, but unfortunately, instructor Pixie Harvest was replaced by Yogi Sergeant Terri, who apparently considers yoga a competitive sport.

"OH, COME ON, IT'S JUST FIFTY MORE SECONDS IN THAT HEADSTAND! MY GRANDMOTHER HAS A STRONGER CORE THAN YOU PEOPLE!! ARE YOU A WARRIOR OR JUST A DAMN CORPSE?!!!"

Anyway, it occurred to me during this class that Sergeant Terri has a job and I still do not, so I've decided I'm going to update my résumé tomorrow!

JUNE 15
10:15 P.M.

I still have not updated my résumé. Instead, I stayed in bed and watched YouTube videos about hoarders and their extraordinary obsessions for four straight hours. I have no idea how I got here.

Stacey, Susan, and Lisa came over for Bachelorette Night, finally forcing me to leave my bedroom at six. The ladies were dressed in matching red pumps, which is their alternative to the famous red hats.* I watched the TV in horror as the remaining contestants each professed their undying love to the Bachelorette, who would later invariably say to the camera/producers, "I don't knowwwwwwwww. Jeff is, like, so smart and so funny."

"Mark is, like, so smart and so funny."

"Brad is, like, SO smart and SO funny."**

After an hour of wreaking havoc on my brain cells, I was faced with the deplorable reality that I had spent an entire day doing nothing but watching YouTube and *The Bachelorette*. *Come on,* Lou! If these fifty-something ladies can find the chutzpah to leave the houses before noon in sexy red shoes, then you sure as hell should! Where is your work ethic? Your pride? You did NOT spend the past twelve years busting your ass to watch ditzy Pilates instructors eclipse your career by making out with random men and crying!!

Enough. I am a college graduate, dammit. Time to pose like Wonder Woman. Steve Jobs, Shonda Rhimes, Martha Stewart, *Me*.

---

*The Red Hat Society was a movement that emphasized "friendship and fun after fifty." The Red Hots have a similar message: "friendship and fun; age not disclosed."
**Susan has a hunch that she's going to choose Brad.

JUNE 16
9:30 P.M.

We have a brilliant idea.

After taking an emergency planning session disguised as a hike, Val and I have decided to use subtle intellectual manipulation to delicately influence Mom's opinion about my boyfriend. Basically, if Val can plant a few good seeds about Theo in Mom's mind, then we might just be able to eventually harvest a garden of love and acceptance. Like *Inception* or a weird form of gaslighting.

Luckily, Val was in a few Gap commercials as a child, so she'll do most of the convincing. My job is to play it cool and try to not laugh nervously.

I have a good feeling about this. If all goes well, my family will be having Theo over for dinner by this time next week! Maybe even earlier. Between Val's acting skills and my minor in psychology, there's no way this could go wrong!

JUNE 17

 Natasha McPatterson

— 😷 feeling sick

Dearest friends,

I initially refrained from speaking publicly about my current ailment, in the hopes of preventing unnecessary panic, but I've received messages from the universe indicating that it's time to be inclusive. Since arriving in the magnificent city of New Delhi, I've been suffering with parasites, and though the case is only minor, it is enough to cause me much discomfort and distress. Some of the symptoms I am experiencing

(continued)

include (but are not limited to) abdominal pain, nausea and vomiting, diarrhea, fatigue, stomach pain/tenderness, gas, and dysentery.

I am in the presence of a Reiki healer who is determined to return me to health, as well as a sound specialist and two midwives I met in the airport. Please send your best vibes. I look forward to reporting a full recovery.

32 , 3 😀, 4 😕

Alicia Marie: Oh honey!! Feel better soon!! <3

Chris Sterling: Gas AND dysentery? Damn.

11:45 P.M.

Everything is falling apart.

For reasons beyond my understanding, Tash decided to make her fake ailment PUBLIC, resulting in the concern of our entire graduating class. Not to mention Theo, who's highly troubled by the fact she's theoretically been inflicted for almost two whole weeks. UGH, she is easily the dumbest genius I have ever met. But instead of getting caught up in her foolishness, I decided to focus all my attention on tonight's master plan, which resulted in the following shit show:

Dad made us dinner, as he does most nights since Mom refuses to cook with butter, oil, spice, sauce, or anything else resembling flavor. We had grilled chicken breast with a cauliflower puree, which is supposed to be some sort of sick substitution for mashed potatoes. Val and I kept eyeing each other from across the table, like two CIA operatives secretly signaling in enemy territory. Mom occasionally would sneak chunks of chicken under the table to the pugs, who've made a habit of scratching our legs until we deliver the goods. Finally Val reached into her pocket and yanked her phone out, the way one might in a telenovela.

"Hold on—I have to check my Facebook!" she announced.

No one seemed to find this behavior odd, despite our "no phones at the table" policy. To be fair, I was the one who implemented this policy back in high school after reading a study about the significance of undisturbed family dinnertime . . . and I was also the only one who took it seriously. Val continued with her performance: "Oh, *wow*, look at this cute boy!"

Mom's head snapped to attention. "Who? What? Where??"

The wisp of a smile appeared on Val's lips as she shoved the phone up to Mom's face. Val was pleased with her own performance, and so far, I was, too.

"The one in this picture with Lou! Isn't he *so* hot? You know, in a hipster kind of way?"

Mom grabbed the phone and held it away from her, squinting to see clearly. A moment passed before recognition crossed her scrunched-up face.

"Wait, I know this guy. Lulu, isn't that the serial killer I saw walking with you the other day?"

I all but choked on my chicken. Dad looked up from his plate, confused.

Val jumped right back in, her volume a little too loud. "Serial killer?! No, not at all! He's just so *artsy*. He looks, like, *super* smart. Like socially conscious and stuff. Like Lou!"

Bless you, Valentina. You are the single greatest sister of all time. I will never correct your grammar or ask you to stop saying *like* inappropriately ever again.

Mom cackled. "Oh boy, are you going to turn hipster on me now? I swear, one of you has to bring me home an athlete, and I had my hopes high for you!"

I dropped my fork. Val face-palmed with two hands. The giggles were upon me in an instant, forcing me to feign a coughing fit to keep myself contained.

Dad butted in. "Shelly! What on earth are you teaching our children?"

Mom snorted and waved a hand.

"Come on, Charlie, I'm just kidding! They know I'm just kidding! Tell him, Lulu."

I stopped coughing for long enough to let out a sort of half grunt. Val shot me an apologetic look. Baguette continued scratching at my leg, completely oblivious to my agony. Oh god, the horror. The pure, familial horror! How could we underestimate Mother so terribly??

Dad shook his head, clearly upset with Mom's outrageously shallow declaration. *Go on! Let her have it, Charlie!*

"Whatever he looks like, he's clearly Lou's friend, and that should be enough. Hell, when I was her age living in Queens, half of my friends *were* serial killers, for Christ's sake."

I almost asked, but I didn't.

He kept on, "Not all of the kids' friends have to be supermodels, Shell. And besides, it's not like she's dating the guy. Right, Lou?"

The manic laughter that burst out of me was taken as confirmation.

Seriously considering my double life option, here. Maybe England? Thailand? The moon??

JUNE 18

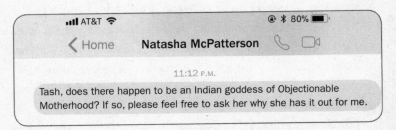

Tash, does there happen to be an Indian goddess of Objectionable Motherhood? If so, please feel free to ask her why she has it out for me.

> **11:14 P.M.**
>
> But more significant, PLEASE explain to me why it was a good idea to publicly give yourself parasites ten days after the initial incident? The world thinks you're sick, and Theo now thinks you're dying. What happened to karma being a bitch??
>
> **11:15 P.M.**
>
> Speaking of Theo, I really do want to hear your thoughts on my current crisis, since I'm very much on the verge of fleeing to Alaska and becoming a bush person. Unless you want to see me wrapped in layers of fur (and I KNOW you don't), please respond at your earliest convenience.

JUNE 19
2:20 P.M.

Since Mom is still in trouble for hiding her shopping receipts and espousing morally questionable ideals at the dinner table, Dad decided to take me on a much needed father-daughter brunch date. After arguing with the waiter for several minutes about whether his eggs were in fact properly over medium instead of over easy, he turned his full and undivided attention toward me.

"So. How've you been holding up?" he asked, hands laced together on his extended belly. At least I know whose metabolism I inherited.

"Um . . . I'm all right," I mumbled, twisting the silver band that decorated my index finger. "Actually, I've been better. Mom can be a bit . . . much." I don't know where the sudden dose of honesty came from, but it felt so good to say something true. Dad nodded knowingly and waited for me to go on, which for reasons unknown, I did.

"I just wish she would give me a little space; that's all. Or treat me even remotely like an adult."

His bottom lip pressed up into a frown. Oh no—the dreaded frown.

"Well, are you an adult?"

I paused, taken aback. Was this a trick question?

"That's what it says on my ID."

"No, it says you're twenty-two on your ID. Does that really make you an adult?"

I stared at him, baffled. What kind of question was that? Of course I was an adult! I AM an adult! I'm a college-graduated, twentysomething, 100 percent fully, completely, totally grown-ass woman adult! HUMPH!

"I mean, uh . . . yes?" was all I could muster. The corner of his mouth pressed down further, and I slumped deep into my chair. HUMPH again.

"Okay, fine. I believe you. Then what are you waiting for? Get a job. Find a place. Live your life. I know you're capable."

I opened my mouth to say something about the failing economy and housing market and my personal lack of direction, but the pressure of his parental gaze kept me silent. This man was missing part of a toe from the neighborhood gardening business he started at ten years old. Excuses were futile.

"I guess I don't know where to start."

Dad's frown softened a bit, turning into a thin line. "Start by getting a job. At least you'll be busy all day, and not sitting around like a goddamn worry target for your mother."

He made a good point. He always makes good points. For a moment, I entertained the idea of bringing up Theo, but then our waiter came back over with "two goddamn golf balls" for eggs, so I decided to keep quiet. Once our server had left with Dad's plate for a second time, I reached into my purse and pulled out my phone.

Twelve unread messages from Mom.

I groaned and slammed my phone on the table, pushing it toward Dad.

"Here, exhibit A."

Dad saw the litany of messages and sighed empathetically. YES. The defense rests.

"Look, I'll talk to your mother. I see that she's on your back a lot. But you have to step up, too. How's this: when you send out your first job application, I'll convince her to delete Find My Friends. Sound good?"

If there really is an Indian goddess of objectionable motherhood, there is also a god of reasonable, level-headed fatherhood, to whom I am deeply indebted. With my new assignment and restored hope, I left brunch a grown-ass woman adult on a mission.

•   •   •

Mama Shell

11:12 A.M.

MS   Hi

MS   Hi, Lulu

MS   Hey, honey

MS   Where did you and Dad go?

11:18 A.M.

MS   Why are you in West Hollywood?

11:20 A.M.

MS   Oh, you're at Agora Café! Great! Have fun 🖤

11:26 A.M.

MS   What are you eating?

11:30 A.M.

MS   Hello?

MS   What is Dad eating?

MS   Make sure he doesn't eat any bread, okay?

11:35 A.M.

MS   Call me

MS   Instagram your food so I can see it.

JUNE 20
9:30 A.M.

SHOOOOOOOOOOOOOOOTTTTT Mom brought me a cup of coffee this morning while I was still in bed and before I knew what I was doing I took a sip of it which isn't fair because you can't think about avoiding coffee before you've had a cup of coffee ughhhhhhhh anyway I figured the seal was broken so I had five more cups in a row since I'm going to quit again tomorrow and this might be the last time I have coffee ever and THERE'S SO MUCH I HAVE TO DO!!!

1:00 P.M.

Bathroom is clean. Sock drawer is organized. Résumé is finished. Pug shit discarded. I'M ON A ROLL, BABY! Bless coffee. Why did I ever give up coffee? Coffee is my goddamn blood type.

1:30 P.M.

I'm never drinking coffee again. Can't move my body. Nothing's in focus. Head feels like it's been trampled by elephants. UGH. Caffeine's a sickness. Caffeine's a disease. Who's the devil who discovered coffee, anyway??

1:35 P.M.

Just learned that Kaldi the Ethiopian goatherder discovered coffee. Ugh, damn you, Kaldi! Henceforth calling coffee *goat juice*. And I don't mean the "Greatest of All Time" juice. Hold on, Mom's calling for me.

1:40 P.M.

Mom just asked if she could die from eating three-day expired yogurt. I told her at the very worst, she might throw up. She proceeded to eat the rest of the yogurt.

9:15 P.M.

I have no idea what century I'm in. Passed out sometime around two. Mom just woke me up to make sure I wasn't dead. Told her about the goat juice. She said I should try Adderall instead.

ELOISE LAURENT HANSEN

<u>EDUCATION</u>

Columbia University

Both useful choices.

Majors: art history and philosophy with an emphasis on modern Western thought.

Minors: corporate strategy, psychology.

This would have been impossible, had I not convinced Natasha to attend and record certain classes for me to watch later.

- Top Ten Outstanding Senior Award Recipient
- John Pakozdi Undergraduate Award for Outstanding Academic Achievement
- Larry Widenbaum Honor for Scholarly Integrity
- Dean's Merit Honor Scholarship Recipient

Every semester, mind you.

<u>WORK EXPERIENCE</u>

TIME WARNER | Assistant Strategist

- Facilitated and participated in the brainstorm and implementation of comprehensive company strategy.

This means nothing. This is barely a sentence.

- Analyzed and determined strategic opportunities for growth through data and trend research.

This is the time I fell asleep at my desk.

J. PAUL GETTY MUSEUM | Cultural Coordinator and Curator

- Assisted with museum planning, as well as Getty exhibit management.

Made sure little kids didn't try to touch the Picassos.

- Wrote comprehensive profiles of various artists for permanent exhibitions in the museum.

  I wrote the little beige squares that pretentious people stare and nod at.

- Provided administrative support and assistant duties including covering phones, scheduling and organizing meetings, and arranging for shipments and messengers.

  Bitch work.

ENVIRONMENTAL PROTECTION AGENCY | Intern

- Made comprehensive reform to the environmental protection policy within the program's community.

  I put recycling bins in all the bathrooms.

- Provided full-time members of the EPA with tools necessary to make an environmental impact.

  Bought coffee

<u>INVOLVEMENT</u>

- Art History and Culture Club—President
- Kappa Delta Kappa—Standards Chair
- Environmental Protection Club—Vice President and Outreach Coordinator
- Young Philosophers Alliance (YPA)—Active Member/Contributor
- *Columbia Daily Spectator*—Contributor/Cultural Columnist
- Political Advocates of Columbia—Active Member

<u>SKILLS</u>

- Microsoft Office: Word, Excel, PowerPoint, Outlook
- Adobe Photoshop and Premiere

  Thanks to Mother.

- Strategy development and competitive analysis
- Superior editing and proofreading
- Demonstrates leadership
- Task management
- Collaborative; works well with others

Honorable mentions include:

- *Being the most awkward dancer in your mother's Zumba class.*
- *Eating an entire bowl of mozzarella sticks and not throwing up.*
- *Holding the top five solitaire scores on Delta Air Lines for two years running (my record is 38 seconds).*

JUNE 21

2:43 P.M.

Lou-Bou-Digeridoo, I'm so sorry for the late response and for your current distress. Have you visited the healer I told you about? She lives at an artists' community in Venice, in the most adorable little bungalow. You'll love it! Her living room is decorated solely with 100% recycled materials and/or items found on the street.

I also encourage you to keep an open heart and perspective. My status, of course, was written with the purest of intentions! I was only trying to add a layer of believability to your story, since you are such a gloriously open book/terrible liar.

2:51 P.M.

As for the situation with Theo . . . I'm conflicted. On the one hand, I understand trying to protect your relationship from any unnecessary darkness, but you also must have faith that your love will endure. Your mother is a wise woman—odd as she may be—and her love for you will surely outweigh any concern she has about him. As long as he's good to you, she'll return the goodness. Such is a mother's nature, in all animals except polar bears, who often eat their young.

Regarding the serial-killer comment: it's my understanding that many sociopathic killers are often quite charming. Perhaps she meant to invoke that comparison? Remember: open perspective!

Love to you always, Me.

2:56 P.M.

PS: there is no goddess of objectionable motherhood, but I'd suggest burning sage in all the corners of your bedroom, or wearing amethyst.

2:58 P.M.

PPS: if you're going to flee to Alaska, please feel free to contact my cousin Mason, who lives there now with his wife. It's a beautiful place, and I highly recommend doing shrooms there, but if you're looking for something more permanent, might I suggest a state that isn't melting?

JUNE 22
11:50 A.M.

After taking a few days to lick our wounds, Val and I have come up with an alternative approach, called Operation Suck It Up and Suck It In.

Here's our logic: we figure the happier Mom is with me, the better she'll receive any unexpected news. When is Mom happy with me? When I'm losing weight, of course! Ipso facto, if I lose the seven pounds that Mom is constantly nagging me about, she'll be happy enough with me to accept the fact I've been harboring a secret boyfriend for more than half a year. Boom. Foolproof.

1:15 P.M.

Just mentioned my new weight-loss goal to Mom, who almost threw herself to the floor in mania.

"OH, HONEY! I'm so proud of you!! This is so exciting . . . You're already so beautiful, of course, but a good five to seven pounds and you'll be a Victoria's Secret Angel! I'm going to buy you a whole new wardrobe. Trust me, once you take off that inner thigh, you'll be *begging* me to take you shopping. Let me get the protein powder!"

Though I'm certain no amount of weight loss or sorcery could turn me into a Vickie Secret Angel, her enthusiasm is good news for Theo. Speaking of Theo—despite working there for only two and a half weeks, he is already getting noticed by the higher-ups at Farmhouse. The head of the LA branch (aka his boss) recently complimented him on his unique vision for food, before saying she'd "keep an eye on his work." Not only is he making a great professional impression, but his new nickname around the kitchen is apparently "Hot-Food Hottie" . . . a fact that would bother me, were it not excellent leverage to be used against Mother later.

JUNE 25

Update: I've decided that goat juice is a necessary evil if I'm going to lose any weight. It was a tough decision and took a lot of deliberating, but ultimately, it's just too much to give up gluten, dairy, sugar, AND caffeine without surely collapsing into a state of catatonia. Don't we all deserve a vice? And anyway, a little caffeine kick-starts the metabolism . . . or at least that's what "they" tell my mom.

FOOD JOURNAL

- Breakfast: 2 eggs, 2 pieces of turkey bacon, 1 piece gluten-free toast, goat juice with sugar/dairy-free cream—380 calories (good)
- Snack: Celery—negative calories (more calories burned digesting celery than are in celery)
- Lunch: Salad with grilled chicken, cucumbers, tomatoes, onions, and goddess dressing—400 calories
- Snack: A scoop of organic almond butter—90 calories
- Snack: Another scoop of organic almond butter—90 calories
- Snack: A finger dip's worth of organic almond butter—approx. 50 calories (it's healthy fat!)
- Dinner: Turkey burger with gluten-free bun, lettuce, onion, pickle (good for digestion), ketchup (considered a vegetable by the US Congress), and sweet potato fries (much better than the usual russet potato fries)—600 calories (okay, b/c I burned calories earlier with celery)

- *Dessert: Piece of chocolate (had great day, so I deserve it)—a piece of chocolate is 155 calories?? Seriously?? That can't be right... I'll just say 100.*

Total calories: approximately 1,700.
Notes: A good start! This isn't so hard at all!

JUNE 27

missmeganmitchell
Paris, France
...

452 likes
missmeganmitchell Bonjour, Paris!
Merci for the time of my life 🌍
#travel #fun #wanderlust #Europe
#besttrip #notallwhowanderarelost

JUNE 28

Alberto (H.E.L.P.)

1:17 P.M.

SOS, Al. — Lou

Al — Yes?

Mom can't figure out how to turn the fire alarm off. — Lou

Al — . . . Why is the fire alarm on?

She tried to cook a petite filet without using oil and it was a disaster. — Lou

Al — Did you open all of the doors?

Yes, of course. — Lou

Al — Use a rag to fan the alarm system until it stops.

1:19 P.M.

It worked! That's such a great trick! — Lou

Al — Yup. Smoked a lot of weed in college.

. . . Wait, what? — Lou

JUNE 29

10:15 A.M.

One week into my health and fitness binge and I've gained exactly half a pound.

I don't understand what I'm doing wrong! I've been exercising, I've been writing down everything I eat. Maybe my body is holding on to its fat because it instinctually knows we're going into the cold season? Wake up, body! This is Los Angeles! There is no cold season!!

However . . . it IS possible that I've just been gaining muscle, which of course weighs five times more than blubbery fat. Yes, that's definitely it. All of my days with Sergeant Terri are turning me into a muscular body builder type. Any day now, my jeans will start falling off me.

Anyway, June is almost over, so I'm taking a quick inventory of my progress thus far. In terms of goals—

Good news: I finally found my label maker! Turns out Mom mistook it for a food scale, so it was in a kitchen drawer this whole time.

Bad news: my average wake-up time is 9:45, I have no leads on an apartment or a job, and I'm compulsively lying to my parents.

Two steps forward, one step back.

I'm spending the night at Theo's again, and Mom is starting to become skeptical. When I told her I was sleeping at Natasha's for the third time this week, she crossed her arms and narrowed her eyelash extensions at me. "Jeez, you guys are like teenagers. At least tell me you paint your nails or something. And I mean a color *other* than black."

Anyway, I want to spend the night at Theo's because he and Jett are leaving on a California road trip! They're spending Fourth of July weekend with Jett's family up north in the Bay Area, which will be a much-needed break from work for them. Also a much-needed break from sneaking around for me.

PS: Recently learned that Alberto was a stoner in college?? Huh. You think you know a guy.

Month Three

Codependence Day

Ahhh, July! The glorious month in which America fought valiantly against British forces to establish its independence! A concept I deeply relate to: revolutionaries desperately fighting for freedom from a looming mother nation, which is taxing the hell out of their tea/my sanity.

Theo is having a marvelous time up north, enhanced by the fact that he's staying in a twenty-million-dollar estate in Palo Alto. As it turns out, Jett's family is ridiculously wealthy because his mom is the creator/CEO of some beauty enhancement app for smartphones. Theoretically, it's supposed to remove any lines or blemishes from a client's face, making them appear flawless and youthful in their precious Instagram pictures. In reality, this app makes you look like an airbrushed alien, and I highly discourage its usage.

Anyway, while Theo has been taking private helicopter tours of San Francisco, I've been busy organizing the annual Hansen Fourth of July Barbecue: a task that's done miracles for my deteriorating psyche. I love having an assignment of any kind . . . even if it means dealing with Party Planner Mama Shell.

No one in this world can throw a bash quite like my mother, who's convinced she missed her calling as an event coordinator.* Every year she goes completely overboard by booking a full staff and bringing in tables, chairs, decorations, heating lamps, and even party favors. This year, however, Mom has kindly (and questionably) decided to save money by arranging the whole barbecue without the help of professionals, appointing me as her second-in-command.

Surprisingly, organizing events is my favorite activity to do with Mom. It employs both of our hobbies and strengths: she gets to be

*Other missed callings include actress, hand model, sorority house mom, dog walker, personal stylist, personal shopper, spiritual counselor, and a rosé-specific sommelier.

social and to beautify the house, while I get to create structure and make extensive lists. It's a win-win for all involved, except for Dad, who still has to pay for it.

GUEST LIST

- Shelly and Charlie Hansen
- Stacey and Buck Hoffman
- Susan, Simon, ~~and daughter~~
  (Apparently, Mia is now in college and is spending the summer abroad in Madrid. Isn't she, like, twelve??)
- Lisa and the Viking twins
  (a dreadful set . . . must find ways to keep them contained)
- Val and rest of the "Swaggin' Six"
  (can't remember their names on account of them all being the same person)
- Rosa, Marco, and the Adorable Seven Dwarves
- Alberto and Aubrey Rodriguez
- Me

JULY 2
3:12 P.M.

This weekend is shaping up beautifully!

Mom bought these gorgeous red, white, and blue centerpieces, as well as recyclable plates and utensils, cute little mason jars for drinking glasses, and long-lasting multicolored sparklers for the guests. She also got twinkle lights to hang above the porch, brand-new white tablecloths with silver runners and candles, a giant pool swan for no apparent reason, and an American flag scarf to wear for the occasion.

She also purchased patriot-themed dog collars that play the national anthem whenever the pugs shake their heads.

Meanwhile, I went grocery shopping for all the necessities: burgers, turkey burgers, veggie burgers, hot dogs, kosher dogs, vegan dogs, buns, gluten-free buns, flaxseed buns, cheese, vegan cheese, condiments, sugar-free condiments, chips, baked chips, gluten-free baked unsalted chips, soda, diet soda, all-natural sugarcane soda, sparkling water with hints of fruit to make it taste like soda, and salads.

Oh, and ten bottles of rosé.

In preparation for Lisa's twins, I bought two Nerf blasters and a first-aid kit, just in case they try to bring their BB guns again. I imagine the Swaggin' Six will probably spend the entire party on their cell phones, so I bought little party hats and cutout signs for potential Instagram pictures. I even bought a new Captain America shirt for myself, and a giant cutout of Lady Liberty wearing sunglasses.

There is nothing we're not prepared for.

JULY 4
4:00 P.M.

THREE CHEERS FOR THE RED, WHITE AND BLUEEEE!!!

Almost time for the big party!! I've been decorating the house since eight this morning. The tables are set, with the centerpieces out on display, the candles have been lit and strategically placed for enhanced lighting, the twinkle lights have been hung, the swan has been inflated, and the snacks are on the buffet table with plates, napkins, and utensils. Nerf guns: check. Photo station: check. New Captain America shirt: check.

The guests should be arriving in one hour! Hold on, Mom needs me to turn the music on.

Mom isn't letting me wear the Captain America shirt. According to her, "This is a house party, not Comic-Con," which is very unfair since seventeen-year-old Val is wearing a shirt that says *Political Party*, with the Founding Fathers playing beer pong on it. Whatever. I'm not going to waste time arguing. Instead, I'll wear a blue-and-white-striped T-shirt with jeans. This should be fine.

4:20 P.M.

Mom doesn't think the shirt is flattering. Horizontal stripes "accentuate the wrong areas." Changing into a white tank top with a red scarf.

4:25 P.M.

Apparently I wore the tank top and red scarf last year. Who would even notice?? Somehow Mom remembers every outfit I've ever put on my body, but she can't remember how to turn the house music on. I am settling on a red shirt, blue jeans, and white Converse. That is my final offer. SHOOT. Only half an hour before the guests arrive! I'm going to put the drinks out.

4:30 P.M.

Oh god, somehow the pugs got onto the table and ate all the chips and guacamole. UGH. Where is Val?! She's supposed to be on pug surveillance!! Dammit, I'll be right back. Have to run to the store and buy more.

4:45 P.M.

Okay, I got the chips but somehow the store was OUT of guacamole, so I have to make the entire thing from scratch in less than fifteen minutes. Why, WHYYYY is this happening?? Checking Pinterest for good guacamole recipes.

4:47 P.M.

Why are all the recipes on Pinterest so weird?! Guacamole with cubed eggplant, grilled cheese bacon and guacamole, triple-layer guacamole with Reishi extract and matcha powder . . .

FINALLY. Basic guacamole. Let's go.

5:00 P.M.

The guac has been made, and it's absolutely delicious, I'll have you know. Pinterest always has the best recipes. I'm so happy with my culinary prowess. Theo would be proud!

Okay, I'm keeping ALL chairs away from the buffet table, to avoid another dog debacle. The guests should be showing up any minute now!

5:15 P.M.

Fifteen minutes past five and still no guests. Had I known people would be running so late, I'd have taken my sweet time whipping together this delicious homemade Mexican treat for American Independence Day, instead of recklessly throwing ingredients together like a contestant on *Chopped.** Humph.

---

*This is easily the best show on television, according to Theo. It's his secret dream to one day be a *Chopped* champion.

OH! The doorbell! Someone is here!! All right, here we go . . . let the festivities begin!

7:10 P.M.

So far, so great!!

The Red Hots were the first to show up, carrying various kinds of store-bought treats. The only exception was Lisa, who made a feta watermelon salad that tasted like mushy salt. But bless her for trying.

Dad was thrilled to see Buck and Simon, who were kind enough to bring beer instead of rosé. The Viking twins made a beeline for the Nerf guns and ran straight outside to abuse each other in peace.

It was SO nice to see Rosa and her family, even though they could only stop by for an hour or so to say *hola*. Apparently, Rosa's supposed "family emergency" was actually her niece's quinceañera, which Mom mistook for some sort of disease. After explaining to her that it's a cultural celebration not dissimilar to a bat mitzvah, Mom gasped and exclaimed, "OH! *COMO SE DICE* 'MAZEL TOV'??"

Al and his wife, Aubrey, show up a bit later, and to my shock, they were on a Harley-Davidson. Admittedly, my relationship to Alberto has mostly been limited to frantic text messages and emails, but the vision of him in my head does not wear a fringed leather jacket. Maybe a nice button-down shirt, or a cape?

Regardless, I have wonderful news!! Lisa is giving me the contact into of her friend Tyler Jacoby, who works for a prominent public relations agency in West Hollywood. All of the ladies agreed that I'd be fantastic in PR . . . though anything with the word *public* does not sound too promising. Regardless, this would be an amazing job opportunity, and I'd be working with the best and brightest in the business. What else could I possibly ask for?? I'll email him this week!

The Swaggin' Six are all taking Snapchats and sending them to one another in the backyard with the little hats I purchased. Dad is cooking some seriously delicious burgers on the grill, and Mom can't stop me from eating any of it. Yippee!! I love this holiday!!!

7:45 P.M.

. . . That was terribly uncomfortable.

A few drinks in, Susan called me over to where the Red Hots were congregated, gossiping about something that was clearly me. When I got there, Susan brought me into the circle and draped an arm over my shoulders, holding me hostage.

"Lulu, I completely forgot to mention! My nephew is coming into town soon, and he is such a doll. Twenty-seven. Tall. A doctor. Oh! And I hear he's going to be on one of those medical reality shows!!"

I felt the whole group staring at me.

"Oh! Well . . . no kidding!" I said in my best excited voice. Susan nodded proudly.

"I know, he's *very* impressive. I'm telling you, he's a total catch!"

Seeing as "I secretly have a boyfriend" was not a usable excuse, I was forced to scroll through the many Facebook profile pictures of Aaron Levin, nodding and smiling at Susan in artificial interest. After a solid minute of mimed enthusiasm, I excused myself to go to the ladies' room, but Susan caught my arm before I was able to make my escape.

"Would you mind if I gave him your number? He doesn't know anyone in Los Angeles, and I'm telling you, Lou, he's so cute!"

I racked my brain for potential excuses, looking around at the circle of excited ladies around me—Mom included. Finally, I was forced to agree before running away to the kitchen, where I stuffed my face with more Pinterest guacamole and another glass of sparkly pink wine.

Why? Why, Lord? Why must everything go to hell in a handbasket??

As it turns out, vegan cheese isn't necessarily SOY free, which caused Lisa to break out into psychosomatic hives.

"Am I blotchy??" she'd ask every five minutes.

"You look fine, Lisa," I'd reassure her.

"No, I think I'm blotchy. My nutritionist tells me my soy sensitivity is off the chart. Are my lips puffy at least? Somebody get me a Benadryl!"

I went to the bathroom to get her some drugs, only to find three of the Swaggin' Six locked inside, sneaking sips of rosé. Instead of reprimanding them for the underage drinking, I grabbed each of their cups and gulped down the remnants in order to deal with Susan's doctor nephew, who was now making his way into every conversation.

"You know, my nephew is environmentally conscious, too." "Did you hear that Susan's nephew graduated from Penn?" "I heard Susan's nephew's television show is going to be a hit!"

By the time I came back out with two Benadryl in hand, a tipsy Stacey had bumped into Val, sending her precious cell phone flying into the pool. Without missing a beat, Val dove headfirst in to save it, cradling it in her arms as she rushed out of the water and into the house, soaking wet. "HELP! HELP! SOMEBODY GET ME SOME RICE!!!"

Meanwhile, the Viking twins had tied all of the sparklers together with lit matches and shot them out of the Nerf guns—all of which landed in the rosebushes and started a small fire. Without a change of expression, Alberto emptied his mixed drink onto the grass, lightly jogged over to the pool, filled his mason jar with water, and calmly poured it over the tiny flame, extinguishing it faster than it started. I would normally be amazed, but Alberto makes a living putting out various Hansen fires, so I suppose he was only doing his job.

Is there more to drink? Did the kids take the last of it? I'm sure there must be something in the liquor cabinet. Let's see what's in the liquor cabinet.

11:30 P.M.

Mmmffffd thiss was a ggrreeaattt party!!! Sndonno why I was sooo uptigghtt. Thrs sooo mch alccohols in the cabbnets hahaha yes. I shoddd prolly go to shleepp I'm ttiiiirreds. Haappttyty forrh og Julyyyy, bitfchessss!!!! <3<3<3<3<3

JULY 5

Theo 🩶

8:15 A.M.

Th | Well, good morning to you, too!

Th | Were you drunk last night?

??? How did you know that?? | Lou

Th | You left me a voicemail at 3:30 in the morning saying, "Fuck Aaron Levin! I love you smmmuchhh!!"

. . . | Lou

I'm never drinking again. | Lou

JULY 6

 Email

TO: **Tyler Brian Jacoby**
From: **Lou Hansen**
Subject: **Introduction**

Mr. Jacoby,

First of all, I hope you had a wonderful Fourth of July weekend filled with family, friends, and plenty of food! Second, I'd like to formally/virtually introduce myself. My name is Lou Hansen, and I'm a recent graduate of Columbia University. I'm also a close family friend of Lisa Van Williams, who was kind enough to pass along your information.

As Lisa will tell you, I've always been fascinated by the world of public relations, and have been looking at different companies that I might consider applying to. As someone who is also deeply committed to health and fitness, Holistic Public was a natural choice, since it's easily the best health-food PR firm in North America. If you're willing, I would love to meet with you to learn more about your work, as well as the company that you work for.

Thank you for your time, and I hope to hear from you soon!

Best,
Lou Hansen

1:40 P.M.

If I'm going to meet with Tyler Jacoby at Holistic Public to discuss my apparent deep commitment to fitness, I better get back on the health horse. My regimen was completely blown over the Fourth of July weekend . . . but to be fair, holidays don't count as cheating, and the plate of cookies I managed to eat were both gluten-free and vegan, which has to count for something.

Speaking of food: Theo comes back from the Bay Area tonight, so I'm going over to the Treehouse for road-trip stories! Apparently Jett's mother loved Theo so much, she gave him an Apple Watch—just for the hell of it—as well as a free subscription to her beauty app.* How crazy is that?! Now if only my own mother would love him enough to just accept his very existence. Ugh.

---

*I'd like to be this rich someday. Rich enough where I can give virtual strangers Apple Watches without thinking twice. I'd add this to my list of long-term goals, but I should probably focus on finding a paying job first.

This is ridiculous. I have to tell Mom by the end of this month. Natasha is right—it's silly to spend all of this time terrified of her disapproval. And why? Because it might burst my little happy relationship bubble? Pshh! That bubble was popped long ago with the serial-killer comment. And besides, if I love him, then she'll love him, too.

. . . that being said, I doubt losing a little weight will hurt my cause.

FOOD JOURNAL

- Breakfast—Oatmeal with walnuts, honey, and apple slices (perfect).
- Snack—2 bags of Skinny Pop popcorn (okay, because it's skinny.)
- Lunch—Turkey burger with only half the bun, side salad instead of fries (excellent)
- Snack—Celery with garlic hummus (celery negative calorie effect should counteract the hummus)
- Dinner—Veggie and brown rice stir-fry with low-sodium soy sauce (thank you, Theo).
- Dessert—Skinny Cow ice cream bar (once again: "skinny")

Notes: I've decided that counting calories is both a dangerous and ineffectual way of losing weight, so I'm going to try "listening to my body" instead. As of today, my body is telling me that Skinny Cow is a sad excuse for ice cream. Blegh.

Another day, another existential crisis.

I spent all morning and afternoon with Mother . . . again. Unless I'm spending the night at Theo's or working out with Val, I am pretty much always in Mom's company, which is making it increasingly difficult to stay rational. Wow, Mom was never this crazy while I was growing up. I mean, she was always a bit unusual; after all, she did have me on my first apple juice cleanse at age ten. But she was also dedicated to pickups and drop-offs, science fairs and choir rehearsals . . . even "twice-a-year temple," as our rabbi affectionately put it. Sure, she has always been a helicopter parent, but now she's more like a party chopper with a neon searchlight on me at all times.

Even my sister has noticed the difference. Ever since Val started applying to college, Mom's insanity level went from a 6 to a 15.5, and has only gotten worse from there. Luckily for us, we have Dad, who is a perfectly normal and rational person.

What am I even saying?? Of course he isn't! I once heard a rumor around my elementary school that Dad could build a house using nothing but super glue and a thumb tack. It was also rumored at some point that he marinated steak with the tears of his real estate enemies. When I asked him about this, he reassured me that the rumor was ridiculous, and that it was with blood, not tears.

I really need a job. Dad's right: living at home would be a lot easier if I had somewhere to go every day. In the meanwhile, I suppose I'll focus on getting fit . . . That way, if nothing else, she'll have one less reason to nag me.

missmeganmitchell
Capri, Italy   ...

530 likes

missmeganmitchell Ciao Bella!
The Kappa Ladies send you all love
from Italia! ☀️🙏 #amazing
#vacation #girlstrip #postgrad
#eurotrip #food #friends #life
#beauty #blessed

JULY 10

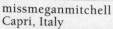

📎 **Email**

From: **Tyler Brian Jacoby**

To: **Lou Hansen**

Subject: **RE: Introduction**

Hi there, hun—

So glad to hear from you and your talented self. Columbia, huh? What a
spectacular school! Me? I never went to college, but the university of life
will teach you quite a bit, let me tell ya! ;)

Lisa, Lisa, Lisa . . . she is such a riot, isn't she? Of course she is! Get
this: Lisa told me to expect an email from you an *entire day* after I'd

already received yours. Says something about you, doesn't it? Clearly
ahead of the game, li'l missy!

Fabulous that you want to come join us here at Holistic Public. Would
love to chitchat. How does coffee sound? A little conversation over cold
brew? I can tell you a bit about our company, our vision, and your
potential place in our fam bam . . . so long as you're not too good for us,
Miss Columbia Grad. ;)

Does July 17 work for you? At Bud and Bean. Let me know!

Ciao,
Tyler B. Jacoby

Associate at Holistic Public, PR
Health—Happiness—Holistic

                                                              3:15 P.M.

I GOT AN INTERVIEW! I GOT AN INTERVIEW! I GOT AN INTER-
VIEW! I GOT AN INTERVIEW!!!!

Well, it's actually just coffee, but IT MIGHT AS WELL BE AN
INTERVIEW!!!

Take THAT, Megan and your Parisian Instagrams! Next week, the
seventeenth, I'll be meeting with Tyler B at Bud and Bean (never heard
of it!) to discuss work possibilities. OH, GOODNESS, THIS IS SO
EXCITING!! Time to do some research. The more I know about
Holistic Public, the better I seem to my potential employers.

I'm back, baby!

JULY 12

5:20 P.M.

Things I now know about Holistic Public:

- The PR firm specializes in health-oriented food products.
- They are frequently mentioned by various blogs and health gurus, including a coveted shout-out from Gwyneth Paltrow.
- Holistic's CEO, Phoebe Rietz, is an ex-model, and though she does not have a degree in nutrition, she is responsible for most of the fitness fads of the past decade.
- Holistic was once sued for claiming that their client's turmeric products cure cancer. However, they won the case, arguing that "can cure cancer" doesn't mean "will cure cancer."
- As an employee, I would receive free food products from the companies they represent (score).
- Skills desired as a potential employee: a degree in communications or PR (drat), experience in brand relations (check), strong writing skills and good grammar (YESSSS!), and a love for the world of fitness (sure).
- Key phrases to know:
  - Activate your potential.
  - Flush out toxins.
  - Radiate.
  - Glow.

JULY 15

5:41 P.M.

I need more friends.

Mom is going to Red Hot Mah-jongg Night at Stacey's, Theo and Jett are grabbing drinks after work with a few catering buddies,

Megan is wasted somewhere in Europe with her sorority sisters 4lyf, and Natasha has probably started a local meditation circle in an abandoned warehouse in New Delhi . . . all of which is making me nostalgic for the days when I too talked to other human beings.

I miss college, where being social required no more than stepping outside my dorm room and walking half a block. Now, all my friends are either on the East Coast or going to graduate school, leaving me a completely isolated introvert in La-La Land.* This is pretty much the equivalent of dropping a blind person in the Sahara and asking him to find water.

Ugh, I am so bad at initiating contact. It makes me feel so desperate and sad. Why can't more people just reach out to *me*? It's really not that hard!!

. . . Unless I have to do it. Then it's really hard.

All right. Officially replacing "clear out closet" with "make new friends" on my list of short-term goals.

JULY 16

Mama Shell

2:15 P.M.

MS Have you picked out your outfit for your interview tomorrow?

I was just going to wear my black slacks and white blouse. Lo

MS . . . No. Just no.

MS When you get back from Natasha's, we're going into my closet and putting together an outfit.

Mom, I can't really fit in your clothes . . . Lo

MS You're going to have to try. Didn't Megan once buy you Spanx??

---

*Unless, of course, you count people from high school, which I do not, because they've seen and know too much.

JULY 17
4:15 P.M.

That went . . . er . . . well?

As it turns out, Bud and Bean is a coffee shop/weed dispensary that Tyler often frequents. He frequents it so often, it would appear, that the barista knew both his coffee and cannabis orders: a black Ethiopian cold brew, and something called "Girl Scout Cookies."

Tyler was alarmingly handsome for a PR person. Had I seen him on the street, I definitely would have taken him for an actor or a model or personal trainer or something. But I guess that's everybody in Los Angeles . . . everyone is unnecessarily pretty and has a "personal brand."

"It's all about your brand, hun," he explained, leaning back in his chair, one foot crossed over his knee, hands behind his head.

"Everyone, everything, *everywhere* needs a brand. Actors, writers, dogs, breads, restaurants, TVs, bubble gum, water . . . If it exists, it needs a brand, and that's the way we like it at Holistic. How many followers do you have on Twitter?"

I stiffened.

"Um . . . eight?"

Tyler's mouth tightened into a sort of grimace.

"No, no, that won't do. You're a brilliant young voice who needs to be heard in the Internet space! You're so authentic, so real . . . Real is such a great sell these days."

He took a sip of his cold brew before continuing. "So if you were to describe your personal brand in two sentences or less, what would you say?"

I opened my mouth twice before any words came out. "My brand? As in my personality? What I like to do?"

He leaned forward with a clenched fist, shaking it to the sky like a preacher. "No, no, I mean your *brand*. Your trademark. Your style. Your niche. Here: What three words do people use to describe you?"

I thought for a moment. "I would say driven, thoughtful, intelligent—"

"BOOM." He slammed his fist down on the table, spilling my latte. "Sexy bookworm. I like it. That's real hot right now: geek chic. Tell me: have you ever considered dying your hair red?"

"Uh . . . red?"

"Yes, red. Blond screams, 'fun, carefree, bright-eyed bombshell,' while red whispers, 'quirky, smart, intriguing. Reads *Nee-chee*."

I contemplated this idea for a moment, ignoring the fact he had mispronounced Nietzsche. What did my hair color have to do with PR?

"Right. Red. Maybe. So . . . in terms of the company—"

"The company is all about the new wave. It's taking old products and flipping them on their head. Ice cream? Who eats ice cream in Los Angeles anymore? No one, that's who. But what if it's made from all-natural, organic ingredients? If each batch is hand-churned every morning by a group of ten-year-old spiritual exchange students from Japan?"

I considered. "You'd have a violation of labor laws?"

"What you'd *have* is a new angle. The hip man's ice cream. Artisanal, thoughtful, totally sellable."

He leaned back again, his point made. I nodded slowly. "Right . . . but it's still just ice cream?"

"Exactly."

"Huh."

The idea was compelling. Anything can be sold if it has a brand, huh? Including me?

"When I was working with the Getty, I was in charge of their on-line marketing . . . My primary job was to make art and art history more accessible to young people. If I can do that, I can definitely build a brand for myself."

He smiled with blindingly white teeth. "I like you, Lou. I think you'd make a great addition to Holistic. Let me have a chat with the higher-ups about ya . . . and I expect to see your application in my email inbox soon, yes?"

He gave me a wink and downed the rest of his cold brew before walking to the counter to get another prerolled joint.

JULY 19
5:15 P.M.

What on earth is my brand??

I've been wracking my brain for the past twenty-four hours, and I can't decide on my personal package. Why didn't I learn about this in college?? I know that a tesseract is a convex regular 4-polytope, but was blissfully unaware that my career would be contingent on the way I describe myself in three words.

I brought up the question at Theo's tonight, while he was rummaging through his collection of LPs. I sat on the couch, therapist style, while he pulled an album from the pile.

"Theo, what's my brand?"

"Your brand?"

"Yeah . . . Like, if you were to sell me, what would my description be?"

He chuckled, sliding the record from its case and checking both sides before gingerly placing it on the turntable.

"First of all, I wouldn't be selling you, because that's human trafficking." He lowered the needle onto the LP and the Decemberists started to play. "Second, why are you asking this? Did your mom secretly submit you for modeling jobs again?"

I shook my head. "No, it's just this interview I had with Tyler yesterday. I can't stop thinking about it. He's right: everything has a brand."

"But you'd be working at a desk. It's a behind-the-scenes job, not one in the public eye. Why would you need a brand?"

I bit on my lower lip, lost in thought. Theo walked back to the couch and plopped himself next to me, kissing me on the cheek.

"Do you think I'd look good as a redhead?" I asked.

He pulled back, brows knit tightly together. "Red? Like, fire-hydrant red?"

"I don't know. Like 'reads Nietzsche' red."

He snorted before grinning, then kissed me on the other cheek. "I think you'd look good with red, brown, blond, black, pink, or blue hair, or no hair at all." He ended with a kiss on my lips and I giggled, which is gross. Giggling is definitely off-brand.

"Come on, I'm serious. What about you? Do you have one?"

Theo thought for a second.

"I'd say I'm a health-conscious chef with a personal emphasis on farm-to-table cuisine and a geometric aesthetic."

I blinked at him. His grin grew more lopsided.

"Basically, I make healthy food look pretty."

"I got that, smartass." I threw myself across the couch face first, shoving my head between the cushions.

"Ughhhhhh, WHY am I so bad at real life??"

"You're not bad at real life! Tyler said he liked you, didn't he?"

I sighed before mumbling yes into the cushions.

"Then don't worry! Look, if you really want to work on a brand, why don't you talk to Val? Isn't she an Instagram celebrity?"

"I'm not asking my little sister for career help. Besides, she would just try to teach me how to duck-face."

"Okay, then . . . why not talk to your mom? She's probably great with this sort of thing."

The idea struck me as crazy until I suddenly realized it was true. Mom *is* great at this sort of thing . . . After all, she once convinced Cher to buy a uniquely gaudy property of Dad's by framing it as "Versailles's humbler cousin." If she can do that within forty seconds of seeing a house, I'm sure she can successfully package me, whom she literally created from loose cells roaming around her uterus.

JULY 20

<u>GRADUATION GOALS</u> (~~REVISED~~) (RE-REVISED)
Short Term

- ~~Establish new living-at-home rules/expectations with parents. (Should probably reiterate these).~~ (I tried.)
- ~~Rid closet of all unnecessary and unprofessional outfits.~~ (Thanks to the Mama Shell Bedroom Purge of 2017.)
- ~~Email Professor Richmanson about job opportunity!!~~ (UGHHHHH.)
- ~~Buy more ink for label-maker. (Can't find label-maker itself,~~ ~~also~~ ~~thanks to the Mama Shell Bedroom Purge of 2017).~~ (YES! Now if only I had something to label.)
- Start waking up at ~~7:30 AM (Will be tough without coffee, but must stay strong.)~~ (Was impossible without goat juice. Now aiming for 7:45.)
- <u>TELL. MOM. ABOUT. THEO.</u>
- Work out ~~thrice~~ twice a week. (Realistic goals are key.)
- ~~Murder Megan Mitchell~~ (Holding grudges is immature and prison is not on my list of long-term goals.)
- ~~Substitute coffee with lemon/cayenne water.~~ (Never again.)
- Make new friends.
- Create a personal "brand."

Medium Term

- Move out of parents' house within 4 to 10 months. (How has it been 3 months already??)
- Secure a job in a field that I can commit to for the rest of my life. (Possibly PR?)
- ~~Learn how to cook something that isn't cereal.~~ (Can now make a mean Pinterest guacamole.)
- Lose 5-7 pounds (soon).
- Find a one-bedroom apartment that's reasonably priced.
- ^That Mother will approve of.

Long Term

- *Forbes* 30 Under 30 article (still within reach).
- Modern-style house in Pacific Palisades.
- My very own NPR segment (~~nonnegotiable~~). (Will settle for 60 Minutes special.)
- Have kids: one boy, one girl. (Amendment: a boy and a girl for each one of my double lives.)
- . . . ?

JULY 21
4:20 P.M.

Mom and I took the pugs on a much-needed walk this morning, after finding a trail of sofa stuffing that led to the living room armchair (RIP). We showed Rosa, who sighed and mumbled "diablo" under her breath, which Mom still thinks means "Muffin" in Spanish. About ten minutes into our stroll, I casually asked Mom if she had an opinion on personal branding and was met with a gasp.

"Are you kidding?? Lou, it's my missed calling! I've been told I'm downright gifted at it," she said, tossing her lob behind one shoulder. "Why? Are you finally thinking of going on Jdate??"

Baguette tried to sit down, clearly tired from the whole three blocks we had journeyed. I gave her leash a gentle tug . . . Pugs need the cardio.

"No, but Tyler Jacoby said that everyone needs a personal brand, so I thought I'd come to you for advice."

Mom beamed with pride.

"Oh, this is my best day! I already know the answer to this. You are a sexy-meets-smart, badass boss bitch. Beauty and brains, all in one. You *could* be a model, if you really wanted to, but the industry is just *so* beneath you, since you're too busy saving the world. Think Amal Clooney."

I'm not sure what about my eggplant-shaped body continues to read *model* to Mom, but the idea of saving the world appealed to me. Also, being Amal Clooney.

"Do you really think I come off that way? Or are you biased, because I'm your daughter?"

Mom snorted, flipping her hair again.

"Trust me, I am not blinded by affection. Half of your father's success is because of my branding. Did I ever tell you the Cher story?"

"Yes, I remember it well," I assured her. She smiled fondly at the memory.

"You know, your dad was hardly the strapping baron he is today when I first met him."

My ears perked up. "Really?"

"Sure! In fact, he was quite a fixer-upper back in the day. Do you know what he was wearing the night we met?"

"The neon panda sweater, I know."

She laughed and shook her head. A few feet ahead of us, Muffin started digging into someone's flower beds, ripping up roses left and right. Mom paid no attention, twirling a strand of blond hair with her almond-shaped fingernails.

"It was quite a challenge, getting his look together. The first year we were dating, he only owned three shirts! THREE! A travesty. But what could I do? He was adorable, and in the end, I married for love."

I suddenly thought back to Natasha's comment about maternal instincts, and felt a pang of guilt deep in my chest. How could I be so wrong about my own mother?! Maybe Tash wasn't so crazy after all: if I love Theo, then she'll love him, too.

"Wow. That's beautiful, Mom. In fact, I—"

"Just don't make the same mistake, Lulu," she said, snapping out of her nostalgia. "Whoever you marry, get him all packaged up, nice and ready for delivery. Remember, it's just as easy to fall in love with a rich man as it is to fall in love with a poor one. The same goes for looks and good fashion sense."

My mouth hung open, the remnants of my almost confession gurgling a bit before dying in my throat. Well, so much for *that* theory. Apparently, Mama Shell's mothering style resembles that of a polar bear, only she would never eat her young . . . way too many calories.

"What was I saying? Oh yes! Back to your brand. I'd say you're like Audrey Hepburn meets Katharine Hepburn . . . Oh my gosh. You're the third Hepburn!!"

Muffin ran back to us, covered in mud and rose petals. Baguette lay down next to him, rolling over on her back, officially declaring her walk over. I stayed mostly silent as I carried her for the remainder of the walk, listening to Mom blabber on about the importance of well-fitting black dress pants.

I've got to get out of here, fast. Help me Tyler B. Jacoby: you're my only hope.

JULY 23

Alyssa 👑

> Hey, Alyss! It's me, Lou!   Lou

> Just wanted to reach out and remind you of my existence!!   Lou

> Hey, Alyss! It's me, Lou!   Lou

> Just wanted to say that I'm so very lonely and am in desperate need of a friend!   Lou

> Hey, Alyss! It's me, Lou!   Lou

> Just wanted to check in and see if you're as hopeless and miserable as I am! Ha-ha-ha-ha!   Lou

> Hey, Alyss, it's me, Lou!   Lou

> Just wanted to catch up. Let me know when you're free!   Lou

delivered

JULY 24
9:10 A.M.

I woke up at 8:30 this morning (better), poured myself a cup of blessed goat juice, and am now going straight to work on my job application.

Theo has been stressed as of late, what with August just around the corner. August is a ferociously busy month for the catering company, since there's a birthday party virtually every single day thanks to the love children of Christmas. As a result, my boyfriend is facing a tidal wave of work . . . Personally, I would settle for a small splash of work, or even a little sprinkle would do.

Failed First Draft of My Holistic Public Application

Legal Name: Eloise Laurent Hansen
Preferred Name, if any: Lou Hansen
Desired position: Administrative Assistant

How did you hear about Holistic Public?

I was first made aware of Holistic Public by my mother's best friend, Lisa Van Williams, who mentioned the company after consuming a bottle and a half of Whispering Angel rosé. Thankfully, she was kind/drunk enough to give me Tyler's personal information.

In two sentences or less, describe your personal brand.

Smart, sexy, badass boss bitch who is secretly the third Hepburn.

What are some of your personal strengths, and how will they contribute to our company?

First and foremost, I am a tremendously hard worker, and will accomplish any and all tasks that are put in front of me. Assuming I have at least one cup of goat juice in the morning and unlimited access to Red Bull, I am pretty much an unstoppable specimen.

Second, I am able to grasp difficult and complex concepts quickly and effectively. For example: I recently placed second in my mother's monthly mah-jongg tournament, after being taught the complex and multifaceted game only an hour before the event.

Third, I am a master of memorizing odd and unnecessary facts, and can recall these details at any moment's notice. For instance, did you know there are more sheep in New Zealand than there are people? Or that a giraffe's heart can weight up to twenty-three pounds? Now you do!

As an employee of Holistic Public, I would be sure to apply all of these talents to the rigorous job of alphabetizing Mr. Jacoby's legal marijuana containers.

JULY 26
6:45 P.M.

After two days and thirteen drafts, I have finally submitted my completed Holistic Public application to Tyler Jacoby's inbox at 12:35 this afternoon. My room is drowning in abandoned coffee mugs and crinkled-up balls of rejected paper, but the resulting product is completely flawless! If all goes well, I will be starting my new job by the end of next month.

Since I've been sedentary for the past forty-eight hours, Mom is making me walk around our pool with her to "get steps in." She refuses to go to bed until she's hit at least ten thousand steps, which sometimes requires a whole hour's worth of pool circling. She's been out there for twenty minutes, checking her Fitbit every two or three.

Ugh, she just saw me. All right, here we go . . . time to join the March for Family Fitness. Wish me luck!

JULY 27

Alyssa 👑

12:31 P.M.

Al | ELLA SQUEEZE!!! Baby girl, I've missed you!

Al | How's life at home treating you, girl? How are Theo and those precious puglings??

Al | I've never been so busy in my whole. Damn. LIFE.

Al | Law school orientation is in a MONTH, and I already have FIVE assignments. 🙈

Al | PS: Did you see this article about Natasha?! That chick is crazy. I hope she's okay! [columbiaspectator.com/news/20 . . .]

★ COLUMBIA DAILY SPECTATOR ★

Recent Columbia Grad Suffers Month-Long Illness Abroad

One humid evening in a small but authentic New Dehli hostel, recent Columbia graduate Natasha McPatterson noticed an odd gurgling sensation in her stomach, followed by nausea and a fever that ran long into the night. What at first appeared to be food poisoning turned out to be a month-long case of intestinal parasites, a battle that has tried the scholar both physically and mentally.

This is McPatterson's first visit to India, though she "feels as though [she's] been here in another life." After a particularly vivid dream she had a week before her commencement ceremony, Ms. McPatterson was inspired to book a one-way ticket to New Delhi, intending to write a journalistic report about the country's culture of violence against women. Her research was halted abruptly, however, when she became aware of her sickness. According to her reports on social media, Ms. McPatterson has been suffering with almost every possible consequence associated with parasites, including extreme fatigue and even dysentery.

Interestingly, McPatterson has refused to see a Western doctor, relying solely on Eastern medicine to cure her ailment.

"I see no need to take medication in my current state," McPatterson told The Spectator in an email. "Parasites, like any living creature, are simply seeking a way to live and thrive. I prefer a more natural, humane way of ridding myself of them."

Ms. McPatterson expressed her gratitude toward the community of her alma mater, who've made their well wishes known on a Facebook page entitled #PrayForNatasha.

"I'm just grateful for the outpouring of support I've received from my Columbia family. I have every intention of continuing with my research, just as soon as these darling worms find a more nurturing host."

The *Spectator* wishes Natasha McPatterson a speedy recovery, and hopes to get a full interview once she is healthy and back in the States.

2:15 P.M.

WHAT. THE. ACTUAL. FUCK?!?

Who is in charge of the *Daily Spectator* now?? How could anyone allow this story to run without ANY LEGITIMATE PROOF that Natasha McPatterson is in fact inflicted with goddamn motherfucking parasites?? WHAT EVER HAPPENED TO JOURNALISTIC INTEGRITY?!?

I absolutely MUST call and berate the bastards in charge about the consequence of dishonest and inaccurate reporting . . . or at least I would, were I not entirely responsible for the wretched lie that inspired the article in the first place. UGH UGH UGHHHH-HHH.

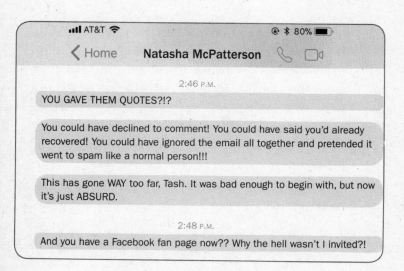

‹ Home   **Natasha McPatterson**   📞 🎥

2:46 P.M.

YOU GAVE THEM QUOTES?!?

You could have declined to comment! You could have said you'd already recovered! You could have ignored the email all together and pretended it went to spam like a normal person!!!

This has gone WAY too far, Tash. It was bad enough to begin with, but now it's just ABSURD.

2:48 P.M.

And you have a Facebook fan page now?? Why the hell wasn't I invited?!

JULY 28
2:30 P.M.

Great. Mom has requested that we go to the beach tomorrow, since it's prime bikini season and we've yet to "strut our stuff." Personally, I've been avoiding said strutting, since I haven't been able to reduce any jiggling, that might accompany it. However, Val is insisting that we go for the pictures, so Mom is making me try on my old bathing suits.

2:45 P.M.

I would honestly rather wrap myself in a woolen straitjacket and lie out in the sun than wear any of the bikinis in my closet tomorrow. I look like a water balloon that's being strangled on both ends by a rubber band. Also, my bikini region has been neglected for so long, I'm starting to resemble the missing link. I haven't gotten a bikini wax since last summer. Why don't I ever shave?? I'm going to have to shave.

3:15 P.M.

OWWWWWW OH MY GOD, RAZOR BURN.

Ugh, this is absolutely revolting. It's like I took a cheese grater to my poor defenseless thighs. How did I get so many ingrown hairs? And why are all female razors so much more expensive than men's razors when they're basically a defective lawn mower of the legs??

That's it. I'm not going to the beach tomorrow. I refuse.

JULY 29
10:30 A.M.

Did the whole damn state of California decide to come to the beach today??

We woke up early so we could beat the morning traffic to Malibu, which is about a forty-minute drive from our house. Malibu is what I call the "bougie beach," and though I humbly requested going to Venice instead, I was vetoed because Mom can't stand public beaches or anywhere she might have to talk to strangers. Besides, Mom LOVES Malibu. It's her personal paradise. Everyone in Malibu has a service dog and wears flip-flops that somehow cost $600 and pays for overpriced sushi that was imported from a different ocean. It's tremendously beautiful, and so are the people, who are probably all Ralph Lauren models who somehow achieved spiritual enlightenment by surfing and investing in shabby chic bedsheets for their beachside bungalows.

My mom's number-one dream in life is to buy a house here, where she can finally attain the lifestyle and even the tan that she deserves.

We made our way to Cross Creek, which is the community hub where the locals congregate. This place is so filled with celebrities and good-looking people, there are literally signs prohibiting paparazzi from entering the premises. It's like a watering hole for the physically superior.

Mom and Val are off doing a photo shoot along the shoreline, so I guess I'll take the next hour to . . . relax? There's not much else to do here. The problem with beach life is that it's entirely unproductive. I suppose I can play count the celebrities, or even more fun: count the celebrities with service dogs.

Mama Shell

12:00 P.M.

Lou, where are you??

I'm sitting next to the hottest guys on the beach and they are wearing Yale shirts. Get your ass down here. I told them my hotter younger sister is coming down. Don't blow this. #wingwoman

Currently hiding in the dressing room at an Intermix, pretending to try on clothes that another customer abandoned. Until Mom gives up on the sunbathing Yale boys, I'll just sit here and sift through the thousands of dollars' worth of clothing that this client almost bought.

My God, how old was this person, ten? Seriously, do these shirts come in adult sizes??

Oh boy. One of the attendants just came over and asked how I was doing.

"Hi, Tiffany, how's everything working for you? Do you need anything in another size?"

. . . *Yes.*

"Er—no! This is great, thank you!"

I heard the sound of her heels click-clacking away. Shoot, how am I supposed to escape if the store now knows I'm in here? Was Tiffany able to sneak out unseen by her assigned attendant?? Impossible. No one leaves a store empty-handed without having to shamefully admit to their loss, explaining that either they or the clothes were simply too ugly to purchase. Walking out without buying so much as a pair of Hanky Panky's can feel downright criminal.

Wow, Tiffany really liked sparkly clothing. There's a sequined jacket here that has "whatever" sewn in silver glitter on the back. Wretched. I have to try this on and send a picture to Theo. This could *not* be more tacky!

Turns out Tiffany had not left the store. Tiffany was just grabbing a few more floor-length skirts from the back. Tiffany also happened to be one country star turned pop sensation Tiffany Swan.

She was so startled by me, who was decked out in her tight-fitting shimmering apparel and taking selfies in the mirror, that she dropped her purse and screamed for her bodyguards, who descended on me before the shutter on my iPhone clicked. As it turns out, hiding in a celebrity's dressing room and imitating their person makes you seem a bit like a stalker, so without being able to change back into my clothes, I was apprehended by the Cross Creek security team and taken to the holding center. Apparently, "I was hiding from hot Yale guys" didn't seem like a legitimate excuse.

Once in detention, I was finally able to call Mom and explain what had happened . . . but instead of running to the holding center to save me, she and Val sprinted to the Intermix and grabbed a photo with the still-recovering Ms. Swan. Thankfully, Mom is friends with the general manager at the Malibu Intermix, so it only took a quick phone call to clear me of all possible charges. That being said, nothing will ever clear me of the humiliation I endured while sitting in the security center, unable to lift my arms because the shirt was so snug, the sequins from the skirt irritating my bikini razor burn.

Dad is so pissed. This is the second time this summer a Hansen woman has been detained for questionable behavior. He's so mad that he's completely revoked the offer to rid me of Find My Friends, seeing as I "clearly still need to be monitored." This is the worst beach day of my entire life. Even worse than the time I got hit by a rogue boogie board and had a chipped tooth for five days. Ugh.

Tiffany Swan
@TiffanySwan

When your dressing room stalker turns out to be @SoCalSoVal's older sister! Val is such a sweetie, and her mama is just fabulous! #funny

Month Four

Endless Summer

Email
From: Holistic Public
To: Eloise Hansen
Subject: Application Results

Eloise Hansen,

Thank you for applying for an administrative assistant position at Holistic Public Relations. We appreciate your interest in our company, and in a healthier, more wholesome community. The application process for Holistic is very competitive, and unfortunately, we've decided not to move your application forward.

Holistic Public will be advertising more positions in the coming months. We encourage you to apply again if you see a job posting for which you are suited at a later date. We wish you the best of luck with your professional endeavors.

Regards,
HR, Holistic Public Relations

11:42 A.M.

Oh, look! There it goes! The last of my self-esteem, flying headfirst out the window along with my dignity and any semblance of self-worth!!

I can't believe it. A flat-out *rejection*? How could that be?? I was absolutely *positive* I'd get this job!

Maybe I'm missing something in the email? Maybe I just *think* it's a rejection, but really, it's an acceptance in disguise??

No. It's still a rejection. Even after the twelfth time reading it.

This is so humiliating! I can't believe I didn't get so much as an interview to a company that sells veggie chips. Tyler and his bosses are all probably sitting in a fancy corporate conference room somewhere, sipping goat juice out of fancy, corporate goat juice mugs, laughing at the silly nerd girl who dared to apply for an entry-level office position without a decent Internet presence while not being a size 2. UGH.

Hold on, I'm getting a call.

OH MY GOD. DON'T PANIC. IT'S TYLER JACOBY.

What do I do?

Should I answer?!

I don't think I should answer.

What on earth would I say to him, anyhow??

"Oh, don't worry, Tyler! I'm fine! I'll just continue spending my days trapped in Mother's house like feminist Rapunzel, getting topknot tutorials and passive-aggressive comments about my ever-growing unibrow!"

Unless . . .

Of *course*! There must have been a mistake. A clerical error; a contact mix-up! Why else would he be calling me on a Saturday morning? I bet he's calling to correct the unfortunate blunder, assuring me that whoever's responsible has just been fired, and that I will be filling his/her position starting first thing next week. HOORAY!

SCREW YOU, TYLER B. JERKFACE.

"Hello?" I answered after three and a half rings, trying not to seem too eager.

"Lou! Thrilled you picked up. It's Tyler here. From Holistic Public."

I cleared my throat and sat upright, putting on my best "professionally indifferent" voice. "Oh yes. Hello, Tyler! So lovely to hear from you."

I leaned forward on the edge of my seat, eagerly awaiting the upcoming apology: *I'm so sorry for the inconvenience, Ms. Hansen. Can you start on Monday? Your desk will be right next to the snack table!*

"Listen, hun, I'm sorry this didn't work out . . ."

Would you prefer your pens to be ballpoint, or—wait, what?

". . . It's tough, I know, but you can't take these things personally. It's the nature of the marketing beast, babe! And as long as there are no hard feelings—"

"Hold on . . ." I interrupted, my feeble brain finally catching up, "so just to clarify, you're saying I *didn't* get the job?"

Cricket. Cricket. Cricket.

"Did you get the email?"

I looked down at the opened email on my desktop. "Er . . . no?"

I heard Tyler blow air through his closed lips, like an old dehydrated horse. "Then I hate to break it to you this way, hun, but it's a no."

I bounced his words around between my ears, desperate to find the order in which I'm offered an administrative assistant position and an explanation for this awkward encounter. But all I could hear was:

. . . *it's a no.*

No!

No?

No.

Noooooooo.

NO.

". . . but I have to tell you, Lou—you are SUCH a superstar. Really! I read your brand concept, and it's genius. Genius! The third Hepburn? Gold!"

Hang up. Hang up on him, Lou. You don't deserve this kind of pity. Why should you have to listen to this half-wit sad sack, smug-face, good-for-nothing—

"So when I saw 'overqualified' on the HR report, I can't say it surprised me, but it's still disappointing nonetheless."

—deadbeat pretty boy . . . WHAT??

My mouth bobbed open and closed for a whole minute, like a fish gasping for water. "I—I'm sorry?" I managed, voice cracking.

"I know, I know—it's an annoying policy, and legally I'm not supposed to be telling you, but I figured you're Lisa's lady, so you'll keep it hush-hush, yeah?"

"Hold on, you said I'm . . . what did you just say I am?"

Tyler let loose a few coughs before answering. "Oh. You're overqualified, hun."

I heard the pitter-patter of pug paws creeping up the hallway, which meant Mom wasn't far behind them. Shit.

"Overqualified?" I repeated flatly, the word tasting sour in my mouth.

"You know, too damn good. Better elsewhere. Overdressed for success. The company can't have you dumping us for some other job!"

". . . But I don't have another job."

Tyler chuckled lightly. "Ah, but you *will*, sweetheart, and we can't have you breaking our hearts once you do!"

Is this a prank? This has to be a prank. No, this is worse. This is the Twilight Zone. This is the parallel universe that Dr. Richmanson wrote his third book about.

"So . . ." I started tentatively, "you're not giving me an interview . . . because I might quit for a better job that I don't have yet?"

I heard him inhale sharply and hold it, as I've seen Jett do a million times. *Oh! He's getting high. Excellent.*

"See? Smart meets sexy." He exhaled what was definitely marijuana smoke. I could feel Mom's looming presence through the door, her ear undoubtedly pressed to my shaded window.

"Anyway," Tyler said, clearly not interested in what I might have to say, "if something more appropriate opens up, I'll one thousand percent call you first. No question. And if you ever wanna grab coffee or talk shop, just shoot me a quick email. Sound good?"

I could hear his obnoxiously white smile through the phone. I rolled my eyes so hard it hurt. The pugs started scratching at the door, and I heard Mom's gentle *shhh* from the other side.

"Sure, Tyler," I conceded, my shoulders slumping forward.

"Great! *So* glad we had this chat. Best of luck to you, hun! Ciao."

The phone beeped twice, ending the phone call, and I let my head fall onto my desk with a thump.

Mom finally opened my door and poked her head inside, as though she hadn't just been eavesdropping. The pugs pushed their way into the room and sat down on my feet.

"I didn't get the job." I groaned. Mom gasped in feigned shock. "What? NO! What do you mean? What did they say??"

I kept my forehead on the desk, not wanting to look up at her.

"They said I'm overqualified," I repeated blankly.

"Over-*what*??" Mom yelled, this time genuinely outraged. I let out a low moan as she started pacing back and forth furiously, shifting into Mama Bear Mode.

"But that's ridiculous! That's *absurd*! What kind of stupid excuse is that supposed to be? *Overqualified*. Please! I didn't send you to Columbia for you to be overqualified! What a *schmuck* that Tyler is. You know what? I'm calling Lisa right away and telling her that—"

"No, don't!" I said, lifting my head an inch off the table. "He wasn't even supposed to tell me. Just . . . leave it alone." I let my head slam back down on the desk too quickly. *"Ow."*

"Oh, honey." Mom sighed, tenderness softening her voice. She walked behind my chair and gently wrapped her arms around my hunched body, enveloping me in a tight cocoon. "I'm so sorry, sweetie," she cooed, giving me a kiss on the nape of my neck. "Rejection always hurts. But they're missing out on someone *brilliant*. It's their loss, baby. I promise."

I pulled her arms tightly around me and closed my eyes, surrendering to the hug. I took a deep breath in, my disappointment fading slightly as the pugs licked my feet in support.

"Thanks, Mama. I'll be okay."

Mom gave me one last squeeze and a kiss before letting go. I sat back up and rubbed my throbbing head.

"I just don't know what to do," I said hopelessly. "I have no direction. And without a direction, I can't get a job. And without a job, I can't make money. And if I can't make money, how am I supposed to move out of the house?"

The instant the words left my lips, I regretted them. Excitement glimmered in Mom's eyes as the realization dawned on both her and me:

"Well, Lulu," Mom started, "the good news is, you always have a place to live! Your laundry is taken care of, you have free food, you have full access to my wardrobe. There's no hurry to leave! In fact, this could be a good thing for us!" She giggled, bouncing slightly on the balls of her feet.

I raised a finger in objection. "Wait a second . . . *us?*"

"Oh, shoot!" she yelped, checking the time on her phone. "I forgot, I'm supposed to meet Susan at yoga! Sorry, Lulu, but I have to run. We'll talk about this more later, okay?"

I raised my hand higher.

"Okay, sure, but about the 'us' thing—"

"It's all going to be okay, sweetie!" Mom assured me as she spun around to leave. "Take as long as you need to recover. There's no rush! You can stay here forever!!" She gave a little wink and ran down the hallway, the pugs trailing behind.

. . . *Forever??*

The word echoed in my head like some sort of trippy demonic hallucination. Images of me at fifty, sitting in my bedroom as eighty-year-old Mom picks out an outfit for my first colonoscopy, are flashing before my horrified eyes. Oh god, I *have* to get out of here!!

What day is it? August first?! *Shit!* Where did the dreaded time go? Only two more months until my updated self-imposed move-out deadline, and I still have no job, no apartment, no prospects, and no clue.

Back to square one. Freaking fantastic.

Val

1:10 P.M.

Val LOU, HELP

What? What's going on?? Lou

Val Mom showed up to my yoga class with Susan, and her boob popped out during warrior two.

NO Lou

Val YES

Did anyone see? Lou

Val The whole class stopped and applauded for her.

NO Lou

Val YES

Yoga is ruined forever. Lou

AUGUST 2
8:10 A.M.

Woke up in a full sweat from a hideous nightmare in which I'm be-ing chased by Tyler Jacoby and Dr. Richmanson into a jail cell made of nail files and round brushes, only to realize that my eternal pris-onmate just happens to be my topless mother. Decided I'm not going to sleep ever again.

8:25 A.M.

Just stepped onto the scale for the first time in over a month. Then stepped off, removed all articles of clothing and stepped back on. Then stepped off, did twenty crunches, and stepped back on. Ugh. Does rejection make you retain water? I bet it does.

8:39 A.M.

How am I out of fresh underwear? Doesn't Rosa do my laundry? Or do I spend so much time locked away in my room that she forgot I'm even here?? Ugh again. I could borrow a pair of Mom's or Val's . . . No, that won't do. The admission that I've been reliant on someone else to wash my own panties is too shameful to be uttered aloud. Also, I hate thongs, and that's all they seem to wear.

The only reasonable solution here is to go to the mall and buy some new pairs.

8:46 A.M.

After some digging, I managed to find an old pair of booty shorts from my brief stint in middle school volleyball, which I'll be wearing to the mall instead of underwear. They're much, much, much too tight, but it's better than going commando or wearing inside-out granny panties or, god forbid, whipping out the dreaded Spanx.

9:15 A.M.

Crisis averted. Found a pile of my freshly folded underwear in a basket by the front of the house. Bless you, Rosa! I will never take your work for granted again.

Huh. I wonder what Rosa thinks of my family? Dad's never home, Mom walks around all day in a bathrobe, occasionally covered in bruises and/or bandages from various surgeries or Botox . . . Does she think we're battered? Gravely ill? Victims of domestic abuse or a tragic disease that keeps us at home in pajamas?? Curious.

7:50 P.M.

Useless, useless, *useless*. I can't believe another whole day went by, and the only productive thing I did was organize my newly washed unmentionables by color and cheek coverage. To be fair, Mom kept me plenty busy, constantly asking for help with every home appliance we own:

"Lulu, could you help me turn on the TV?"

"Sweetie, why isn't the garbage disposal working?"

"Why is the dishwasher making that noise? Should it be making that noise??"

"My computer is doing the little rainbow spinny thing and it won't stop. What? What's wrong with keeping thirty tabs open??"

Oh, well. I guess we're all entitled to a lazy Sunday . . . but tomorrow is when I officially get my shit together. No more excuses. It's Monday, and Mondays are the perfect time to refresh and reboot.

AUGUST 3

Mama Shell

12:15 P.M.

> Mom, why are our couches covered in bedsheets? Lo

MS Muffin scratched holes in the upholstery and Rosa needed something to cover them up with.

> . . . Lo

> Mother, you HAVE to train your animals. Lo

MS Oh, hush! He's only a puppy!

> He's five years old. Lo

MS Don't judge my parenting! I raised you, and you turned out fine!

> . . . What's your definition of fine? Lo

11:37 P.M.

I hate Mondays. Everyone goes off to work but me, stuck watching two hours' worth of TED Talk videos about productivity and "living your best life" while choking down an algae shot Mom bought with a ginger slice to "aid my digestion and prevent bloat." Ugh.

I'm just salty because of tonight's airing of *The Bachelorette,* which thankfully has reached its season finale. Somehow the Red Hots will have to suffer through *two whole* Bachelor-*less weeks* before the return of *Bachelor in Paradise,* which is sort of like the original, if it were on steroids soaked in vodka.*

Seeing as tonight was the big climactic finish (THREE HOURS!!! Most people can't sit through a Shakespeare play if it hasn't been cut down to two! What is wrong with humanity?!), the ladies each dressed as the profession of their favorite contestant this season. Susan sported

---

*How are there so many incarnations of this stupid show?? How many different ways can we watch these people make out and cry?!

a zookeeper outfit for an "animal lover," Lisa wore an apron and gloves as a "former oyster shucker," and Stacey kept it simple with the hat and wand of a "magic enthusiast."

Mom borrowed Val's old Coachella outfit for "music festival roadie," which consisted of ripped jean shorts, a lacy white crop top with a plunging neckline, five different chokers, and a flower crown.

The Red Hots gathered eagerly around the TV on our bedsheet-covered couches, all screaming and laughing and weeping and cheering as the artificial drama unfolded before them. Just as the Bachelorette was selecting an impressively large diamond ring for her future ex-fiancé, Susan slammed a hand down on the arm of the couch and gasped. "Lou," she said excitedly, "*you* should be the next Bachelorette!"

Rosé shot out of my mouth and nose, spraying the sheets and burning holes in my sinuses.

"What??" I exclaimed, trying not to choke from my spit take.

"Oh, come on, you'd be so great!" Susan insisted. "You'd be, like, the quirky, self-aware girl!"

"Yes!" Stacey agreed, her top hat bobbing as she nodded. "They'd fly you all over the world, and I'm pretty sure they provide your whole wardrobe!"

"Um—thanks, but no thanks." I dismissed the notion immediately, my pride cringing at the very thought.

"Why not?" Mom asked, crossing her arms and legs. "Have you seen the men on this show? Of course you wouldn't have to marry one, but it's *great* exposure."

I closed my eyes to keep from rolling them.

"Mom, I don't need exposure. Or a fake engagement. I need a job."

Lisa snorted. "Honey, have you seen our outfits? You can turn anything into a job these days. And exposure is just the key." The ladies all murmured in agreement.

"You know, my *nephew* was thinking of doing *The Bachelor*," Susan casually slipped in, "but then he was offered the medical reality show. By the way, he's moving to LA soon. Just saying." She winked at me. I forced a smile and took another long swig of rosé.

"See? Even doctors are celebrities now!" Lisa proclaimed, waving her oyster-shucking knife around. "I'm telling you, Lou, just post a picture of your hoo-ha online and you'll have three job offers by the end of the week."

"PLEASE STOP TALKING." Dad's muffled yell emerged from behind the closed bedroom door. The ladies howled with laughter as I sank deeper and deeper into the couch cushions.

I must have sucked down an entire bottle of rosé myself as this year's Bachelorette kick-started her career as an assistant kangaroo wrangler by choosing Brad over Mark in a deluge of sand and tears.* *Ugh.* Lisa and Tyler are right: it's not about the *job,* it's about the *image.* It's about the *exposure.* A college degree means nothing if you aren't willing to dance a paint-covered samba in the middle of Times Square while juggling penis-shaped sparklers . . . and even *then* you're competing with nudist protesters and janky Elmo. In fact . . .

Maybe that's the key to success! Maybe I need to become more Internet savvy! Having a brand means nothing if it's not paraded publicly. After all, how is anyone supposed to know that I'm the Third Hepburn if my Instagram doesn't make it obvious?

Anyway, it's just posting pictures and writing clever captions. How hard can it be?

AUGUST 4
10:05 A.M.

Coming from a person who has dabbled in string theory, I can confidently say that social media is the most complicated development of the twenty-first century.

---

*Susan was right about Brad.

Nothing about it makes sense to me. When are you supposed to post? And how many posts should you post?? And of what? And with whom? Why is anyone supposed to care about the way my coffee cup looks against a brick wall?!

Thank goodness I'm meeting Theo at the farmer's market to do some shopping today. That should lift my spirits! Plus, I can finally rant about Tyler with someone who isn't Mom. She's been unusually perky as of late, and has even started calling me "roomie."

12:42 P.M.

Drat. I've been so consumed with Tyler and *The Bachelorette* and my wounded ego, I almost forgot that Mom still thinks Theo is a creepy hipster lunatic bent on killing innocents by the masses. Ugh. I don't know what to do! I'm starting to lose faith she'll ever accept him. Anytime I come close to confessing, Mom says something absolutely horrid like "buckteeth are only tolerable with an accent," or "real men don't wear V-necks." Most recently, she hung a sign in my hallway reading:

WARNING: NO MEN UNDER SIX-FOOT-FIVE BEYOND THIS POINT.

Meanwhile, I suspect that Theo is starting to grow . . . well . . . suspicious. We spent our morning weaving through the farmer's market, surveying various vegetables and making justifications for my disastrous rejection.

"It's the excuse that really gets to me," I told him for the fifth time. "*Overqualified?* Please! I'm not overqualified for anything. Just ask Rosa! I'm twenty-two years old, and I still have someone changing my bedsheets."

"Right, of course," Theo teased, closely examining a peach. "Because graduating with honors from Columbia makes you tragically stupid."

"Exactly!" I agreed, ignoring his sarcasm. "I don't know what Tyler is talking about. I'm a total incompetent!"

Theo chuckled, trading in the fuzzy fruit for another seemingly identical one. I let out an exasperated sigh.

"I just feel so helpless," I said, leaning onto the rickety plastic table. "It's a total catch-22. I apparently don't have enough job experience, yet somehow I'm overqualified for the jobs that would *get* me the experience. What, am I just supposed to be the perfect amount of mediocre?"

Theo frowned, bringing the peach an inch from his face. "These feel a bit underripe," he concluded.

I snatched the perfectly good fruit from him and put it back with the others. "Earth to Theo!" I said, waving a hand in front of his face. "It's your girlfriend here in the middle of a massive panic attack. Do you copy?"

Theo looked me up and down incredulously. "If this was a real panic attack, you'd be whittling holes in your fingers with your jewelry," he asserted. I stuck my tongue out at him and he smiled back impishly.

"Okay! You want my undivided attention. Roger that," he said with a firm salute. "So. We hate Tyler, and you feel helpless. How can I make it better?"

I sighed again, bitterness dripping off me like a much-too-young Norma Desmond. "You can't make it better," I lamented. "It's not your fault that I'm a complete loser."

"Louie, come on, you are not a loser."

"It sure feels that way."

"Don't you think you're being a bit dramatic?"

"In what way am I being *dramatic*?" I asked, dramatically.

Theo shook his head. "You're living rent free. You got rejected from *one job*. This is hardly the end of the world."

He was right, which ironically annoyed me even more.

"I know," I mumbled, crossing my arms. "I just would like for my life to start already."

"You're only twenty-two. You have plenty of time. Everyone goes through this!"

"*You're* not going through this."

Right on cue, Theo's Apple Watch vibrated with yet another work email.* He let go of my hand to look down at his technologically enhanced wrist and frowned.

"Jeez, the kitchen is a freaking beehive right now," he said, squinting down at the tiny print. "This month is going to be a killer. We better get a family dinner on the books before my schedule fills up."

My stomach did a triple axel flip and landed in a weird pool of guilt/anxiety. *Shit. The dinner!* I quickly grabbed onto Theo's arm to keep from any suspicious ring fiddling.

"Oh, don't worry about that! You've just been settling in!" I squeaked, my unease very apparent.

Theo frowned. "Don't be ridiculous. I've been here for two and a half months," he said, using a finger to find the calendar app on his watch. "It's time to meet your folks. Now, when are you all free? I can do the eighth or the fourteenth, or if weekdays work better—"

I put a hand over his watch, suppressing whatever nervous giggles were trying to surface. "You know, right now might not be the best time. Dad's so busy, he's barely home these days! Also, my house is super messy. Also, we might have mold."

That's enough, Lou. Theo cocked his head to the side, letting wavy locks fall into his face.

"Your house might have *mold*?"

"Maybe! Who knows? It's hard to tell with these things."

---

*Theo *finally* started wearing the watch that Jett's mom gave to him, just to keep up with the onslaught of work emails. He loves it, because it makes him feel like Captain Kirk.

Shut up shut up shut UP. One of Theo's brows raised up so high, it was hidden by his bangs.

"Louie, is there something you're not telling me?"

"WHAT?!" I yelled, laughter banging at the top of my esophagus. "Of course not! I just don't want to expose your lungs to potentially dangerous bacteria!"

The brow remained raised. *Think, Lou, THINK.*

"Oh!" I exclaimed, the realization hitting me like a rock to the head. "Val is going away to summer camp next week!"

Theo crossed his arms, not understanding my point. "So?"

"So, I *really* wanted this to be a family dinner. With all of us. To-gether."

"There will be other dinners . . ."

"Yes, but I want the first one to be special," I said, giving his arm a firm squeeze. "She's only gone for three weeks. Then we can have as many dinners as you want."

Theo ran a hand through his chin-length hair. "Are you sure? I can move some stuff around this week . . ."

"I'm positive," I said, putting a finger to his lips. "You know how close I am to my family! I want this to be perfect."*

Theo gave me one last suspicious look before shrugging and push-ing his hands into his pockets. He gave my finger a small kiss, signi-fying my victory. "All right, I understand that. Just so long as your parents don't think I'm stalling."

I shook my head furiously, declaring with complete confidence: "Trust me: it won't even cross their minds. Now, help me take a pic-ture of these berries that will increase my social media following."

---

*Or at the very least, not a total disaster.

its_lou_hansen
Farmers Market ...

7 likes

its_lou_hansen Sunday at the farmer's market! BERRY-licious! #berries #farmersmarket #puns

theo_green Nature's jewels 👌
socal_soval Lol #puns I'm crying 😭
therealmamashell Did you edit this? Always ask your sister to help edit your pics. Call me 🙄

AUGUST 5

 Megan Mitchell

— 😊 feeling excited

Today was my last day in the Ay-bay-Bay! My AMAZING friends were so, so, SO sweet to throw me such a PERFECT going-away party. So, so, SO blessed to be moving to La-La Land to pursue my LIFELONG DREAMS!!!

(continued)

#friends #party #goingaway #adventure #LA #dreams #bestfriends #bestjob #bestlife

253 👍, 13 ♥, 10 😟

 Sabrina Ward: We love you, Megan! <3

 Hillary Alvarez: Go get them, beautiful!

 Marianna Breton: I guess it really is the City of ANGELS!

9:30 P.M.

Oh, joy! How could I forget? My favorite Miss Silicon Valley pageant winner is moving to town!

As if I needed any more stress in my life. Now I also get to deal with the Queen of Passive-Aggressive Slights herself, sitting in her glorious West Hollywood castle on her royal throne of full-time employed-ness, rubbing it in my face with her scepter of unnecessary abbreviations and too many likes. *Ugh.*

As if this weren't enough, Val leaves for Camp Sycamore next week, which means I'll have to fend for myself against the Mother/Mitchell Monstrosity . . . an experience I'm not sure my ego can survive. And to top it all off, I lost three followers on Instagram today because apparently I used the wrong hashtags.

Can't I catch a break?

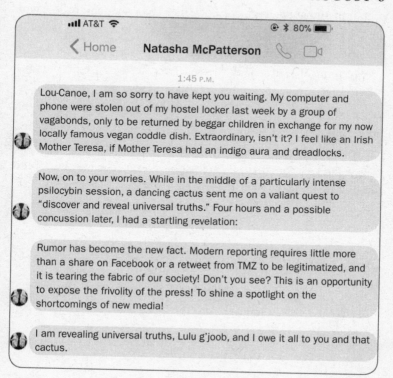

all AT&T 🛜   ⊕ ✳ 80% 🔋

‹ Home   **Natasha McPatterson**   📞 📹

1:45 P.M.

Lou-Canoe, I am so sorry to have kept you waiting. My computer and phone were stolen out of my hostel locker last week by a group of vagabonds, only to be returned by beggar children in exchange for my now locally famous vegan coddle dish. Extraordinary, isn't it? I feel like an Irish Mother Teresa, if Mother Teresa had an indigo aura and dreadlocks.

Now, on to your worries. While in the middle of a particularly intense psilocybin session, a dancing cactus sent me on a valiant quest to "discover and reveal universal truths." Four hours and a possible concussion later, I had a startling revelation:

Rumor has become the new fact. Modern reporting requires little more than a share on Facebook or a retweet from TMZ to be legitimatized, and it is tearing the fabric of our society! Don't you see? This is an opportunity to expose the frivolity of the press! To shine a spotlight on the shortcomings of new media!

I am revealing universal truths, Lulu g'joob, and I owe it all to you and that cactus.

11:15 A.M.

Mom is right. Natasha is a completely ridiculous person who is depressing and wears way too much black.

Somehow she now fancies herself a "truth crusader" because she's publically perpetuating a lie that I fabricated in the first place. It's incredible. If irony were a person, she'd be dancing the Tash Tango.

Feeling very depressed. Can't seem to shake the impression that I'm doomed to be a hopeless failure whose glory days are far behind her . . . even though my glory days were far from glorious. Being a balding caffeine addict should NOT have been my peak. I should just pack it in and apply to grad school, like Theo said, and collect random degrees until I'm so old and broke the only way I can possibly pay off my student debt is by dying.

Speaking of grad school: Alyssa Carter starts classes at Harvard this month for a joint degree in law and government. Her "rough plan"—as she puts it—is to become a senator for the state of Vermont by the time she is thirty-five so she can eventually run for president by fifty.

This is a lot better than my rough plan, which is to murder Megan and go to prison so I'll at least have a set schedule with three carbo-loaded meals a day.

socal_soval   ...

5,732 likes

socal_soval Did you know that global warming could make avocados go extinct? It's true!
That's why I'm off to environmental camp, aka #CampSycamore to help save our brunches and our planet. I'll be gone for 3 weeks, but don't worry! I'll be back ASAP! 💕 🥑
#camp #summer #SaveTheAvocados #SaveTheWorld

julesdean Don't leave, Valentina!!!
playwithjax Ur so philanthropic
catieryan_ Pls flw me back @Socal_Soval I luv u

AUGUST 10

3:33 P.M.

I never thought I'd say this, but I wish I were a teen again.

I'd give anything to be headed to Camp Sycamore with Val today. Camp was easily my favorite part of summer growing up . . . It was where I discovered my love for the environment, where I planted my first tree, and even where I had my first kiss.* It's three wonderful phoneless weeks of gardening, arts and crafts, DIY projects, and rope courses . . . Sure, it's a millennial's nightmare, but it looks *great* on college applications.**

Mom, Dad, and I drove Val to the drop-off point and helped load her belongings into the bus. The Swaggin' Six were already there, taking farewell Snapchats in their matching jean short-shorts. Mom cried as we said our goodbyes and waved theatrically as the buses left the parking lot, as though Val were on a ship headed for the New World instead of a bus to summer camp in Topanga.

On the way home, Mom gasped dramatically from the front seat, nearly causing Dad to swerve into oncoming traffic.

"Lulu! Did you see Megan's Facebook post? She just moved to LA!"

I pressed my forehead against the cool car window, trying not to get sick from the motion and/or Megan's presence.

"Yes, Mom, I did see it," I said sharply.

"That's so great! Isn't that great, Charlie?"

"Who's Megan again?" Dad asked, shooting a quick wink at me over his shoulder. I smiled broadly to myself from the backseat. *I love you, Dad.*

---

*It was during Spin the Ecofriendly Bottle. Jason Marrs licked my face, and I went in the bathroom and cried.

**The campers are forced to leave their phones at the front desk upon arrival. Val once argued that she needed her phone for occupational purposes, which did not go over well with the counselors.

"Oh, you know, Stacey's niece!" Mom reminded him, landing a playful slap on his broad shoulder. "The one who went to Vanderbilt? Dark hair? Super fun? Oh, Lulu, she is *such a good friend for you!*"

Dad slammed down on the brake for two seconds longer than necessary, causing me to bang my head against the window.

"Jesus Christ! What the— Choose a lane, asshole!"

"Charlie, that man has to be eighty-three years old."

"Then he should know how to freaking drive by now! Stupid son of a—"

Megan this, Megan that, Megan, Megan, MEGAN. When did Megan suddenly turn into the Golden Child? It was bad enough when she was just cooler and skinnier than me . . . Now she has to be more successful than me, too? What's the point of growing up geeky if you don't have an awesome life to show for it??

I need to do something, and fast. I can't face Megan while I'm holding bubkes and she has a royal flush. There *must* be a job that fits all my criteria that I can apply for and be admitted to in the next week, right?

AUGUST 12

Alberto (H.E.L.P.)

Al   Hey, Lou, I just received a receipt from Apple saying you've purchased five seasons' worth of Buffy the Vampire Slayer in seventy-two hours.

Al   This seems excessive, so I wanted to check that you weren't the victim of identity theft.

  *Identity crisis.

  This isn't a theft. It's a crisis.

AUGUST 13
9:20 P.M.

Help. Currently in the throes of a full-blown quarter-life freak-out.

I spent the day helplessly scrolling through Craigslist for possible job opportunities, noting that I'm not qualified to be a gorilla-costumed street dancer with sign because I lack the necessary coordination. Meanwhile, Theo is catering a party at Charlize Theron's house.

Happy birthday, Charlize! Enjoy the tiny kimchi tacos! I'll be here, spending my night deleting embarrassing pictures of myself that may tarnish my aspired brand off Facebook.

AUGUST 14
4:17 P.M.

I'm starting to wonder if Mom's behavior could be deemed "cruel and unusual" in a court of law.*

The two of us went on an afternoon walk to the juice bar, since Mom needed another four thousand steps on her Fitbit. Also, Lisa told us we just *had* to buy this new mushroom powder that tightens your eyelids or something.

"They say mushroom is the new algae," Mom explained, walking at a brisk pace. I nodded.

"That's cool. Does it taste any better?"

"Oh, you don't drink this powder. You snort it."

Of course you do. I shook my head as Mom performed an unconscious visual scan on me from top to bottom—a process that occurs every ten to fifteen minutes and usually results in a nagging comment. This time her eyes fixated on my greasy scalp, her nose scrunching up in disapproval.

---

*Remember to ask Alyssa about this later.

. . . Three . . . two . . .

"Lulu, your hair looks oily," Mom declared. "When's the last time you washed it?"

I sighed heavily. "Sunday."

"Sweetie, it's Saturday."

"And?"

"And it's starting to look like you used car grease as hair spray."

I rolled my eyes, not nearly in the mood to take her criticism. "Please don't get on my case. I'll take a shower tomorrow."

"Fine. Just so long as you wash it by Monday."

"Why? What's happening Monday?"

"You're going over to Megan's!"

My head snapped back so quickly, I almost lost consciousness. "I am? Since when??"

"Since I told Stacey you were free on Monday."

"What if I'm *not* free on Monday?"

"Of course you are! You don't have a job!"

Ouch. Mom tossed her perfectly clean blown-out lob over a shoulder.

"According to Stace, you weren't returning any of Megan's calls, so I made arrangements for you."

"Don't I get a say in making my own plans?"

Mom waved her hand at me, as though this notion were ridiculous. "What's the big deal? I thought you'd be excited! Megan is such a—"

"—*good friend for me,*" I growled. "I know."

Mom pulled the tiny Fitbit out of her bra and checked the number, frowning. She started walking in zigzags to increase her step count.

"I just think she's a good influence, is all. She has a job, an apartment, she's in such great shape . . . I like to see you around winners, Lulu."

I had a quick flashback to the time Megan did my makeup using a Sharpie instead of eyeliner. "Yup. Real winners."

"Plus, she's always so cheerful and fun!" Mom gushed on. "And it'll be good to have another friend in town besides Natasha. I know you like her, but she can just be so—"

"Dark?" I offered from the list of commonly used Tash adjectives. "Unconventional? Eccentric?"

"Yes," she confirmed. "Also, kind of crazy."

Oh, you have no idea.

Theo 🩶

5:40 P.M.

> SOS.

> I have mushroom powder stuck in my nostrils and my eyelids don't look any tighter.

Th . . . is this something all the cool kids are doing?

> I need a sanctuary.

> Are you free tonight for dinner? Can I escape to your place??

Th Shoot, I wish I was! 😔 The company is working some film premiere, so I'll probably be working real late.

> Seriously? What premiere?

Th I think it's Leonardo DiCaprio's?

> Oh. That's casual.

AUGUST 16
10:00 A.M.

Today's judgment day.

I'm supposed to be at Megan's by noon, which gives me an hour and a half to eat breakfast, choose an outfit, take a shower, do my hair, get dressed, and leave while still giving me a fifteen-minute cushion for parking and any unexpected traffic. I have plenty of time!

What's for breakfast? Do we have any more cereal?

10:10 A.M.

Rough start. Poured cereal into bowl, only to realize we are out of almond milk. Now I have to awkwardly shimmy the cereal back into the box and decide on something else to eat.

10:15 A.M.

Why is there never any food in this house? The only breakfast options in the fridge include egg whites, half an apple, and a few scoops of some questionable yogurt.

Oh, wait! There's protein powder! I'll just mix it with some water . . . That should be fine!

10:25 A.M.

OH GOD. HEINOUS. It tastes like watered-down chocolate milk that was produced at a nuclear waste site. BLEGH. How can I fix this?? Let's throw in that apple, the yogurt, maybe some almond butter, and . . . vanilla extract? Cinnamon? A handful of the cereal?

10:30 A.M.

SHIT SHIT SHIT. Forgot to put the top back on the blender before starting it. Disgusting protein concoction/cereal pieces are all over the kitchen/myself. *Ugh*.

Towels! I need paper towels!!

10:42 A.M.

All right; kitchen's clean. I used the pugs as mini makeshift Swiffers by letting them lick the sticky remains off the floor. Also managed to gulp down the remaining protein shake by using coffee as a chaser of sorts. Now it's time to get dressed.

10:55 A.M.

How on earth are all my jeans so tight?? HOW?! What evil curse was cast upon me to keep my metabolism from working?!?

11:02 A.M.

UGHHHHHHHHHHHHHHHHHHHHHHHH!!!!

11:10 A.M.

Finally found a pair of pants that fit me. And by pants, I mean leggings. I don't really have time to take a shower, so I'll have to use Val's dry shampoo instead.

11:02 A.M.

Shit. Val's dry shampoo is meant for brunettes only. Now I have an awkward brown streak running down the middle of my shiny scalp.

Hmmm. Maybe if I cover more of the top, I can pass it off as ombré?

11:09 A.M.

My head is a biohazard.

I reek of aerosol and protein powder and god knows what else. My hair is a nasty mess of dirt brown and white powder, like a post-erupted Mount Vesuvius. Revolting. Where are all my beanies?

11:16 A.M.

Mom hid all my beanies because they are "strictly winter wear." Only floppy hats are allowed until October at the earliest. UGH. I don't have time to wash my hair in the sink. Putting it up in a ponytail and leaving.

12:03 A.M.

. . . You've got to be kidding me.

Pulling up to Megan's apartment complex, I was only slightly shocked to see a complimentary valet service out front. I banged my head on the roof of the car as I made my way out, sending a puff of powder into the air from the dry shampoo. I marched through the steel revolving doors and into the elegant art deco lobby that I'm in now, with sweeping high ceilings and smooth marble floors. Light is pouring in through the tall glass windows, which are adorned with golden leaf-shaped spandrels, and the whole room glows a beautiful copper.

It's perfect. It's freaking perfect. All the apartments in West Hollywood, and Megan had to find the PERFECT ONE. There's no way she appreciates this majesty! I bet she doesn't even know what a chevron is!!

1:35 P.M.

I give up on literally everything.

After I'd waited in the lobby for fifteen minutes, the elevator let out a sharp *ding* as the metallic doors opened wide. Out walked Megan—arms outstretched, hip popped, and pink jumpsuit customized with a golden *MM*—sending a shudder of self-consciousness down my slightly slouched spine.

"AAAAAAHHHHHHHHHHHHHH!!!!! YOU'RE HEEERREER-ERRREEE!"

Her piercing shriek echoed against the marble-and-concrete walls. I tried not to cringe as she ran toward me and threw her arms around my waist, subtly grabbing at my back fat.

"Yeahhhhh!" I imitated with the exuberance of Stephen Hawking.

Megan rocked back and forth with me in her arms, throwing me off-balance so that I was forced to hug her back.

"I'm so, so, SO happy to see—*EEK!*"

Megan gasped and ripped herself away from the hug, covering her mouth in horror.

"OMG, is that dandruff??" she asked, pointing to my snow-covered shoulders.

My cheeks burned as I tried to brush my shirt clean with one hand. "No, it's dry shampoo," I muttered to the marble floor.

Megan breathed a heavy sigh of relief. "Oh, thank goodness! I was wondering why you smell like great-aunt Gerty."

Ugh.

We made our way into the elevator and pressed the button labeled PH: penthouse. She started fiddling with a cursive golden necklace that spelled *Megan* hanging from her neck, and I wondered how many other items she owned that were embroidered with her name/initials.*

"Isn't this place, like, totes retro? Daddy says it's from the Golden Age of Hollywood," Megan bragged, as if I couldn't tell that from the fluted woodwork. "I know the lobby's, like, a little dingy, but the room is totes redone!"

I took a deep breath and put on a strained smile as we arrived at

---

*So far, the count is at two. A symptom of narcissistic personality disorder? My minor in psychology says yes.

the fifteenth floor. We walked across the hallway and to the corner apartment, where we stepped into possibly my worst nightmare.

How could she?! All the charm of the lobby was ruined, replaced by freshly painted, sterile white walls that nearly rendered me blind. There was faux fur *everywhere,* with dangling twinkle lights and mini lanterns hanging from the ceiling. There was so much pink, I felt dizzy. Even the dreaded Moroccan poufs were present.

That, and the massive window overlooking the skyline of Los Angeles.

Megan threw herself onto her white denim couch, tossing fluffy pillows in all directions. I walked over to the window, wondering if there might be some way to jump out.

"Soooooo? What do you think?" she asked rhetorically.

I took another look around Barbie's Dream Suite before answering. "It's . . . I mean, this view is magnificent."

Megan gave a satisfied squeak and stretched her arms overhead, her contour-enhanced abs peeking through. "I knew you'd love it! I'm so obsessed. It was, like, *such* a pain pulling out the old tiles 'cuz of all the permits and stuff, but it was *so* worth it. You wouldn't even know it was in such a stuffy old building."

I suppressed a gag. "Right. So, how was Europe?" I asked, desperate to change the subject.

Megan gasped and swung her legs to the floor, sitting upright. "OMG, Lou. Europe was, like, SO incredible, I can't even."

I nodded, as if this sentence made any sense.

"Obvi I've been to Europe before, but not as, like, a *real human,* you know? Like, over eighteen and stuff. I'm *totes* a different person now. Like, I'm awakened or something. I just understand the world so much better."

I put on a thoughtful expression and leaned against the giant window, half hoping it would break. Megan kept going:

"Just like: why are we so lazy in America? It's so gross. *Everyone* walks *everywhere* in Europe. And the food is, like, SO much less processed. I ate bread every day and didn't gain a *pound*."

"You know, actually," I interjected, "in Japan, it's customary to slaughter the animal at the table to verify the freshness of the food."

Megan blinked at me. "Ew."

I leaned a little harder against the window. "So, anyway," I said, clearing my throat, "I'm glad you had a good time!"

Megan put a hand on her heart and closed her eyes theatrically. "For real, though, if I didn't have my new job and this new apartment, I, like, *never* would have left," she declared.

The smile plastered on my face was starting to hurt. I walked across the room and took a seat on one of the pink poufs. "Speaking of your new job: How is it?" I asked, though I didn't want to know.

"AMAAAAAAAAZING!!!" she belted out, her voice only slightly lower than Stacey's. "The vibe is so chill, and Elysie is *such* a queen— she's, like, my spirit animal. Every day at my job is, like, a dream come true."

She brought her moisturized legs onto the couch, crisscross style. "OMG, but what about you, Lulu? Did you . . . hear back from Holistic yet?"

She smiled slyly, arrogance already painted onto her made-up face. Oh my god. She *knew*! She knew, and she was asking me anyway! I bet her auntie Stacey had told her allllll about my little rejection, but she just HAD to hear me say it. I could feel her smugness radiating like the rays of a bratty, bitchy white sun.

"Actually, I have an interview at a different job," I spat out defiantly.

Megan's haughtiness wavered. "Really?" she asked suspiciously. "What job?"

My body tensed up. I hadn't gotten that far. "It's this . . . uh . . . you know . . . it's a start-up," I lied.

Megan's smile turned vicious. She crossed her arms and tilted her nose up at me, narrowing her beady brown eyes. "Oh? What's the start-up? Have I heard of it?"

My fingers itched for something to fiddle with. I grasped the edges of the pink pouf for comfort.

"It, well, um . . ." I fumbled along, frantically looking around the room for inspiration. My eyes bolted from pink object to pink object until they finally landed on an M-shaped clock.*

". . . it has to do with time. Time management. It's a start-up that helps with time management," I quickly decided.

Megan seemed unconvinced. I stumbled on: "Yeah, so, it's a start-up that helps people who are, you know . . . disorganized. It helps disorganized people learn to manage time. It's an app! It's a time-management app for smartphones that's in early development, but the company hopes to launch it in the fall. I'd be consulting. I have an interview this week."

I buttoned up my story with a confident nod. I couldn't believe how smoothly the lies were pouring out of my mouth! How long does it take to become an expert in something? Ten thousand hours? I must be pretty far along!

Megan gave me a quick up-down and clucked her tongue before uncrossing her arms, defeated. Her smirk went sour while mine became genuine for the first time since parking the car. Ha-*ha*! After years of putting up with Megan's abuse, I finally found the secret to defeating her: unabashed, pathological lying.

"Well, then . . . congrats, babe." Megan sneered. "You just *have* to tell me how it goes."

I tossed my ponytail to one side—the way my mom always does—and gave a small shrug. "Thanks, Meg! I'll let you know right away," I threw back at her.

Megan's gaze wandered down my body, and she scrunched up her

---

*Three.

nose. "Do you know what you're going to wear?" she asked, the judgment oozing from her invisible pores.

I looked down at my striped T-shirt and leggings. "Uh—I'm not sure? I'll ask my mom," I answered flatly.

The snooty smile swiftly returned to Megan's face. *Shit.*

"Ooooo! Come with me! I have *just* the thing."

· · ·

Mama Shell

1:20 P.M.

MS You got another job interview?!?

??? Lou

How did you know about that?? Lou

MS Megan told Stacey and Stacey told me! Why didn't you say anything?

It just happened. In the car ride to Megan's. It's no big deal! Don't tell Dad. Don't tell anyone. Lou

MS Oh, everyone knows already! I texted all the ladies. We're so proud of you! 🤍

MS What's the app called?

MS How much does it pay?

MS Do you think you could work from home??

AUGUST 18
2:15 P.M.

Once again I tried taking a selfie this morning to spice up my Instagram page, but all I did was waste fifteen perfectly good minutes attempting to find an angle in which I only have one chin. Ugh.

I have acquired a serious newfound respect for Valentina and her social media aptitude. Never again will I judge the countless hours she spends planning, executing, and editing what I once called "silly pictures." Every brightly lit salad bowl or shadowless floppy hat shot is a goddamn work of art as far as I'm concerned. If he were born a millennial, Da Vinci probably would have been a blogger.

Officially replacing "create personal brand" with "learn how to use social media" on list of short-term goals.

AUGUST 19

Unknown Number

3:30 P.M.

UN Hey, is this Lou Hansen?

UN This is Susan's nephew, Aaron Levin. My aunt gave me your number! She says you want to get drinks. ;)

3:52 P.M.

Sorry, you have the wrong number. Lou

AUGUST 20

12:40 P.M.

Guess what? Today is my super exciting marketing interview! What a wonderful time to be me!!!

Just kidding. Today, I am getting dressed up in a frilly, slightly snug white blouse and pink blazer that my nemesis picked out for me, and lying to both of my parents about a job interview that I don't have for a start-up that doesn't actually exist.

I've never felt like more of an idiot.

The supposed interview is taking place at Viva Grenada—an Italian/Spanish fusion café in Hollywood—so that's where I'll be getting lunch today. I'd invite a friend to join me, but I still don't have any, which means I'll be eating alone.

Thrilling.

1:12 P.M.

FINALLY found parking. I had to circle the café seven times in the hopes of avoiding valet. Fifteen dollars for an hour? Theft, I say!

1:14 P.M.

Wow, the restaurant is pretty busy! I should have known. I've heard Theo talk about this place at least a dozen times, so it must be great. All right, I should probably eat something healthy. A nice salad? A piece of fish, perhaps? Let's look at the menu . . .

1:16 P.M.

Oh my god, house-made pasta with a Bolognese sauce?! I *must* have it. It's Thursday, so it's pretty much the weekend anyway!

1:20 P.M.

The waiter just asked if I was expecting someone else. I mumbled no under my breath and watched his face twist with pity. Ugh. Going to restaurants alone is humiliating. I'm never doing it again.

1:25 P.M.

Actually, going to restaurants alone is kind of nice! No food restrictions, no pesky conversations to keep up with . . . Maybe I'll do this more often!

1:31 P.M.

I. AM. SO. BORED. And I'm positive everyone in this restaurant thinks that I'm being stood up. Writing in the journal is helpful, though, since it looks like I might be a writer or poet or something. Damn, I should have brought my laptop! No one questions a girl in a café with a laptop.

How long would this interview normally be? Fifteen minutes? I feel like fifteen minutes is more than acceptable. I'm turning down this theoretical job, anyway. I'll leave as soon as I finish my pasta.

1:35 P.M.

CODE RED. CODE RED. THEO JUST WALKED IN WITH ANOTHER WOMAN.

Currently hiding under my table to keep him from seeing me. What is he doing here? Isn't he supposed to be at work?? And who is *she*? Must investigate further.

1:40 P.M.

Okay, I ran to the bathroom with a dessert menu covering my face and caught a glimpse of the mystery woman. She has to be thirty-five at LEAST, with the most stunning curly red hair I've ever seen. Wow. I bet she *does* read Nietzsche. UGH. I can't believe it. Come to think of it . . . Theo *has* been unusually busy as of late. Working late hours with "Charlize" and "Leonardo" . . . Oh god. Am I being cheated on?? I'll die if Theo's cheating on me with a freckle-faced older woman who may or may not have an interest in nihilism. And after protecting him from my mother all this time?! I'm going back in there, dammit!!

As if today could get even more humiliating.

I crept out of the bathroom toward my lonely corner table, nose shoved deeply into the menu, still trying to steal looks at my boyfriend and the anonymous redhead. While craning my neck backwards, I managed to walk straight into a particularly short counter stool, tumbling over it and into a rolling cheese cart with a *clank*. The cart barreled forward, crashing into an empty table, sending cheeses flying in every direction. Rolls of Brie and Gouda rained down onto the floor and me, still on the ground, frozen from shock and mortification. All eyes whipped in my direction.

"Lou?!"

Theo's voice hit the back of my head harder than the cheeses hit the floor. I slowly turned around and choked on a fit of nervous giggles, trying to smile as though nothing had just occurred.

"Theo?!" I managed in a surprised manner. Both he and the redhead were staring wide-eyed at me. Waiters were rushing to pick up the fallen mold while customers uncomfortably tried to look away. Theo jumped up and ran over, kneeled to my level, and placed a caring hand on my knee.

"Are you okay?" he asked, worry lacing his furrowed brows. I peeked over his shoulder at the human version of Ariel, who was gaping at me as if I were an actual train wreck.

"What, me? Of course I'm okay! I'm fine! I'm great! Just clumsy, as usual! Ha-ha-ha-ha!"

The giggles escaped in an awful burst as Theo hoisted me to my feet. I brushed myself off, picking both the menu and my journal off the floor as the restaurant returned to its usual bustle.

"What are you doing here?" Theo asked as though *I* had something to explain to *him*. "And, uh . . . what are you wearing?"

I looked down at my frill-covered white blouse, which I realized had several red pasta stains on it. I frantically buttoned up the blazer and crossed my arms across my chest.

"I had a job interview," I swiftly lied. "I was going to tell you later."

Theo's face lit up with excitement that filled the entire café. "What?!" he asked, grabbing me by both arms. "That's amazing! How'd it go??"

Suddenly the ridiculousness of the situation washed over me like a tidal wave. I am *such* an ass! That's not the face of a cheater! That's the face of a loyal and loving boyfriend who's yet to realize that his girlfriend's a complete dunce.

The mysterious redhead approached us timidly from behind Theo—her round face assessing the sad scene. "Is everything all right over here?" she asked. Theo spun around and nodded a little awkwardly.

"Yes, everything's fine! Lou, this is my boss," he said. "Jackie, this is Lou. Lou is my girlfriend."

Jackie's hesitation melted away and she smiled at me, extending a freckle-covered hand. I took it limply, all but dead from embarrassment. She gave it a firm shake.

"Well, hey there, Lou!" she said. "It's nice to meet you! You took quite a tumble there, didn't you?"

I laughed a little too loudly and crossed my arms again, trying to shrink into the floor. "Yeah, well . . . you know. These stools just come out of nowhere!"

I am so stupid. Why am I so stupid?

Jackie put her hands on her hips and grinned over at Theo. "We've all hit the deck once or twice," she said sympathetically.

"Or a hundred thousand times, if you're me," I half joked.

Jackie let out a hearty laugh, and I chuckled along with her. I tried putting my hands on my hips confidently, like her, but the buttons on my blazer popped off and flew across the room. She laughed even harder. I turned as red as her hair/my pasta stain.

"So," I said, trying hard to divert their attention, "you work in the kitchen with Theo?"

Theo shook his head. "Actually, Jackie's one of the owners of Farmhouse Catering," he explained. "She's in charge of the LA branch."

"Oh, wow! That's impressive!" I said, declaring the obvious.

Jackie seemed charmed by my simplicity. "Well, thank you. I try to be." Her eyes glimmered with amusement. "But the person who's really impressive here is your boyfriend. He's quite the talent, as I'm sure you know."

Theo blushed and stared down at his shoes, which I noticed had purple laces.

"Trust me, I do," I quickly agreed, nodding emphatically. "I'm honestly just dating him for his ricotta toast."

Theo sent a loving smile my way. Jackie's grew wider.

"Well then, maybe we add ricotta toast to the menu, huh?" The question was directed at Theo, who was turning into the lankier version of Bashful from the Seven Dwarfs. I, on the other hand, had somehow morphed into Dopey.

"The menu?" I asked, looking back and forth between the two of them. "What menu?"

Jackie checked her watch, probably deciding if her time was well spent answering a sauce-covered plebeian like me.

"I'm opening up a new restaurant next month," she graciously explained. "Farm to table, primarily Mediterranean. I've been scouting some of the young caterers at Farmhouse, and after watching him work for a few months now, I'm asking Theo to be one of my chef de parties."

My chin dropped to the frills of Megan's blouse. "WHAT??" I yelled much too loudly. "Wait. Isn't that a sous chef position? I could be wrong. I think that's what they said on *Chopped*. I can't remember exactly. We watch a lot of *Chopped*."

Jackie laughed again, patting Theo on the back. "You've got a funny one here, huh, Theo? Yes, he'd be a sous chef. And frankly, my right-hand guy. Assuming he takes the position."

For a moment, I forgot all about my embarrassment and was overcome with pure, unmitigated joy. Theo was being asked to work as a CHEF! A real-life honest-to-goodness *Chopped*-level sous chef!! My heart soared with pride as Jackie looked back over her shoulder to their food-adorned table.

"Well, our lunch just got here, so we should probably get to it."

"Yes! Of course!" I said, nodding furiously. "Go and eat! Just don't get it all over yourself, like I did." I pointed with two fingers toward my multiple pasta stains. Jackie squinted at my chest.

"Oh, look at that! I hadn't even noticed!"

And with that, she turned around and walked back to her booth. Theo grabbed both of my hands in his and squeezed them tightly, his buckteeth fully out.

"This is such a good day! I can't wait to hear about your interview . . . I'll call you in the car, okay?"

"Okay," I croaked.

He gave me a quick peck on the cheek and skipped back to the table, where Jackie had already bitten into her fresh chopped salad. It took me a minute to remember what on earth I was even doing there, covered in pasta sauce in a ruined blazer alone on a Thursday. All the pieces fell into place as I slowly made my way back to my cold bowl of Bolognese.

Wow. So this is what bottom looks like: pretending to interview for a fake job while almost ruining your boyfriend's offer for a real one.

Could this day possibly get any worse??!?

Megan Bitchell 🍦

3:30 P.M.

MB Soooooooo? How'd it go?

> Great! Excellent. In fact, they offered me a job right on the spot, but I don't think I'm going to take it.

Lo

MB OMG, why not???

> The headquarters are in Cambodia, so I'd have to move there for at least five years.

Lo

MB Awww, that's such a bummer! But don't worry . . . something will turn up!

MB PS: can you return the outfit ASAP? It's Prada, and I, like, REALLY need it for a charity event.

AUGUST 23

12:16 P.M.

Mom stormed into the kitchen this afternoon carrying four canvas bags stuffed with multicolored bottles. They clinked together loudly as Mom set them down on the kitchen counter, Dad trailing behind her, arms crossed.

"Mom? What is that?"

She began pulling glass bottles out of the bags one by one, placing them on the countertop. The pugs trotted over and sat on my feet, anxious to be part of the action. Dad shook his head and disappeared into the pantry.

"These are our meals for the next week!" Mom chirped, opening the refrigerator door. I pulled one of the bottles from the bag and read the label.

"Aloe vera ginger juice?"

She nodded, her blond hair bouncing just above her shoulders. She began filling the fridge with the strange elixirs.

"That's right! You and I are juicing for seven days, Lulu!"

I picked up another bottle: charcoal Reishi root blend. Ugh. "So we're drinking these juices for the next seven days?"

"That's right!"

Muffin and Baguette stared up at me, desperate to be included. I lowered the bottle to their level, giving them a sniff. Muffin licked it twice, violently snorted, and then ran into the other room. Baguette growled. Not a good sign.

"Okay, Mom, that's fine. But where's the food?"

"This is the food!"

I cocked my head and frowned. "I think we have a very different definition of food."

Mom started removing half-empty Diet Cokes from the back of the fridge to make room, spilling them into the sink. "What's the big deal? You've done plenty of cleanses before."

"Yeah, but normally they include some sort of chewing. Four ounces of protein. A carrot stick. Anything."

A plastic bag popped open in the pantry and was followed by the distinct crunch of potato chips. We have potato chips?? Since when do we have potato chips?!

"That's the whole point of a cleanse, honey! Solid food is too harsh on the stomach. They're saying it's the best thing to do for your digestive system . . . Prepare to flush out those nasty toxins!"

My whole body shuddered. No food for seven days? Surely this was banned by the Geneva convention. I rolled my eyes as more crunching sounds emanated from the pantry.

"Why isn't Dad doing it?" I asked.

The crunching abruptly stopped. Mom shook her head. "Because it would be too expensive to add a third cleanse for the week, and your father is addicted to food."

"I am not!" Dad protested, his mouth half full.

"You are, too!" Mom and I shouted back in unison.

Dad growled words like *whipped* and *browbeaten* as he sulked back into the kitchen, the dust of fallen chips spattering his guilty chest. Mom shoved the bottles deeper into the fridge, the entire shelf dominated by vibrant juices and alkaline waters.

I quickly considered my options as Mom yelled at Dad about the evils of processed foods:

I could refuse the cleanse altogether, but that would put me in terrible standing with Mom. I'd end up a pariah in my own home, which would be difficult considering it's where I spend 99 percent of my time as of late.

I could subtly cheat throughout the cleanse, but that's a preposterous waste of money and my mother would find out. She always does. It's like she has a sixth sense that detects whenever carbs come near my face. She would hear the crunching of a single snap pea from a mile away if I dared to attempt a nibble.

Then of course I could . . . just do it? Why not? It's not like I have any dinners or social events planned this week. And if all goes well, I'll be a few pounds lighter, which is on my list of medium-term goals and of course will make Mom happy. Maybe this is the secret weapon I've been looking for! Maybe, just maybe, this will lead to . . .

"All right," I conceded as Dad ran out of the room to escape the nagging. "Seven days of juices. Sounds great! I'll look at this as an experiment. And hey, it's great that the bottles are recyclable!"

Mom smiled wide. "That's the spirit! I'm so happy to see you embracing health in this way! Maybe spending a day with Megan wasn't so bad after all. Now, help me find where your father hides those potato chips."

AUGUST 24
8:30 P.M.

Juice cleanse, day one:

Hunger Level: Surprisingly, the hunger has been manageable. I craved solid food only twice today, and both times I was able to curb it with alkaline water or coffee.* The juices themselves have ranged from pretty good to absolutely revolting, depending entirely on the presence of fruit. I didn't think it was possible to juice plain dirt, but this company may have found a way to do it.

The equation I've come up with is:

$$\text{Taste of Juice} = (\text{Number of Fruits per drink [NF]} / \text{Number of Vegetables per drink [NV]}) - \text{Hunger Level [HL]}$$

Physical Sensations: I have peed approximately three hundred and forty-nine times today.

Mood: Generally unpleasant, but not terrible. Comparable to a light PMS, or a bad encounter with a disagreeable relative. Regardless, I'm going to bed early, so I can be one day closer to the end of this nonsense.

AUGUST 25
9:20 P.M.

Juice cleanse, day two:

Hunger Level: Today was . . . harder. I experienced some tummy grumbling, and I had to hold my nose to choke down certain

---

*Technically I'm not supposed to be having coffee, but I can take only so much abuse.

juices. Luckily, my tongue has started to go numb from all the acid, so it's harder to taste anything anymore. The updated equation is as follows:

$$\text{Taste of Juice} = (\text{Number of Fruits per drink [NF]} / \text{Number of Vegetables per drink [NV]}) - \text{Hunger Level [HL]} \times \text{Number of Juices Already Consumed [JAC]}$$

Physical Sensations: I've started getting hunger headaches and continue to pee like a diabetic who is pregnant with twins. My energy is low, and so is my tolerance for Mom, who continues to call the cleanse "euphoric."

Mood: The mood swings fluctuate from slightly peeved to egregiously annoyed, but I've yet to hit any extreme levels of sadness or rage. All in all, it was a good day.

Only five more to go.

AUGUST 26
9:47 P.M.

Whoever created the all-liquid cleanse deserves to spend eternity in a purgatory so dark and desolate, their souls beg for the sweet escape of toxin-filled hell.

Hunger Level: 40 years stranded in the desert.

Physical Sensations: The headaches are blazing. I can barely lift my arms to write this. It's like someone spray-painted the front of my brain with lighter fluid and lit a match. I started chewing on my own finger just to feel the sensation on my teeth again. Ugh.

Mood: I'm absolutely fucking miserable and downright homicidal. Mother is first on the list. How is she so damn chipper??

"I feel amazing!" she all but sang to me, lightly dancing into the living room. I stared up at her from the couch, a zombielike expression stuck on my face. "What about you, Lulu? Don't you feel amazing??"

I grunted and hiccupped a little. She didn't seem to hear or care.

"Wow, I'm feeling so good . . . I might just extend the cleanse for a few more days! What do you think, honey?"

I choked back tears. Extending? Mom twirled out of the room and I slumped so deep into the couch that I fell off onto the floor. The pugs found my motionless body and licked my face, like fat little vultures feasting on the dead.

Almost halfway there.

AUGUST 27
8:10 P.M.

Day four, and I'm feeling . . . good? Can that be true?? The headaches are gone, even though I didn't drink coffee today, and I've begun noticing subtle complex flavors in the juices. Dandelion has a bit of a bitter taste, doesn't it? Huh. Who knew consuming dirt required such a sensitive palate?? I'll have to discuss the culinary possibilities with Theo later.

Is it plausible that this godforsaken cleanse actually *does* flush out some sort of strange, mental-blocking toxins? I might be able to suffer through this, after all!

AUGUST 28
10:15 A.M.

I. Feel. GREAT!

Day five, and I'm feeling positively excellent. Exultant! Blissfully swimming in a cloud of oxygen and glorious golden light. WOW, energy is bursting from my core!! Where is Mom? I need to find Mom! It's a beautiful day and we're going to go on a HIKE!

1:45 P.M.

I effortlessly ran that entire hike TWICE. I could barely even feel my legs, much less experience pain. I've never seen Mom look so proud of me. She was actually glowing! Or maybe that was the aura that seems to be emitting from objects every thirty minutes. It's hard to tell. BUT SHE WAS SO PROUD!!!

AUGUST 29
10:27 A.M.

Hahaha everything's glowingggggggg. My head feels funny. I think I'm seeing spots. Or polka dots. Polka spots? OOOOOO the pretty colors!

12:30 P.M.

Why's my body tingling? Is that normal? It's like I'm carbonated. Can humans be carbonated?? Whoa.

5:45 P.M.

I don't want anyone to panic . . . but I think the living room lamp might be alive. It keeps dancing in circles, but no one else sees it. WHY CAN'T ANYONE ELSE SEE IT?!

9:12 P.M.

Everything is beautiful. How is everything so beautiful?? I just want to hug everyone in the whole world. I AM NEVER EATING SOLID FOOD AGAIN!!!

AUGUST 30
7:30 P.M.

The Last Will and Testament of Eloise Laurent Hansen

As she feels the grip of death slowly but surely closing around her juice-filled body, Ms. Hansen leaves to her beloved successors the following:

To MAMA SHELL, Eloise leaves all the material possessions found in her closet, oversize as they may be. She also asks that Shelly dresses her for the funeral, since Lou would never be allowed to do it herself.

To PAPA HANSEN, she leaves her cherished book collection, as well as the stash of dark chocolate and pretzels that she kept in the first-aid box below the sink.

To HER SISTER, VALENTINA, Eloise bestows her old ID to be used as a fake, assuming Val does not have a fake already. She also grants Val access to all her embarrassing pictures and journals, to be burned if deemed necessary by the new possessor.

To HER BOYFRIEND, THEODORE, Lou leaves her fallen dignity and deepest condolences, seeing as he'll now know the dark secrets of her wacky family. Also, all her cookbooks, coffee mugs, and whatever succulents he so chooses.

TO HER PUGS, Eloise grants permission for her old bedroom to be converted into a doggy restroom, which it might as well be at this point, anyway.

AUGUST 31

Alyssa 🐾

3:45 P.M.

Al — Girl. Today was the first day of classes, so we had an all-school introduction assembly. Guess who made an appearance as our guest speaker.

> Gloria Allred?

> Ruth Bader Ginsburg?

> Kerry Washington in character as Olivia Pope??

Al — Nope. Dr. Richmanson!

> . . . you're kidding me.

Al — I know! How crazy is that?

Al — We're getting coffee next week.

Al — Apparently, his best friend's law firm is looking for new interns. He's going to write me a rec!!

Al — Isn't that exciting?!?

Month Five

Back-to-School Shopping

Mama Shell

10:35 A.M.

Mom, where are you?

MS Sitting in Val's AP bio class. How did you ever get through this??

Why are you in Val's bio class?

MS It's back-to-school day. I'm so bored . . . no wonder I always played hooky.

MS By the way, Olivia's mom has resting bitch face.

. . . Mom, don't text in class. Lou

11:03 A.M.

Val just spent three weeks in Topanga eating crappy grilled-cheese sandwiches and shoveling dirt, yet she somehow looks like she went through an episode of *Extreme Makeover: Camp Edition*. She's toned and tanned, and I'm pretty sure her butt got even perkier. Seriously, who comes home from camp looking *better* than when they left? Most of us were still finding soil in our near-dreads for three weeks afterward, grateful to be using a shower with hot water that didn't require flip-flops.

Hold on, I'm getting a call.

11:15 A.M.

. . . Well, that was weird.

Mom just called me from the car, hysterically crying.

"My *last* back-to-school day, Lulu!" she blubbered as I stared across the bathroom at the dreaded scale. "It's just hitting me now! No more pickups, no more drop-offs, no more parent-teacher conferences or SAT tutors . . ."

"Isn't that a good thing?" I asked, slowly tiptoeing toward the digital doomsday mechanism.

"Of course not!" she yelled too loudly into the phone. "For twenty years, I've been sitting in the backs of classrooms, listening to your teachers drone on and on about *enhanced curriculums* and *critical thinking*. Because that's what *moms* do! That's who I am!"

Another flood of tears overtook her as I came face-to-face with my inanimate nemesis. I braced myself, hovered one foot over the scale, and then quickly withdrew, too afraid to step down.

"You're still a mom, Mom. That doesn't suddenly change."

Mom's wavering voice came booming through my phone speaker: "But it's not the same! You don't *need* me anymore. You and your sister are strong, independent, fully capable young women."

I lifted my foot again and let all the air out of my body before stepping onto the scale, eyes squinted so that I could barely make out the number.

. . . *Ugh*.

"Yeah, the 'fully capable' thing is kind of debatable right now."

Mom let out a tiny hiccup. "Oh, sweetie, you'll find a job. You have the whole world in front of you! What do *I* have to look forward to? More wrinkles and senior citizen discounts??"

"But you won't be a senior citizen for another ten years."

"ONLY TEN?!"

Even more tears. Dad's low voice mumbled words of comfort on the other end of the line as I contemplated how leftover juice might still be hiding in my organs, keeping me the same exact weight as I was pre-cleanse. Maybe if I start crying, too, I'll rid myself of some remaining liquid.

"I'm sorry you're upset, Mom. Is there anything I can do?"

"Yes, actually," she said, sniffling a bit. "Will you go with me to the doctor tomorrow? Normally I go with a friend, but no one's available."

"Of course! What's going on? Are you feeling sick?"

"No, it's just a routine checkup."

"Okay. Is Dad coming, too?"

"No, he has to work on a very important property tomorrow and he's terrified of needles."

". . . Needles?"

The Han Fam

MS   Pack your bags, girlies! We're going to Santa Barbara!

Val   ?!?!?

> What? When?? **Lou**

MS   Labor Day weekend! Stacey and Buck go every year, and your father thinks a vacation will be good for my psyche.

Val   HELLS YEAH!!!

> That sounds great! **Lou**

Val   Thanks, Dad!

PH   👍

MS   Perfect! We'll leave on Friday morning to beat the traffic and come home Sunday night.

Val   But I have class on Friday . . .

MS   So? It's your senior year! Don't you know "D" is for diploma?

SEPTEMBER 2

3:45 P.M.

If rhinoplasty had a patron saint, it would certainly be saint Saj Kapadia, the most renowned plastic surgeon in Los Angeles. More faces have been broken in his office than at the World Boxing Association—and more money has been spent, as well.

"He's an artist," Mom raved on our car ride over. "He makes sure that each nose is perfectly suited to the person's features. None of that bunny-slope nonsense you see those southern pageant girls sporting."

"I don't want a nose job, Mother," I said, anticipating the question.

"Who said anything about *you*? *I'm* thinking of getting one," she explained, pulling the passenger mirror down and eyeing her already slender bridge.

"Didn't you already get a nose job?" I asked, stealing a look in her direction.

"Of course, but that was a long time ago. And it's not a *Saj* nose. Saj is like the Chanel of the face."

We pulled into the parking lot and walked the eighteen flights of stairs to Saj's office, where Mom was greeted like the Sultaness of Juvéderm.* Everyone in the office knew her by name, including the reverend himself, who was somewhere between the ages of thirty and sixty-five. It's impossible to tell.

"Ahhh, my beautiful Shell." He greeted Mom with a hug so warm, I'm pretty sure a glacial ice cap melted. "We've missed you. Is this your . . . sister?" he said, gesturing toward me.

"Stepdaughter," Mom said with a wink in my direction.

"*Actual* daughter," I corrected. I pointed to my own nose. "*This* is what she looked like with the first one."

Saj laughed so deeply and graciously, I suddenly understood why anyone would allow him to stick needles into their face. He was mesmerizing. Also, oddly attractive for a thirty- to sixty-five-year-old man.

In only fifteen minutes, Mom looked ten years younger. I'm amazed, if not slightly traumatized and confused. I held Mom's hand as Saj worked his magic, like an inverse sculptor at work. It was fascinating. But about halfway through the visit, I couldn't help but wonder: When did Mom stop holding my hand during TB shots and I start holding her hand during Botox shots?

---

*Mom refuses to get in elevators due to her supposed claustrophobia, which I'm convinced is just a ploy to make us take the stairs.

SEPTEMBER 3

Theo 🖤

3:30 P.M.

I think I may have created the most delicious labneh and macadamia scallops the world has ever known.

But the only way to know for sure is if taster extraordinaire Lou Hansen gives it a five-kiss rating.

Is she free for dinner tonight?

Hells YES she is! I LOVE labneh!!!

Boom shakalaka! Jett is joining us, so dinner will be served at seven o'clock sharp.

Great. 😊 I have to help Val write a letter to her dean excusing her from class on Friday, but I'll be over shortly after.

Oh, right, Santa Barbara! What excuse is she using?

"Family emergency." Lou

What's the emergency?

Mom's feeling old. Lou

8:05 P.M.

Theo had meet-and-greet day at the restaurant this afternoon, where he met with the other chefs, the property manager, and, of course, Jackie.

"You must be stoked, man," Jett said through a mouthful of labneh. "Jackie Reid is a culinary goddess. That makes you, like, a foodie demigod, dude."

Theo chuckled, slapping a second round of scallops onto Jett's plate. "Yeah, I'm pretty pumped. Nervous, though. The restaurant opens in less than a month."

"Is this going to be on the menu?" I asked, pointing a fork at my near-empty plate.

Theo shrugged. "Probably not. The menu is already set. I just have to cook what's on it."

"Then they're missing out, man," Jett said, forking another huge bite. "This is unreal."

Theo smiled. "Thanks, guys. It means a lot. It'll be nice to have a set schedule, too, so we can finally plan that family dinner, Louie."

Jett shot us a confused look. "Have you still not met the parents?" he asked, perplexed.

Theo shook his head. "Alas, no."

"Why not?" Jett pushed. "I thought this was happening, like, back in July, or whatever."

I could feel Theo's gaze on the side of my face as I paid particularly close attention to the details on my plate.

"Our schedules just haven't lined up," I explained forcefully. "My dad is a workaholic, Val went to summer camp, you guys were crazy-busy with the catering, the excitement with Theo's new job . . . It just, you know, hasn't panned out."

"Bummer," Jett said, using a finger to lick up some of the extra labneh before plunging it in his mouth. "Well, when you *do* have dinner, you should cook this. If this doesn't win them over, nothing will."

Maybe being three inches taller with a six-pack, I thought.

Theo took a seat next to me, resting a hand on my knee. "Well, once this restaurant opens, there will be nothing stopping me from finally meeting the folks. Right, Louie Love?"

·   ·   ·

Mama Shell

10:16 P.M.

MS What time are you coming home from Natasha's?

MS Call me.

MS Are you sleeping over??

MS I'm not going to bed until I know you're home.

MS Call me

MS I need to know if you're sleeping over so I can turn the alarm on.

MS The pugs miss you. Come home.

MS We'll have coffee in the morning, it'll be fun

MS Call your mother!!!

SEPTEMBER 4

1:14 P.M.

Wow. Mom's not taking this whole back-to-school thing very well.

Not that I blame her . . . I woke up this morning in a full sweat, convinced I had slept through my alarm and that I was late to "Criminal Psychology" or "The Science of Wind Storms" or some other class. It was like the PTSD of PGM.

But Mom seems unusually distressed. Her behavior has been pretty outlandish, even by her standards. When I got home from Theo's today, I found her in the living room, lounging on the couch with cucumbers over her eyes and a bright yellow facial mask on. Classical music sounded through the speakers, and lavender incense made the whole house smell like yoga.

Mom lifted one cucumber to look at me. "How do I look?" she asked.

"Like you have jaundice."

"Good! That means it's oxygenating. Only ten more minutes, and then I'll put in the whitening strips!"

My ears perked up in recognition of the symphony playing around us.

"Is this . . . Mozart?"

"Yes! I used to play it for you all the time. They say that listening to Mozart can help make people smarter."

"Yeah, if they're infants."*

"Must you be so negative? I'm trying to better myself! You should try it, since you're so obsessed with getting a job."

"Is that a bad thing?"

"Don't sass me, I'm your mother. Now get me an algae shot . . . I bought a jar of it for us and put it in the fridge."

Dad's right: Mom desperately needs a vacation. Speaking of which, I should probably make a to-do list for Santa Barbara. We leave tomorrow morning, and I couldn't be more excited!! A weekend away is *exactly* what I need to pull myself out of this fog. Some peace, quiet, and clarity will do wonders for my cluttered-up brain.

LOU'S LIST OF SANTA BARBARA MUST-SEES

- The Mission District/Gardens
- Santa Barbara Museum of Art
- McConnell's Fine Ice Creams (sorry, Mom)
- Stearns Wharf
- The French Press (artisanal coffee shop + bakery, at Theo's recommendation)
- Funk Zone (recommended by Natasha after her California coast bike ride)

Megan Bitchell 💡

2:15 P.M.

MB BAAAAABBBBEEE!!! What are you bringing to SB??

---

*These findings were also inconclusive, but I did not mention this, since it was nice to have music other than Top 40 playing.

MB — I was thinking, like, lots of off-the-shoulder shirts, but I'm worried about tan lines. Also I'm TOTES into maxi dresses right now.

Wait, you're coming? — Lou

MB — OMG YAS! Did your mama not tell you?

No . . . — Lou

MB — LOL SURPRISE!!! I'm staying with Auntie Stacey and Uncle Buck! Which obvi means we'll be in the SAME HOTEL!!!

MB — How fun is that?!?

MB — BTW I'm doing my nails today and I'm thinking classic nude. Thoughts?

4:37 P.M.

Help. My serene Labor Day weekend away just became a lot more laborful.

I stormed into Mom's bathroom, where she was sitting at her vanity, putting curlers in her hair.

"*Megan* is going?" I barked, unable to contain my horror.

Mom barely turned away from the mirror, not noticing my obvious rage. "Yes! I just found out this morning. Isn't that wonderful?"

I pulled my cheeks down with the palms of my hands. "Whyyyyy does she have to come?" I moaned.

Mom rolled another lock of hair into place on top of her head, fastening the curl tightly to her scalp. "What's wrong? Aren't you excited to have a friend on the trip?"

"The last time we traveled with Megan, I ended up missing half an eyebrow."

"She was just trying to help shape them."

"With Nair?!"

"It was an accident!"

I rolled my eyes.

Mom pinned another curl up and swiveled her head back and forth, examining her work in the mirror. "Listen, honey, you've been in a real slump. This trip is just as much for you as it is for me. If you *really* don't want Megan to come, that's fine. You'll just have to call Stacey and explain why her niece is not welcome on their annual trip."

She stuck her chin out and pouted, both literally and metaphorically.

I let out a defeated sigh. "No, of course it's all right. Just—*please* don't ask her to help shape my eyebrows, or give me a facial or anything."

Mom stuck the last pin into place and turned toward me, looking like a blond Medusa. "Of course not! Why would I do that when there's a spa at the hotel? I already reserved a facial for you on day one."

SEPTEMBER 5

Shelly Hansen
@ShellyHansen

#SantaBarbara for the long weekend! Can't wait to soak up that #sun #surf #sand #sangria!!! @SoCal_SoVal @LouHansen @StaceyFHoffman @MeganMitchell 🍷🏄☀️

9:15 A.M.

At last, some good news to report! As it turns out, Megan isn't let out of work until five this afternoon, which means I get one fully Megan-less day of vacation to clear my head. Finally, being unemployed pays off! Funk Zone, here I come!!

OFFICIAL SERVICE DOG CERTIFICATE

K9: Muffin Hansen
Breed: Pug
Handler: Shelly Hansen
Registration #: 2634704

This certificate signifies that Muffin Hansen has been registered as a therapy dog for Mrs. Shelly Lynn Hansen. Mrs. Hansen suffers from anxiety, and is dependent on Muffin to sooth her during times of stress. For this reason, Muffin's presence is a critical factor in Mrs. Hansen's mental health, and should be present with his handler at all times.

* * *

9:20 A.M.

"*Service dogs?*" I shouted from the backseat as Baguette blew snot in my face.

"I registered them on the Internet!" Mom insisted, turning around from the front to face me. "What more do you want?"

"Mom, I know newborn babies who are better behaved than these pugs."

"Oh, it's fine!" Mom dismissed, waving her hand at me. "If anyone has a problem, I can show them my papers."

Muffin pressed his smooshed-up pug face against the car window, his breath sounding like a powering-up chain saw.

"Dad?" I asked uncertainly.

He just shrugged. "It's legal."

"YAYYY!" Val squealed, pulling Baguette onto her lap.

"All right, here we go!" Mom clapped her hands together in delight. "The Official Hansen Family vacation starts: NOW!"

OFFICIAL AAA REPORT

Vehicle Owner: Charles J. Hansen

Report: Flat Tire, Back Left

Time: 10:59 A.M.

Comments: Charles J. Hansen called to report a flat tire on Interstate 101 near Ventura County. Mr. Hansen reported to have hit a pothole at around 10:31 A.M., causing an "extreme jump" from the vehicle. Mr. Hansen, traveling with his wife, two daughters, and two pugs, did not attempt to pull to the side of the road, despite an alert from the car stating "back left tire compromised." According to Mrs. Hansen, Mr. Hansen insisted the alert was "full of shit" and just used out of an abundance of caution.

After driving approximately one mile, Mrs. Hansen and daughters Eloise and Valentina began voicing concerns about a "strange thumping" as they drove down the highway, asking to pull over and check. Mr. Hansen, not wanting to get stuck in Labor Day weekend traffic, insisted that it was "just the goddamn infrastructure" and proceeded to rant about "where the hell his taxes were going."

At approximately 10:40 A.M., an emergency light began blinking rapidly, signaling that the tire pressure in the back-left tire was dangerously low. At this point, the daughters both claim that Mrs. Hansen began threatening Mr. Hansen, holding her expensive sunglasses out the window and repeatedly shouting, "I'll do it!" Finally, just as Mr. Hansen started to pull over, the car came to a halt in the middle of the freeway, causing two cars to swerve to avoid colliding with the Hansen vehicle. Thankfully, no injuries or casualties have been reported.

A truck has been sent to retrieve Mr. Hansen's vehicle and tow it back to Los Angeles. However, Mrs. Hansen is insisting she and her family make it to Santa Barbara for the long weekend, and has requested a rental car big enough to carry the family of four, their dogs, and their unusually hefty amount of luggage. Their car dealership will be sending over a minivan, though this part of the incident will not be covered by their insurance plan.

2:36 P.M.

Well, we made it.

We lost a good four and a half hours of our trip, but we made it.

Pulling up to the beachside hotel in our rental minivan was like entering the promised land after forty years of traveling in the desert by foot. We were cranky, exhausted, and hungry, since Mom had packed snacks only for the pugs. We practically fell into the hotel lobby, kissing the sand-sprinkled floor as fellow tourists walked back and forth in their sandals.

On the bright side: Thanks to a surplus of points on Mom's credit card, Val and I are sharing an ocean-facing suite with two full beds and a completely stocked mini-fridge. It's magnificent! We immediately ripped open the overpriced jar of sea-salt cashews and devoured them within seconds, lying on our military-tight beds with the abandon of newly freed prisoners.

"That. Was. *Hell*." Val groaned, her arms and legs splayed out starfish style.

"I hate the freeway," I agreed.

We both let out sighs of relief as our phones vibrated simultaneously:

Mom: *Meet us downstairs for lunch in five minutes. Your dad's hangry, and the pugs need water.*

"Do we tell her about the cashews?" Val asked me.

"No. Definitely not. Cashews are the fattiest of the nuts," I told her.

All right. So we'll have a quick lunch down at the restaurant, which will give me just enough time to get to the spa for my facial at 3:15. I definitely won't have time to check any items off my list, but I still have two more days. For now, I'm just going to take some deep, ocean-air breaths, and try to relax.

Megan Bitchell 💀

4:10 P.M.

MB Start the party, bitches!!! 😈

MB LOL JK but for real Elysie let me off work early today!!

MB Where are you guys??

4:14 P.M.

MB OMG, this hotel is GORG. I'm DED

4:17 P.M.

MB Found your fam!! You're getting a facial?? YAS girl that'll TOTES get rid of the third eye you had when I saw you 😜

MB hahahaha jk

5:30 P.M.

RIP my face.

I always envisioned spa treatments as a relaxing blend of exotic music and various flavored waters. Instead, I paid money to have a stranger in a lab coat torture me for an hour. It was soothing at first, but then my facialist started poking and squeezing and rubbing oils on me that stung with the intensity of a thousand aggravated bees.

"What's in this mask??" I asked at one point as my skin started to burn. In a thick Russian accent, she replied: "Eet eez honey, essence of laffender, clay imported from ze Dead Sea, and jalap-ey-ño extract."

She proceeded to slap a variety of creams and cleansers onto my face, each itchier and more irritating than the last. After an hour of squeezing, exfoliating, and extracting, she finally dismissed me with a few parting instructions: "So ree-member to stay hy-drated, to keep out of ze sun for ze next four days, and . . ."

"Hold on," I interrupted, stretching my facial muscles so that they might retain feeling. "It's Labor Day weekend. This is Santa Barbara. We're at the beach. I'm not supposed to go in the sun?"

"No, zat will damage ze peel."

"PEEL?!"

I rushed over to the hanging mirror and sure enough: the creases around my nose and eyes were starting to shrivel and flake, revealing raw red skin underneath.

"Oh my god," I choked out, mortified.

"Don't vorry, love," she said. "Eet'll get vorse before eet gets better, but after three dayz yur skeen weel be flawless."

Mama Shell

9:12 P.M.

MS — This waiter isn't getting a tip.

??? — Lou

Why? Did he do something wrong? — Lou

MS — He didn't card me.

. . . Are you serious right now? — Lou

MS — He carded you and Megan and Val! Why didn't he card me?

He didn't card Stacey, either! — Lou

MS — Which is why he won't be getting a tip.

At least he can look you in the face. He keeps avoiding eye contact with me, like I'm some sort of basilisk.

MS   What's a basilisk?

It's a fictional serpent that can kill people with a single glance.

MS   Oh. I thought it might be a cocktail.

Mother put your phone away we're at dinner.

SEPTEMBER 6

socal_soval   ...
Santa barbara, California

6,201 likes
socal_soval Good morning, Santa Barbara! Couldn't ask for a better view. ☀️ 🏖️ #beach #vacation #vibes

hannaahnewmaan Omg😍😍😍😍
amandajartstein SOOO pretty!!!

I cannot believe what just happened.

Actually, that's a lie. I *obviously* can believe what just happened. In fact, I KNEW this was going to happen. Why doesn't anyone ever listen to me except for when I'm saying something stupid or awkward?!

First of all: Heading down to breakfast this morning felt like a scene out of a B horror film, only *I* was the terrifying monster let loose on innocent civilians. *Everyone* stared at me. There wasn't a person Val and I passed who didn't notice my severely peeling skin . . . One kid even gasped and started to cry, pointing at my face and calling me "Snake Lady."

Mom and Dad were already at the restaurant, seated at a lovely corner table facing the beach. They were arguing over how many slices of bacon Dad should be having, which Dad insisted was irrelevant since bacon is "healthy fat." The pugs sat dutifully at Mom's feet, anxiously awaiting their prize bites of breakfast meat, occasionally pawing at her flowy floor-length dress in anticipation.

"I look like a reptile," I said, plopping myself down into a chair.

Mom shook her head in protest. "No, you don't, sweetie. You're glowing! Isn't she glowing, Charlie?"

Dad glanced up from his plate of eggs/giant pile of bacon. "*Oof.* My friend's face was dipped in acid once. It was a very similar deal."

"Ughhhhhhh." I buried my head in my hands as Mom smacked Dad's arm with her napkin.

"It's not that bad. I promise," Mom insisted, turning to Val for support.

Val nodded with an enthusiasm that made it obvious she was lying. "You're Gucci, girl."

"I'm what?"

"So, family," Mom interjected, not wanting to dwell on my distress, "let's plan out the rest of our day!" She tossed her blond lob over one shoulder and pulled out her phone for notes. "I have a massage scheduled at ten fifteen, but after that, I say we shop. The Hoffmans are still asleep, so when they wake up, we should head over to—"

"GET OFF ME, YOU BEAST!!!"

Our heads all whipped around toward the sound of the yelling, and then snapped back in shock. Muffin had somehow made his way out from beneath Mom's feet and onto the lap of an elderly woman, ripping the pancake that she was eating straight out of her wrinkled mouth. The lady pushed Muffin off as she jumped up, banging into the table and knocking a hot teakettle onto her husband's lap, who had been sitting across from her.

"AHHHHHHHHHH!" he cried, leaping to his feet, his pants soaked by the molten Earl Grey. Muffin seized the opportunity to jump onto the man's empty chair and then onto the table, his flat face gobbling up the remainder of the man's granola. Baguette howled at the commotion.

"NO! Muffin! DOWN! SIT!" Mom screeched, as though Muffin has ever heard any of those words. Dad ran over to the table and threw Muffin over his shoulder as the older man hobbled around furiously, his khakis now draped around his ankles, revealing much-too-tight and now see-through tighty-whities. The woman had begun sneezing uncontrollably as nervous laughter took a firm hold of my mother.

"I'm so, *so* sorry!" my mom pleaded between panicked giggles. "This has never happened before! Normally he's so well behaved!"

More crashes filled the restaurant. Baguette had taken hold of the couple's tablecloth and was pulling it toward her, tug-of-war style, shattering the remaining kitchenware on the tiled floor. Muffin leapt from Dad's arms to get to the discarded goodies. Mom laughed even harder.

"Here! Let me find their service papers . . ."

"Get . . . *achoo* . . . your . . . *achoo* . . . dogs out of . . . *achooo* . . . *MY HOTEL!!!*"

Alberto (H.E.L.P.)

11:32 A.M.

> We've been kicked out of our hotel because we have little monsters for pugs.

 Ouch.

> We need help finding another room that can accommodate the four of us + tweedle-dee and tweedle-dumb-ass. Can you help?

On it. Might be tough because it's Labor Day weekend, but I have a few guys in SB who owe me a favor.

Is Airbnb an option?

> Negative. Mom only wants a place where someone else is responsible for making the bed. Lou

Right. Stay tuned.

 Megan Mitchell

— 🔍 looking for recommendations

FRIENDS!!! Where are your favorite places to shop in Santa Barbara?? Me, @StaceyHoffman, @ValentinaHansen, and @ShellyHansen are looking for places!!! #SB #fun #vacay #vacation #staycation #sogreat #laborday #weekend #summer #morefun

125 👍

 Megan Mitchell: OMG and of course @LouHansen oops lol forgot

 Dani Widen: Go to State Street!!

 Kayla Ray: Just stay away from the Funk Zone lol wayyyy too weird

Shelly Hansen
@ShellyHansen

Beautiful weekend away in Santa Barbara with my fav people and fav things: Sun, Sand, and SHOP!!! 🌴 🏖️

Theo 🖤

4:10 P.M.

> Help. Me. Lo

Th   What's going on?

> If I have to try on one more cover-up, I'm going to walk straight into the ocean and never reemerge. Lo

Th   Long shopping day?

> The longest. I haven't done a SINGLE thing on my list. No Mission District, no artisanal bakeries, no Funk Zone. Lo

> Just rack after merciless rack of discounted Labor Day clothes. Lo

Th   Oof. That's rough. 😕

> If that wasn't enough, my face looks like dried-up phyllo dough. I have to wear this ridiculous floppy hat everywhere, and people keep staring at me like I'm a sunburnt alien. Lo

Th   I'm sure it's not that bad.

> Check your Snapchat. Lo

4:15 P.M.

Th   . . . Okay, it's pretty bad.

Alberto (H.E.L.P.)

4:43 P.M.

> Any word on hotels?? Lo

Al	It's been tough. I found a dog-friendly room that your parents can stay in, but it's way too small to accommodate your whole family.

                Well then, what do we do?   Lou

Al	Didn't you say you were traveling with a friend?

                "Friend" is a loose term, but yeah.   Lou

Al	How many rooms is her family staying in?

                . . . no.   Lou

4:55 P.M.

"That's a *great* idea!" Mom shouted as she swiped a credit card through the checkout computer of our twentieth boutique shop. "Megan, you don't mind if Lulu stays with you, right?"

"OMG, of course not!" Megan cheered, clapping her hands together. *"Slumber partay!"*

"Are you sure you don't want me to share the couch with Val?" I asked again in a desperate effort. "I really, *really* don't mind sharing the couch with Val."

"Don't be ridiculous!" Mom said, draping yet another full shopping bag over her forearm. "Why make yourself uncomfortable? Megan has her own room, so it works out perfectly! It'll be such fun!"

Megan flashed me a dangerous smile, like a cat might at a canary. *Shit.*

5:25 P.M.

I am *so tired.* Five and a half hours of shopping without so much as a break. My feet are throbbing. I must have gotten fifteen million steps. No wonder all those mall rats stay in perfect shape. Ugh.

Jeez, I can't believe how messy Megan's room is! Her clothes are *everywhere*: the bed, the floor, the desk, the television. It's as if a small cyclone found its way into her suitcase. Did she even put anything into the cabinets? Let me check . . .

5:30 P.M.

Nope. The cabinets are woefully empty, begging to be utilized. This is positively barbaric. Ugh. It's taking every ounce of my self-restraint to keep from compulsively folding. The bathroom is no better . . . It's practically a war zone of makeup products and assorted creams. Who needs this much product, anyhow? What is the difference between body moisturizer and body rehydration oil?!

Anyway, our dinner reservation is only in half an hour, so my time alone with Bitchell in this pigsty is joyfully limited. In fact, maybe if I just keep writing in my journal and don't make any sudden movements, she won't acknowledge my existence.

Mama Shell

5:38 P.M.

MS　How's your time with Megan??

She's trying to put false lashes on me. Lou

MS　YES! Do it, do it, do it!

Absolutely not. Lou

We made a deal. Megan doesn't get to touch me on this trip. Lou

MS　Oh, come on, Lulu! They'll look amazing!

MS　Just a few extra lashes on the ends won't hurt!

MS　They'll make your eyes look bigger, which will distract from your face!

There is so much wrong with that sentence. Lou

5:45 P.M.

Good news! If, for whatever reason, I am ejected from a plane in the next twenty-four hours without a parachute, at least my new false eyelashes will save me from plummeting to my death!

"They're *huge*," I complained, gawking at myself in the mirror.

"*Psht*. Those are, like, medium length."

"They're poking the tops of my sockets."

"Most lashes do! Yours are just shorter than average."

"I'm taking them off . . ."

"Ooooo, here's the thing," Megan said, scrunching up her nose. "I kinda used like, a *supes* strong glue, so . . ."

"Are you saying that I can't take these off?" I asked, horrified.

"I mean, you *can*, but like—you might take some of your real ones off with them."

I looked back at myself in the mirror. The lashes are so heavy, my eyelids just kind of hang there, half opened, like I'm exhausted or stoned or probably both. Between my flaking skin and these broom bristles that are plastered to my face, I'm starting to resemble the drugged-out zombie of an ex-pageant contestant.

Death, take me now.

9:45 P.M.

Listening to Megan talk about her European adventures was such a snooze fest, I could hardly keep my eyes open. And not just because of the lashes.

". . . but the *best* part about Milan was the fashion show, which was, like, the most *gorgeous* show I've ever been to. Obvi, I wish I were walking the runway like I used to in my pageant days, but being behind the scenes was, like, *so* rewarding," Megan finished with a proud nod.

"That's *wonderful!*" Mom fawned, her martini splashing around in her glass. "Did you meet anyone interesting?"

"Technically we're not allowed to talk to the models, but I totes got to hold Kendall Jenner's boob tape."

Mom beamed.

"So, Lou," Buck interrupted, clearly not interested in the ways Kendall holds up her breasts, "how's the job hunt going? Any luck?"

I strained my eyelids upward so that I could fully look at him.

"Uh—it's all right," I admitted. "I haven't been applying to many places."

"Why not?"

It was an innocent enough question, but the scrutiny made my face flush. I glanced over at Megan, careful not to say anything that might be compromising.

"Well, I'm not exactly sure what field I want to commit to . . ."

"Have you considered going back to school?" Buck asked, leaning forward, both elbows coming onto the table. My potato-peeled skin turned tomato red.

"Yes, but I'd rather not, if I can help it," I said, leaving out that graduating at age twenty-six *significantly* diminishes my chances of being in *Forbes* 30 Under 30.

"The last thing she needs is more school," Mom said, raising the martini to her lips. "I'd like to see her have a little fun for a change."

"What about traveling?" Stacey asked excitedly.

"Or volunteer work?" Dad suggested.

"Or writing a memoir??" Val cheered.

"I'm just taking it moment to moment for now," I said, overwhelmed by the suggestions. "But thanks, everyone."

"I understand," Megan said, her own false lashes fanning the table. "It's, like, *really* hard out there. I have *so* many friends who are totes lost . . ."

"Well, I wouldn't say I'm lost, per se—"

". . . I mean my friend Tata? She graduated two years before me, and she's, like, still a hostess at this diner back in the Bay Area with a degree in finance. It's, like, *so* sad. But just keep trying, you know? You're, like, SOOOOO smart. I'm sure you'll figure something out."

Mom smiled at Megan like she was Delphi's fucking oracle. "That was beautiful, Megan. Thank you."

"Yeah. Great. Thanks," I mumbled.

"Oh my gosh!" Mom gasped, leaning over to take a closer look at Megan's chest. "Where did you get that necklace?"

"Which? Oh, *this*?" Bitchell fiddled with the cursive gold *Megan* that rested on her neckline. "My friend at work makes them. She's, like, SO talented, I can't even."

"It's just like the Carrie Bradshaw necklace!" Mom cheered. "I've always wanted one." She gave Dad a sideways glance, dropping a major hint. Dad shook his head slightly.

"OMG, I can *totes* get you one, Shell! You're, like, *such* a Carrie," Megan said, turning her gaze toward me and puckering her lips. "Hmmm. I'd get you one too, Lulu, but I think you're more of a Miranda."

That's it. I'm not going to let Megan ruin this vacation for me. I don't care how many passive-aggressive *Sex and the City* references she throws at me: this Miranda is going to the Mission District. I have one more day to enjoy myself, so I'm waking up first thing tomorrow morning before anyone else does.

SEPTEMBER 7

7:05 A.M.

Megan's alarm just went off. Apparently, she's going to the gym for an hour. On Labor Day.

"Can't you go later? The sun's not even up yet," I complained, my eyes sealed shut from exhaustion/some residue lash glue.

"No way, José! The early bird catches the rockin'-bod worm."

Seriously. VANDERBILT. There HAS to be a brain hiding between those white gold hoop earrings.

Anyway, while she's doing squats in the gym, I'm going to be sipping an artisanal latte and climbing the stairs of Old Mission Santa Barbara to see the famous murals. Mom was sufficiently tipsy from last night's martini and a half, which means a late morning is surely in store for today. Dad will probably sneak an early coffee/plate of bacon alone, and if Val wakes up, she's bound to use this time as a photo opportunity. This means I should have at least three glorious hours to myself, which is just enough time to see the murals, and possibly even snag a McConnell's ice cream before anyone notices!

. . .

Mama Shell

11:05 A.M.

MS What on earth do you think you're doing?

Hi, Mom! I just went for a morning walk!

MS A likely story.

MS

MS Why on earth are you at McConnell's ice cream at 11 in the morning?!

Why on earth do you have a GPS tracker on my phone?!

MS We're coming over right this minute. If you move, I'll know.

TRANSCRIPT: POLICE REPORT

CT = Call Taker

> **CT:** Santa Barbara Police Communications, how can I help you?
>
> **Woman:** I'd like to file a missing person's report.
>
> **CT:** All right. What is the name of the missing person?
>
> **Woman:** Muffin.
>
> **CT:** Martin?
>
> **Woman:** No, Muffin. Like the pastry.
>
> **CT:** Oh. Uh, I see. Okay. What's the surname?
>
> **Woman:** Hansen. H-A-N-S-E-N.
>
> **CT:** Okay. Age?
>
> **Woman:** Just turned six years old.
>
> **CT:** All right. How long has he been missing?
>
> **Woman:** I went back to the hotel about five hours ago and he was gone.
>
> **CT:** . . . Five hours?
>
> **Woman:** Yes.
>
> **CT:** Ma'am, you realize you have to wait twenty-four hours before filing a missing person's report.
>
> **Woman:** I know, but isn't a year in dog years like seven years? So for Muffin it's been twenty-four hours at least—
>
> **CT:** I'm sorry, ma'am—this is a dog?

Woman: Yes.

CT: You're filing a missing person's report for a dog?

Woman: It's Labor Day weekend in Santa Barbara and we've been searching for hours. Who would you turn to?

CT: I'm sorry, ma'am, but I'm afraid we don't help locate missing animals.

Woman: Then who's the person I need to contact to arrange for a proper search party? Charlie, hold on, I'm on the phone. The police. Well, what was I supposed to do? Oh, that's a LOT coming from a man who wouldn't pull over with a flat tire! Hysterical? What do you mean, I'm being HYSTERICAL??

CT: Uh, ma'am—

Woman: Don't tell me to calm down! My baby is missing! Oh, Lulu, thank goodness you're here. I'm on the phone with the police. What? Of course I did! Why isn't anyone taking my side here?

CT: Excuse me, ma'am—

Woman: I don't care about that! He's been gone for hours and the only—

(Inaudible arguing and phone rustling)

Woman 2: Hello?

CT: Uh, hi? Who is this?

Woman 2: This is Shelly's daughter, Lou. I'm so sorry for the inconvenience this has probably caused you.

CT: Oh. It's all right, ma'am, but I really do have to—

Woman: GET THE NUMBER OF A SEARCH PARTY.

Woman 2: Mother, there is no animal search party! WE are the search party!

Woman: THIS IS WHAT HAPPENS WHEN YOU EAT ICE CREAM.

CT: Lou?

Woman 2: Hello? Yes?

CT: Where was the last place Muffin was seen?

Woman 2: Excuse me?

CT: Your dog, Muffin. When was he last seen?

Woman 2: Uh, he was at my parents' hotel in their room. My family left to meet me at McConnell's on State Street, and when we returned, Muffin was gone.

CT: Were there any other dogs with you?

Woman 2: Yes. Her name is Baguette, and she was sitting on the bed when we returned.

CT: So only one dog is missing?

Woman 2: That's correct. We've searched all around the area and talked to the front desk, but we haven't been able to locate him.

CT: All right. What's the name and address of the hotel? I'll send someone there right away.

Woman 2: Are you being serious right now?

CT: Of course. I have three dogs at home. We can't just let Muffin go missing.

7:31 P.M.

I don't think I've ever been more deeply exhausted than I am in this moment. And that includes the time I stayed up for seventy-one hours and consumed so much coffee that I genuinely thought I had crossed over into a different relative space-time continuum. Muffin was FINE. After hours of running around the hotel and city, asking everyone in our path if they had seen a handsome fawn-colored pug wearing a particularly chic collar, and even filing a police report, we found our little diablo. Apparently, Muffin had caravaned on the bottom of a room-service cart that Dad was hiding in the closet after a late-night cookie order. When the maid came in this morning to remove the cart, Muffin went along with it. Now the specifics of the next four hours are unclear, but somehow Muffin found himself down the street at a neighboring Labor Day cook-off, where he blended in with the band of twelve other party-going pups. It wasn't until Muffin went inside the house and ripped apart an antique leather couch that belonged to someone's great-great-something-or-other that he became the odd dog out.

At this point, we received a call from the party hosts, explaining that they had found our dog and that we owed them five thousand dollars.

Anyway, we're going the hell home. I can confidently call this past weekend the least relaxing vacation of my life. I've basically molted my skin, half of my eyelashes have been pulled off, McConnell's was closed, so I never got my ice cream, and now—thanks to the Mystery of the Missing Muffin—my blood pressure is probably dangerously high. HUMPH.

SEPTEMBER 8

Theo 💚

> Can I stay at your place tonight? I think I've had enough family bonding time for the next month. L

Th Of course! I've missed you 💚 I'll be home from work at around 6, but Jett's home tonight, so feel free to come over at anytime.

> Great. How was your first day of training?? L

Th Freaking amazing. The other chefs are crazy talented, and the menu is top shelf.

Th I just can't believe we open in less than two weeks.

> !!!!! That's so exciting!!! L

Th I know! And nerve- racking. I really have to be on my A game.

> You will be. 😊 In the meantime, can we unwind tonight? Watch the Discovery Channel or play Scrabble or something? L

Th   Only if you want to get your butt kicked again.

YOU DID NOT WIN THAT ROUND. IXNAY IS NOT A WORD.   Lou

Th   Yes it is. It means no. Look it up.

It's in pig Latin, which is a constructed language, making it an unqualified verb, and you KNOW IT.   Lou

12:15 P.M.

Good news to report: I've finally shed the last of the disgusting facial flakes, which have given way to a dewy pimple-free glowing epidermis that is so soft, I can't stop stroking it. My cheeks feel like they've been sandpapered. It's no wonder Megan spends so much money on tiny lotions . . . When your face is this soft, anything is possible.

More good news: Theo is positively high off his new job! He told me all about it tonight over takeout Indian food, which we ordered at my request as a reward for surviving my family vacation—a feat on par with running a marathon, which I'm officially taking off my list of long-term goals. We sat cross-legged on the floor, plastic forks shoved deep into our tikka masala, chatting away over his limited-edition Scrabble board. According to Theo, the restaurant is all about the communal dining experience, so his background in catering has been helpful. Cooking for large groups of people is his specialty. That being said, he can't help but have moments of insecurity when working in such a talented kitchen.

"I'm the youngest of the chefs by far," he said, placing an *A*, a *Q*, an *I*, and an *R* on the board to create *faquir. Damn. Good word.* "The second youngest of us is twenty-six."

"That's only four years," I noted, squinting at my letters to find a decent rebuttal. "Besides, once you're in your twenties, it's pretty much all the same until you hit twenty-eight."

"You think so?"

"Sure! It's all about emotional maturity, right?" I decided, putting a *Z*, an *M*, and an *E* down for *zyme*. Theo's brows furrowed.

"So if you don't get a job until you're twenty-seven, you'd consider it the same as getting a job at twenty-one?"

"No, because an emotionally mature twenty-one-year-old would already be looking for jobs while an emotionally mature twenty-seven-year-old would be looking to have kids."

"Got it." He put down a *J*, an *M*, and a *P* for *jimpy* before ripping off a piece of garlic naan. "But yeah, I feel like I have a lot to prove, professionally speaking . . . my profound and overwhelming wisdom aside." He winked before shoving a giant piece of masala-soaked naan into his mouth. Ugh, he's so cute.

"You proved yourself to Jackie, and you'll prove yourself to the team. And if you're looking to hire a slightly awkward waitress, I'm available," I said with my own wink, which felt a lot less cute.

He chuckled. "You'd hate waitressing more than you hate being unemployed."

"I don't know—I *really* hate being unemployed." I gasped in delight as I threw down a *C* and an *M* to make *cwm*.

Theo threw his hands in the air. "Are you kidding?! That's not a thing."

"It's totally a thing!"

"Really? What does it mean?"

"I have no idea, but I saw it on a Scrabble site once!"

Theo grasped his heart and rolled to the floor in defeat. I shimmied my shoulders in a victory dance, which was hopelessly lame, but who cares? I WON!!!

Wow, I feel more relaxed from one evening at the Treehouse than I did after a whole three days in Santa Barbara. In fact, I'm feeling almost . . . confident? Could it be?? Could a night of spicy foods and spelling for fun be enough to break the dreaded postgrad curse?!

Move over, Megan! I'm back, and with a vengeance! Things are finally starting to look up!

SEPTEMBER 9

Papa Hansen

2:11 P.M.

PH Where are you?

Out with Mom buying some new shower curtains — Lou

PH What's wrong with our shower curtains?

They're "last season." — Lou

PH Right.

PH Anyway, I need to ask you about something.

Sure. What's up? — Lou

PH What's your friend Natasha's last name?

McPatterson — Lou

. . . Why? — Lou

CNN NEWS REPORT

RECENT COLUMBIA GRAD DENIED ENTRY INTO UNITED STATES AFTER REFUSING TREATMENT FOR UNKNOWN ILLNESS

Natasha McPatterson made Columbia headlines this past summer when she fell ill with an unusually bad case of parasites. After catching wind of the story, however, representatives from the Centers for Disease Control and Prevention have expressed concerns regarding the young traveler's health. Now McPatterson is being denied entry back into the United States until she is formally discharged by a medical professional.

"The symptoms she claimed to be exhibiting are not indicative of parasites alone," Marie Brassil, a representative from the CDC, explained. "In fact, they suggest something of a much more serious nature, and until we're certain she's not harboring an unknown bacterium, we simply can't risk opening the doors to a pandemic."

Because Ms. McPatterson refuses to seek Western treatment or even undergo testing, there is no way to determine the nature of the sickness that wreaked havoc on her system for six weeks. However, Ms. McPatterson remains adamant that she will not be visiting a doctor anytime soon.

"I feel much better now," McPatterson told CNN. "Really. I had several healers work with me, and haven't exhibited any symptoms for weeks. This is outrageous!"

Despite Ms. McPatterson's insistence that she is fully recovered, multiple anonymous sources have contacted CNN, claiming that the young American is not being honest with officials.

"I do not believe she is well," an anonymous source told CNN. "One day she came home covered in sweat and spoke of a dancing cactus. Her pupils were very, very large—the size of two raisins. And all that night, she was sick. She is not healthy; take my word for it."

The hashtag #PrayForNatasha has emerged on social media outlets in support of Ms. McPatterson, who will remain in New Delhi until she is cleared by a CDC-approved doctor. When asked whether her family had been briefed on the current situation, Ms. McPatterson declined to comment.

Val

2:20 P.M.

That's it.

Lou: The jig is up.

Lou: I'm finished. Done for. Screwed.

Val: ?????

Lou: Dad knows that I've been lying.

Val: 🙀🙀🙀

Val: What? How? What happened???

2:32

Val: OMG Lou u can't just do that to me SPILL

Lou: Sorry, I'm out with Mom buying new shower curtains, and now she's looking for bedsheets to match them.

Lou: Long story short: Natasha is being held as a detainee in India, and Dad saw it on CNN

Val: Oh, SHIT

Lou: Yeah, I know.

Lou: Clearly, she's not visiting cousins in Silver Lake.

Val: That's legit insane

Val: What did he say??

Lou: Nothing yet. He wants to talk to me tonight after work

Val: Oh damn

Lou: I know.

Val: ugh u seem sus af rn . . . smh

Lou: Does that mean something, or is it a typo?

Val: Idk just tell him ur taking a class in Silver Lake or something

Lou: I can't. Dad has this superpower that forces me to tell the truth . . . Like Wonder Woman's lasso, or torture.

Val: So true.

Val: Ok dw tbh ur gucci this is nbd

Lou: . . . okay, you just sat on your text screen, right?

Val: 😂😂😂 I'm ROTFLMAO

Lou: SERIOUSLY?!

3:15 P.M.

I can't breathe. Everything is ruined. My whole life is flashing before my eyes.

Dad's not home yet. He probably won't be until six o'clock at the earliest. Oh god, that's in *three hours*. Three hours to stew in the pool of dread that is currently drowning me alive. AHHHHHH.

4:05 P.M.

Just hid the shower curtains, new bedsheets, matching kitchen rags, oversize towels, and furry throw blankets that Mom bought for no room in particular. Can't risk upsetting Dad further by reminding him of Mom's compulsive spending habits, or even worse, that I was present during the shopping excursion and didn't attempt to stop her. Oh god, I'M COMPLICIT.

5:10 P.M.

Can't focus on anything. Managed to eat four bags of Skinny Pop popcorn out of stress. I think my adrenal gland is sore. Ugh.

6:34 P.M.

He's still not home. Why is he not home? Is he just trying to torment me by prolonging the anticipation? Or is he so disgusted by my obvious liarhood that he can't come home and look me in my newly peeled face??

OH, SHIT. THE PUGS ARE BARKING. HE'S HERE.

7:00 P.M.

Well. As Val likes to say: "I'm shook."

Besides my usual anxiety, there are only two things in this world that can induce this kind of Code Red level of panic in me: the possibility of a nuclear holocaust and angry Dad.

"Lou?" His even but stern voice came from behind my closed bedroom door. "I need to speak with you."

Oh, damn. Oh, hell. Oh, Jesus, I thought, trying to keep the acid down in my churning stomach. *It's okay! This is fine. This is totally fine. There's no need to make a scene. Just coolly and maturely explain the Theo situation like the reasonable, rational adult that you are.*

I walked to my door like an inmate heading toward the gallows, my heartbeat pounding in my ears, desperate to regain composure as I swiftly pulled open the door.

The temperature must have dropped at least ten degrees the minute Dad's stare met mine. His face looked like a statue carved from the hands of pure disappointment and wrath. Coolly and maturely, I burst into tears.

"*I'm so sooorryyyy!*" I wept like a rational adult. "*I—I—I made such a messssss!*"

Dad stepped into my room, unfazed by the highly irregular display of emotion by his eldest daughter.

"Where's your mother?" he asked, his voice completely unreadable. I swallowed hard, trying to get a grip.

"She's at Susan's for mah-jongg," I told him meekly. "She should be home by nine."

Dad nodded and made his way deeper into my room, turning around to face me only once he found his way to the far back corner. He crossed his arms commandingly and waited: a judge on trial.

After what felt like an eternity of silence, I finally spoke. "I . . . I've been keeping something from you," I admitted, voice trembling.

"Clearly," he agreed. I looked down at my fidgety feet and reached for my rings.

"I just . . . I didn't know how to tell you. I was scared," I started, my stomach churning even harder. Dad remained quiet, so I kept going:

"Well, I *tried* to tell you, but then some unfortunate events made it nearly impossible to—"

"Lou," Dad interrupted, not having my excuses. "Tell the truth. What's in Silver Lake?"

My whole body went numb, with the exception of my heart, which felt like it might burst into flames. The remaining air in my lungs petered out, leaving me nearly voiceless as I croaked out: ". . . my boyfriend."

I squeezed my eyes shut as I braced for the shouting. The last time I was yelled at by Dad, it was in first grade when I tried to put a cast on Val's leg using gauze, socks, and super glue after reading about it in my school's nature survival catalogue. That yell has haunted me ever since, and I live in constant fear of its revival.

. . . But the shouting didn't come. Instead, Dad's lower lip pressed up into his thoughtful frown, the corners of his eyes creasing ever so slightly as he assessed the level of my honesty. "A boyfriend?" he asked, as if this seemed farfetched. I was pretty offended, but nodded quickly.

"Yes. I have a boyfriend."

"For how long?"

Oh no. I considered lying again, but the truth serum of fatherhood compelled me to look down at my fingers and silently count out the number.

"Eleven months?" I squeaked, like I wasn't quite sure.

Dad's piercing blue eyes opened wide, a spark of outrage flashing through them. "You've been seeing this boy for *eleven months*?" he echoed, anger finally rising in his voice. My insides shriveled up.

"I'm so, so sorry, I didn't mean to—"

"You've been lying to us every day for almost a *year*?"

"I was nervous that—"

"Taking the car to see a boy we didn't know existed??"

"I kept trying to tell you, but—"

"But *what*?"

"But MOM!" I finally yelled, unable to hold back any longer. "Mom is so damn controlling, I'm terrified to tell her *anything*!"

Dad looked at me as if I had lost my mind. His top lip curled down into a snarl. "Eloise Hansen," he growled, "how exactly is this your *mother's* fault?"

I heard the pitter-patter of pug paws as they rounded the hallway, curious about the commotion. Muffin trotted over and sat himself between my feet, somehow sensing that I needed backup. I exhaled sharply.

"Okay," I started, preparing my argument like I was back in debate, "so remember at dinner a few months ago, Mom saw a picture I was tagged in on Facebook?"

"No."

"Val had brought it up, and said that the guy in it was cute?"

"Nothing."

"And at that point, Mom looked at the picture and called that person a serial killer?"

Dad thought back for a moment. "Oh, right. Vaguely, yes."

"That was my boyfriend."

The silence that followed was thick enough to cut. Dad's expression fell from heated to stoic as the pieces started rearranging in his head. Muffin started gnawing at my laces, but I didn't dare look down.

Finally Dad let out an empathetic sigh. "Oh, Shelly."

PROGRESS! I gave Muffin a slight nudge with my foot before seizing my opportunity of compassion: "And by the way, that is absolutely ridiculous, because my boyfriend is not a serial killer at all! Not even close. To be fair, that is a pretty low bar, but you get the point! He's the most loving, funny, talented, intelligent, *incredible* guy, and I've been trying to tell Mom about him since I moved back home, but *every time* she says something judgmental and horrible, so I just couldn't bring myself to do it, because if I told her the truth and she didn't approve . . ."

I trailed off, a sequence of possibilities flashing before my eyes ranging from Theo being forced into a sports jersey, to his mouthing "it's over" over the fallen remains of his freshly cut brown locks like a scrawny Samson, betrayed in the middle of the night by Delilah's crazy mother.

". . . let's just say, I don't think it would end well."

Dad's thoughts went inward, his gaze unfocused as the frown returned. Muffin whimpered as he looked back and forth between Dad and me, waiting for someone to crouch down and pet him. My body was stiff as a board as I waited in agony for my sentencing.

"I think you're underestimating your mother," he concluded. Muffin and I tilted our heads in unison.

"I don't think you understood the story."

"And I don't think you understand your mom," he said firmly. I shrank into the floor. "Yes, I recognize that your mother can be a bit extravagant . . ."

I shot a quick glance at the fourth faux-fur blanket that was now strewn across one of my many Moroccan poufs.

". . . but when it comes to your happiness? That's plain and simple: it comes first. No matter what."

Maybe it was the lack of oxygen from holding my breath for five hours, but I suddenly felt faint. That was it: he knew. He knew, and he hadn't kicked me out of the house yet.

I ran a hand through my frizzy hair and shook my head. "Well then, why must she criticize every little thing I do?"

"Because she's your mother. She can't help but smother you. It's in the word."

He made a fair point. Muffin's stubby tail started to wag.

"I'm so sorry, Dad. I wanted to tell you. I really did."

Dad's mouth thinned into a straight line. "Answer me this," he said. "Is he good to you?"

"The best to me."

"Is he a drug addict?"

"Sometimes he takes Advil for headaches, but otherwise, no."

"Does he kill people?"

I actually managed to laugh. "No. Decidedly not."

"Then I'll give him a shot," Dad decided. For the first time since two o'clock that afternoon, I took a full breath.

"So you're not mad?"

"Oh, of course I'm mad," Dad clarified, his hard expression returning. "You still lied to your mother and me for months. But you're an adult now. I can't ground you for hiding a boyfriend. I can just make it clear that I'm very disappointed."

Ugh. This was worse than any punishment I could possibly fathom. I hung my head in shame.

"I'm sorry."

"I know," Dad acknowledged. "And to be fair, this *is* a first-time offense in twenty-two years. I can't say my track record was so good . . ."

I glanced up from the floor, hopeful.

"And it'll never happen again," I assured him. "At least not for another twenty-two."

"But you have to tell Mom," Dad decreed, barely hearing me. "I won't tell her. This is your responsibility. But if you want my advice— and you *want* my advice—you should tell her, and you should tell her soon."

I nodded furiously. "I will. As soon as the moment is right, I will."

"Don't spend your life waiting for perfect moments," Dad imparted. "If I did, Mr. Schivelli would probably be at the bottom of a lake somewhere tied to a cinder block."

And with that, he left the room.

SEPTEMBER 10

Mama Shell

12:15 P.M.

> **MS**   Are you coming with us to temple on Monday??

> **MS**   Let's roll in looking hot as shit!!

> **MS**   We'll get our hair done and wear cute little dresses. It'll be fun!

>> Mom I think you might be missing the point of temple.   Lo

SEPTEMBER 12

8:12 A.M.

Happy Rosh Hashanah, aka the Jewish New Year, aka the perfect time to do some desperately needed self-reflection after months of moral and emotional decay. It's time to face hard facts: I've been a worthless ball of ineptitude ever since leaving Columbia, and though this post-grad me is a bit edgier, sneaking out of my parents' house to visit my secret boyfriend would have been a lot cooler back when I was sixteen. I'm turning over a new leaf . . . or a whole branch, for that matter.

First things first: *I must tell Mom.* Every minute she doesn't know about Theo feels like an eternity of unbearable pressure, especially now that Dad knows. I've already tried to confess four separate times in the past three days, but unfortunately, things with Mother have descended into near madness.

"VAL, HURRY UP, WE'RE RUNNING LATE FOR YOUR AP BIO TUTOR," she bellowed from the front of the house. "DON'T MAKE ME ASK AGAIN. I CAN FEEL MY FROWN LINES FORMING AS WE SPEAK."

The cause of all the hostility is obvious: Mom just received an invitation to the E.N.D., or the Empty Nesters Digest. Basically, it's a group of mothers from our high school who get together once a month to discuss and drink their sorrows away once their youngest children leave for college. To Mother, it might as well be an invitation to the undertaker.

"She hasn't even graduated yet!" Mom shouted, throwing the invitation onto the kitchen table. "I still have a whole school year before I'm eligible for this silly support group."

"It's not a support group, Shelly. It's a club," Dad reassured her.

Mom tossed her hair over one shoulder. "Well, not all clubs are worth joining. Lulu, what's that Woody Allen quote? The one about not wanting to join clubs?"

"It's actually a Groucho Marx quote . . ."

"Oh, always with the corrections. No one likes a know-it-all, Lulu. The point is, I'm not going, so you can throw that invitation in the trash."

Between back-to-school day and the END, Mom's never been more volatile. Last night, she got mad at me for wearing white shorts to the dinner table after Labor Day. She then proceeded to chase three bites of her unseasoned Brussels sprouts down with a martini, casually explaining that "sometimes it's best to drink your calories." Needless to say, I've been hesitant to come forward with my admission. I'm hoping that the abrupt mood swings will calm down within a week or so—once the school year really picks up. That way I can finally remove the anvil that is currently resting on my shoulders, but in the meantime, I'll have to focus on other forms of self-improvement. Seeing as my old goals list was proving to be virtually useless, I'm creating a new, revamped list of my Rosh Hashanah Resolutions, which I'm calling: the Roshalutions.

ROSHALUTIONS

- *TELL. YOUR. MOM. ABOUT. THEO!!!!!*
- *Be more confident in social situations (without the aid of a friend and/or alcohol).*

- *Start waking up at 8:00 A.M.*
- *Focus on finding a suitable job (does not have to be true passion, but <u>does</u> have to pay in something other than "experience").*
- *Lose 5-7 pounds (I mean it this time).*
- *Stop lying to people (especially parents and boyfriend).*
- *Let go of any unnecessary grudges (Megan, Natasha, Dr. Richmanson, and similar).*
- *Improve Instagram average from 12 likes to 50.*

SEPTEMBER 13

10:30 P.M.

Woke up at 7:30 this morning (excellent), meditated for ten minutes (amazing), then went for a twenty-minute run on the moving struggle carpet* (real-world miracle). Instead of going to the pantry and eating away any feelings of guilt or inadequacy, I drank hot water with lemon and cayenne (still wretched tasting, but bearable) and performed deep breathing exercises until I was light-headed enough to forget about my hunger (unconventional, but effective). All in all, a successful first day of the new year.

Meanwhile, Mom was out of the house all day and returned home with freshly painted red nails, perfectly shaped eyebrows, giant candy-apple sunglasses, and her shortest, choppiest, blondest lob to date.

"Those are new." I pointed toward the glasses.

Mom pushed them onto the bridge of her nose to stare down at me. "Do you like them? They're bold, but classic. You could use a pair of glasses like these. I also think you should cut your hair like mine, Lulu. Short hair is so en vogue—it's very French. Also, you could use

---

*Treadmill.

a few highlights . . . Why must you let your roots get so dark? Just promise me that when I'm gone, you won't let your hair go gray. Do you need me to call Tracey? I'll make you an appointment with Tracey for next week. Have you been using your cycling package? You really should, honey; it's expensive and your father has been on me about my spending. If you need me, I'll be walking around the pool."

SEPTEMBER 14

Theo 🩶

3:43 P.M.

Th What are you doing on Friday night?

I think Mom made an appointment for me to get highlights, but that would be during the day. Lou

Why? What's going on? Lou

Th Would you like to be my date to the opening party of PAREA? It's a night for friends and family, which means I won't be in the kitchen 😊

OH MY GOODNESS I WOULD LOVE TO! Lou

Th 😃 Awesome sauce!

Th It starts at 7 and will probably go until 10 or so.

Okay! What should I wear? Lou

Th Nothing too fancy. I'm at work right now, so I shouldn't be texting, but I just wanted to let you know!

Great! I'm so excited. 🩶 Have a good shift! Lou

7:23 A.M.

Someone please tell me when my mother turned into the Jewish second coming of Holly Golightly.

She came out of her bedroom this morning dressed for temple in a short, tight designer black dress and her new red sunglasses.

"Are you really going to wear that?" I asked her, ogling the outfit. She looked down at her exposed legs and shrugged.

"What? My shoulders are covered!"

"Yeah, and that's pretty much it."

"Relax! All the women in temple dress like this. You, on the other hand, look like you're going to a funeral."

"It's respectful!"

"It's matronly."

Dad walked into the living room, rolling up the cuffs of a light blue button-down shirt. I gestured toward Mom's ensemble in disbelief, certain Dad would come to my support.

"Dad, please look at what your wife is wearing."

Dad turned toward Mom, who did a quick turn for show.

"Very nice. Looking good, Mama Shell!"

"You too, Big Daddy," she said, winking behind her shades. I buried my face in my hands.

"Okay, fine, just . . . put a sweater on or something," I grumbled. Val walked into the room wearing a slightly more appropriate "millennial pink" dress that cut off just below her fingertips, nose shoved deep into her cell phone.

"Can I go to Bella's house after temple? She's throwing a party, and there's a rumor Lady Gaga might be there."

"Why would Lady Gaga be at Bella Morton's house party?" I asked.

"Because Bella's dad helped her renovate her cabana house, or something."

"Ooooh, can I come with?" Mom asked, bouncing on the balls of her feet.

"Mom, it's, like, all high schoolers."

"So? Your friends love me! They don't call me Shelly Shakes for nothing."*

Val turned ashen white.

---

*Val's friends call Mom Shelly Shakes because of one particularly horrifying incident during which Mom performed a hoedown on the punch table of their rodeo-themed middle school dance. The school calls it legendary. Val and I call it traumatizing.

"Let her go to the party, Shell," Dad interjected. "You, me, and Lou can go out to lunch. We can have a *nice family talk.* Right, Lou?"

He shot me a deliberate look. I gulped.

"Oh, never mind, I almost forgot!" Mom recalled. "Lisa and I are going urban hiking at twelve."

"Urban hiking?" I asked.

"It's when you hike, but instead of on a trail, you do it in the city."

"Isn't that called walking?"

"Hansens, we have to leave," Dad announced, looking down at his watch. "We're running late, and the parking situation at Stephen Stern is always hell."

"Let me get my purse!" Mom said, running back to her closet. "Oh, and Lulu: mascara or sunglasses. Pick one of the two."

📎 Email

From: **Stephen Stern Valley Temple**
To: **S.S.V. Community (undisclosed)**
Subject: **Temple Etiquette**

Hello cherished community members at Stephen Stern Temple,

First of all, we want to thank those of you who chose to spend the high holiday of Rosh Hashanah with us. It was a beautiful ceremony, and a wonderful way to ring in the New Year.

With that in mind, we at Stephen Stern would like to gently remind the community of what is considered acceptable temple etiquette. As a place of worship, our temple is a sacred space and should be treated with the utmost respect. This means showing up on time and abiding by the dress code, which you can find listed on our community website.

We'd also like to mention that the orange cones in the parking lot are there for a reason, and that moving them to create a personal parking space is out of the question.

Also, while we're well aware of the changes that new technology has made in our day-to-day lives, we strongly ask that you leave social media outside of our services. This includes Snapchatting the rabbi as he blows the shofar, or opening the ark to take Instagram pictures with the Torah. To those of you who were at the eight A.M. service this morning and know which incident I'm referring to: we ask that you kindly keep the story private, so as not to compromise the integrity of our fellow temple-goers. After all, it's a new year, and in the Jewish faith, gossip is frowned upon.

We love you all, and want to thank you for the support you bring to our mishpachah. We understand that some of you may want to share that joy with the World Wide Web, but think of it like Vegas: whatever happens in temple, stays in temple.

Shanah Tovah,
The Stephen Stern Family

SEPTEMBER 15

CULTUREVATE—LOS ANGELES
"Your Online Arts and Cultures Hub"

CULTURE-EATS → RESTAURANTS

New and Noteworthy

PAREA—Somewhere nestled between the relatively quiet San Fernando Valley and the touristy trash of Hollywood, you'll find LA's highly anticipated (if not dangerously overhyped) PAREA. From the genius behind Brooklyn's Tin+Can and the Seattle brunch favorite RECIPE*rocity* comes Jacqueline Reid's newest culinary contribution: a locally sourced, Mediterranean-style restaurant with a California coastal flair. Seem incongruous? Not to Jacqueline.

"I'm just combining deserts, really." The notorious redhead laughed as she gave us a preview tour of the restaurant. "Both are very health-centric and plant-based food styles, both emphasize the importance of communal eating . . . Honestly, it seemed like a natural pairing."

"Communal" was clearly a key factor for Jacqueline, whose new restaurant features several long shared tables and a name that literally translates to "community." From what the Culturevate team could see and smell, PAREA promises to be every bit as deliciously hip and fashionably tasty as Jacqueline's first two eateries, with a full list of California native wines and a particularly Instagrammable dessert called The Palms.

Opening: September 19, aka the autumn equinox
What to get: TBD, upon opening

SEPTEMBER 16
11:13 A.M.

Something is definitely wrong with Mom.

I thought the incident at temple was enough to snap her to her senses (she asked the rabbi to restart the shofar section because her Snapchat glitched in the middle of Tekiah Gedolah), but clearly her antics have just begun.

"We're going vegan," she decreed in the kitchen this morning, arms in the air like Eva Perón.

"Vegan?" I asked.

"*We?*" Dad jumped in.

"That's right," Mom said, slowly lowering her arms so that they rested beside her waist. "Vegan. They're saying it's the secret to anti-aging."

"Who's *they*?" Val asked, her ankles crossed on the kitchen table.

"*People* magazine," I answered.

"Among other sources," Mom confirmed. "Does it matter? Don't you want to discover the fountain of youth?"

"I'll pass," Dad insisted.

"No, thanks," I agreed.

"I'm seventeen," Val noted.

Mom shot her a dirty look. "Must you brag??" She flipped her lob and stormed out of the kitchen, leaving the remaining Hansens to stare after her in confusion.

Is this menopause? Please tell me this isn't menopause. If so, I'll just have to wait another four years before breaking the Theo news to Mother, lest I end up pulverized by the hormonal fury that she would surely unleash like a menopausal She-Hulk.

SEPTEMBER 17

Theo 🩶

Th Tomorrow is the day!

How are you feeling? Are you nervous? Excited? Nervously excited?!

Th All of the above. Some of the biggest chefs and restaurateurs in the country are going to be there, so I have to be on my best behavior. 🙈

Don't worry—I'll try not to embarrass you with my social ineptitude.

Th You couldn't embarrass me if you tried.

. . . Don't tempt me.

Th In all seriousness, though: tomorrow is a very special day for me, and I couldn't be happier to share it with you.

Th I love you 🩶

😊😊😊

I love you, too!! 🩶

You're going to blow them all away. I can't wait to watch you shine!

Th Thanks, Louie Love 😊 Now help me pick out a bowtie for tomorrow—I've narrowed it down to two, but can't decide on the right color scheme.

SEPTEMBER 18

Mama Shell

1:51 P.M.

MS How's your hair??

Exactly like yours. **Lou**

Same cut, same color, same style, same everything. **Lou**

I don't think I've ever resembled you more in my life. **Lou**

MS Fabulous! If you really want to look like me, you should go visit Saj. 😊

Still not getting a nose job, Mother. **Lou**

MS Oh, relax, I'm just kidding! Your dad and I are going out tonight, so I'm also getting my hair done at Tracey's later today. We'll be twinning!!!

MS BTW, have you heard of this app, BeautifyMe 123? It's supposed to get rid of all my wrinkles in pictures. Can you download it for me? Love you 🤍

6:30 P.M.

All afternoon, I've felt like Cinderel-lou with Val as my fairy god-sister, expertly getting me ready for tonight's Restaurant Ball.

"This is like your coming-out party," Val encouraged as she poked at my face with various brushes and sponges. "New Year, New You, New Lou."

"I just want to make a good impression for Theo's sake," I said, readjusting my seat on the edge of the bathtub. "This is his big night. The last thing I want to do is embarrass him by tripping or putting my foot in my mouth."

I cringed as she stuck a dark brown liner pencil right into my eyeball.

"Hold still," she said. "I can't do your makeup if you keep pulling away."

"I'm sorry. I have very sensitive lacrimal punctums."

"Never say that again."

"Are you almost done? My butt is starting to hurt."

"Yes! I just need to add mascara . . . Do you want me to get you some lashes?"

"NO!"

Two coats of nail polish and some eyebrow plucking later, we were ready to move on to the final touch: my gown. Mom has been out getting her hair done, and Dad's been snoring alongside the pugs on the couch, so Val and I had just enough time to sneak into Mom's closet and look for a dress. After much sucking in and a quick hunt for my Spanx, I finally managed to zip up a lacy knee-length size 4 (YES! YESSSSSS!!!!! I don't think I've been a size 4 since my mom's third trimester!) that was such a dark shade of navy, it almost appeared black. As I turned to assess myself in the floor-length mirror, I audibly gasped.

"Holy shit," I said, staring wide-eyed at the vision before me.

"What's wrong? Is it the makeup?"

"No. I'm Mom."

And I was. Between my new hair, the makeup, and her navy dress, I had somehow transformed into the spitting image of my mother. Well, like someone took the image of her on a computer, clicked on the top right corner, and stretched it . . . but nevertheless, the resemblance was uncanny. To date, it may be the most terrifying moment of my life.

But there may be a positive side to this development. My hope is that the more I *look* like Mom, the more I can channel her social confidence. Val is right: tonight is the perfect opportunity to introduce a new and improved me to the world—a me that has good hair and can talk to strangers without admitting that I used to speak fluent Elvish back in high school. I've been researching pointers on "party poise" all week, and I have compiled a list of dos and don'ts for tonight's gala.

At this party, I WILL:

1. Ask lots of questions, making other people feel interesting while subtly putting the burden of conversation on said other people.
2. Act confident: stand up straight, make eye contact, smile, and laugh when appropriate (not nervously or too loudly or at someone's expense).
3. Bring emergency floss and breath mints (will undoubtedly eat something stinky, since it's a Mediterranean restaurant).
4. Make Theo feel special, as it is his night and I am there to support him.

I WILL NOT:

1. Pretend to be on my phone to avoid conversation. In fact, I won't look at my phone at all. Turning it on silent mode now.
2. Fidget with my rings (won't wear any to ease temptation), look down at my feet, or engage in any other insecure body language.
3. Make excuses for why I don't have a job. Instead, I will use the explanation "I'm taking some time for myself."
4. Lock myself in the bathroom.
5. Cry.

All right, it's time to call my carriage/Uber. Look out, Jackie Reid! I'm coming for my redemption!

6:12 P.M.—MISSED CALLS: (4) Mama Shell

Mama Shell

7:16 P.M.

Are you at Dad's new restaurant???

MS

MS   Honey, are you at PAREA? That's Dad's property!

MS   Lulu?

MS   What are you doing there? Are you at the opening party?? I thought you were going to Natasha's?!

MS   We're on our way there right now!

MS   Hello?

7:22 P.M.

MS   In line for the valet! Goodness, there are so many people here!!

MS   Does Natasha know someone at the party? Why are you there??

MS   Did you valet? You better have valeted, I don't want you walking to your car at night.

MS   Just gave them the keys. We'll see you in a minute! 😊

INJURY INCIDENT REPORT FORM

Incident Date: September 18, 2017
Time: 11:18 P.M.
Injured Person's Name: Theodore Greenberg
Injury Type: Strained posterior longitudinal ligament
Details of incident: Sprained neck resulting from sudden twisting of the spine. MRI concluded no strains or fractures. Minor tearing; two days in neck brace.

SEPTEMBER 19
11:15 A.M.

Here I was, thinking I had hit rock bottom. That was not rock bottom. That was somewhere twenty feet above rock bottom, dangling by a thread of lies that accidentally twisted around my neck like a metaphorical noose.

Now *this*? This is most definitely rock bottom.

The party was going splendidly. I walked in as confidently as I knew how to: shoulders back, smile plastered on, hands glued together in front of my stomach to hide any bloat. These are tricks I picked up from years of witnessing Mother at parties, effortlessly navigating through crowds like Tarzan through a thick forest of socialites. I kept this image in mind as I scanned the crowd for Theo, who almost didn't recognize me and my newfound poise. He glanced in my direction, looked away, and then swiveled his head back in surprise, which normally happens only when there's something gross on my face.

"Excuse me, miss," he whispered in my ear once he made his way to me, "I shouldn't be saying this since I already have a girlfriend, but I couldn't help noticing how freaking stunning you are."

I snorted, because it's still me.

There were enough guests in the restaurant that each social interaction was kept to about three minutes per person, which significantly limited my chances of being awkward. It was like speed dating, only instead of convincing people to date me, I was trying to prove what a sophisticated and put-together unemployed person I was. And it was working!

"Yes, I graduated from Columbia this past spring. Hmm? Oh, I'm just taking some time for *myself* right now. So what do *you* do?"

Theo couldn't stop smiling—at me, at the partygoers, at the food he'll soon be cooking. Jackie introduced him to some of her more prominent chef friends, who all commented on the impressiveness of his age/his awesome veggie-patterned bow tie. When I excused myself to the bathroom an hour later, I let out a triumphant sigh: one hour down, three to go. I popped a mint into my mouth and reapplied Val's lip gloss before pulling my phone out of my purse for a quick check.

Four missed calls. Eleven text messages. All from the same person: Mom.

I started skimming the texts, thinking she must need help turning the TV on or something. It wasn't until I read the words *We're on our way* that the reality struck me like a blow to the back of the knees. Before I could compose myself, I was ripping open the bathroom door and dashing to the dining room, slapping strangers out of my way with my clutch purse. I spotted Mom's identical blond lob from across the crowd, her back turned to me as she chatted with Dad and Jackie. At the same moment, I caught sight of Theo excusing himself from a conversation with the main dessert chef.

It all happened so fast.

I watched in slow motion as Theo glanced over at the lob, pivoted slightly, and walked the five steps over to where my parents and Jackie were standing. Without fully turning to look at her, Theo wrapped a loose arm around Mom's waist, spun her around, and to my unmitigated horror, pulled her in for a kiss on the lips. Mom yelped and leaned back just enough to avoid mouth-to-mouth contact as Dad instinctively grabbed Theo by the arms, flung him around into a wrist lock, and slammed his torso onto the hors d'oeuvre table with a thud. The entire restaurant came to a grinding halt as Dad pinned a squirming Theo against the wooden panels of the communal table like an officer making an arrest onto the hood of his elegantly decorated car.

"Get your hands off my wife!" Dad yelled at Theo, whose face was smashed into a plate of sriracha deviled eggs.

"*Wife?!*" Theo yelled back with a face full of spicy yolk cream. "What are you—*OW!*" Theo cried out as Dad tightened his grasp, expertly pressing Theo's thumbs into a knot behind his back.

Phone screens started popping up left and right as the partygoers began documenting the incident. Mom was in hysterics, her hands covering her mouth to hide the fits of nervous laughter that had taken hold. People were scrambling. Jackie was cursing. I felt faint.

"DAD!" I yelled, my voice finally catching up to my brain. "STOP!"

No one could hear me. The whole restaurant had erupted into roars of excitement and gossip, more and more people livestreaming the fight from their phones. I sprinted toward Theo as fast as I could in Mom's size 4 dress, wiggling my hips around like a discount Marilyn as I pushed through the rambunctious crowd.

"DAD! LET GO!"

This time he heard me. Both he and Theo froze as I reached them, panting from the effort and adrenaline. Mom sobered at the sight of me in her lacy dress, her giggles dissipating as I put my hands on Theo's shoulders.

"Dad, *please* let him go, this was a mistake!"

"Louie, how did you—*SHIT!*" Theo tried craning his head up toward me, but yelped in pain. Dad finally relinquished his grip, letting Theo's hands fly to the back of his aching, bow-tie-wrapped neck. I crouched down to table level, frantic.

"Are you okay? Where does it hurt??"

"I can't turn my neck."

"I barely touched him!"

"YOU THREW HIM ON THE TABLE!"

"Everyone, CALM DOWN!" Jackie bellowed, her face as red as her hair. "Please, everyone, we all just need to relax . . ."

"DON'T MOVE!" One of the restaurant critics jumped to the front of the crowd, his pinstriped sleeves rolled up to his pointy elbows. He rushed over to the table and gently laid a hand on Theo's back, careful not to apply pressure. "Don't move a muscle! We need to check to see if your spine is compromised."

"What? My spine is not—"

"IS ANYONE HERE A DOCTOR?!"

"Lulu, what the *hell* is going on?" Mom barged in, ignoring the critic. "What are you even doing here?"

"She's here with me!" Theo shouted back from his folded position on the table.

"And who are *you*?"

"I'm Theo!"

"Theo? You mean physics friend Theo?"

"Physics?!"

Theo tried standing up, but Pinstripes grabbed his neck and held it rigidly against the platter of eggs.

"OWWWW! *What the*—"

"Someone go into the kitchen and get some ice!"

"HE DOESN'T NEED ICE."

"Can everyone *please* put their phones away!" Jackie yelled.

"Lulu, I'm confused," Mom kept on. "You told me you were spending the night at Natasha's . . ."

"*Natasha*? OW! Sir, *please* let go of my head!" Theo pleaded.

"Do you feel any tingling in your appendages??"

"No!"

"Are you seeing spots?"

"Oh, for Christ's sake . . ." Dad groaned.

"Is Natasha at this party, too?" Mom asked, turning to the crowd. "Did you three come here together?"

"I thought Natasha was still stuck in India!" Theo hollered.

"Natasha is in *India*??"

"I have ice!" Some girl in a pencil skirt handed a towel full of ice cubes to Pinstripes, who thanked her and pressed the wrap deep into Theo's sore neck.

"SHIT! JESUS, that's cold!"

"Breathe into it!" the man ordered.

"You're going to give me freezer burn!"

"It's better than a severed spine."

"This is fucking ridiculous," Dad said, crossing his arms.

"Do not make light of this!" Pinstripes threatened, pointing a finger at Dad. "I could have you arrested! This is assault!"

"*Assault?* He kissed my wife!"

"*I thought she was Lou!*"

"You were trying to kiss *Lulu*?"

"THERE'S NO NEED TO CALL THE POLICE!" Jackie shouted to the crowd, anxious to maintain order. "And will everyone PLEASE PUT AWAY THEIR PHONES?!"

Suddenly Dad looked down at poor Theo with wide eyes, clarity finding its way into the creases of his hardened face. "Wait a second— *you're* the boyfriend?"

"You're the WHAT?!" Mom shrieked, silencing the rowdy party-goers. I could feel blood rushing away from my brain and to my cheeks as Jackie seized the momentary silence.

"THANK YOU! Now if I could please have everyone . . ."

"*Your boyfriend??*" Mom yelled over Jackie as I stood with my feet nailed to the floor. "Did he just say your *BOYFRIEND*?!"

Whatever poise I'd managed to fake earlier in the evening had disappeared entirely, making way for my usual mess of anxiety. I was sweating straight through Mom's dress, turning patches of the navy to a sticky black. My makeup was smeared down my cheeks, and I could almost feel my hair starting to frizz. This was it. My clock had struck midnight. Cinderel-Lou was exposed, and the whole kingdom was watching as her gown turned into rags.

"I—I tried to tell you—" I started, barely able to breathe.

"She still doesn't know about me??" Theo yelled out, all different kinds of hurt. "But you said—OWW! Son of a—"

"Can you wiggle your fingers and toes?" Pinstripes requested.

"Get off him or you'll be lying next to him," my dad growled. Pinstripes slowly removed himself from Theo, who immediately tried standing up straight, egg still smeared on the right side of his face. I rushed over to help him, but he quickly pulled his arm back, recoiling from my touch.

"How long has this been happening?" Mom asked in disbelief. I went to answer, but Theo did it for me.

"Almost eleven months."

"ELEVEN?!" Mom started pacing back and forth, the realizations hitting her one by one as my story fell apart like a Jenga tower. "So all this time you've been 'seeing Natasha' in Silver Lake, you've actually been lying to me and going to see Theo?"

"I know it sounds bad, but—"

"And *you*, Charlie!" Mom turned suddenly on Dad, whose frown had grown deeper than the hole I was trapped in. "You knew about this? You knew that our daughter had a secret boyfriend and you didn't bother telling me??"

Dad's lip thinned into a tight line.

"It's not his fault!" I interjected, stepping forward. "He wanted *me* to tell you, but I couldn't!"

"But *why*?" she pleaded. "Why on earth wouldn't you tell me? What have I done to deserve . . ." Mom gasped, hands flying to cover her face as it suddenly dawned on her. "Oh my goodness. I've been calling him . . . Oh no . . ."

"Been calling me what?" Theo caught on. "What has she been—OW!" He tried turning his head to look at me, but a surge of pain kept him locked in place. Pinstripes extended an arm out with the towel of ice, which Theo took with his free hand.

"I think this is something we should discuss in the car," Dad said pointedly.

"Oh, I'm not going back in the car!" Mom announced. "I'm taking an Uber home."

"No, wait, Mom, please—"

She ignored me, swiftly turning on her heels and stomping out the front door in a huff. Hushed murmurs echoed through the restaurant as Dad quietly followed after her, shooting me a disappointed look before he stepped outside. I stood motionless, staring after them, unable to comprehend the shitstorm that had just hit the collective fan. Finally someone from the back of the dining room yelled out: "So, does this mean the drinks are free?"

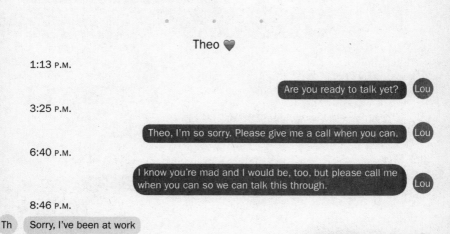

Theo 🖤

1:13 P.M.

Are you ready to talk yet? Lou

3:25 P.M.

Theo, I'm so sorry. Please give me a call when you can. Lou

6:40 P.M.

I know you're mad and I would be, too, but please call me when you can so we can talk this through. Lou

8:46 P.M.

Th Sorry, I've been at work

Oh! Right! Of course! Lou

Lou: How was it?

Th: Well, I'm in a brace for two days and everyone is calling me Turtle Neck, so there's that.

Lou: Shit.

Th: Also, the restaurant could have been shut down on night one, so Jackie isn't exactly thrilled with my performance.

Lou: That's not your fault, though . . .

Th: Also ALSO, my girlfriend has been hiding me from her parents for almost a year now, which isn't exactly doing wonders for my ego.

Lou: Theo, I'm so, so, so beyond sorry.

Lou: Can we talk on the phone? Please?

Th: Honestly, Lou, I still need a few days to think about this.

Lou: You have every right to be angry, but please give me a chance to explain this mess.

Th: This isn't just about being angry, Lou. This is about trust.

Th: You lied to me. You lied to your parents.

Th: Jesus, you lied to Natasha!

Lou: I never lied TO Natasha! Just about her . . .

Lou: And to be fair, she's lying to two separate countries, which is a lot worse comparatively speaking.

Th: I'm being serious.

Th: Louie, are you embarrassed of me?

Lou: What?? NO! Of course not!!

Th: Then why were you so afraid to tell your mom?

Th: 8:55 P.M.

Th: Hello?

Lou: I don't have a good answer for that.

Lou: I'm so sorry.

Th: Well then, I should go.

Th: I'll call you in a few days, once I've had some time to think.

9:14 PM

Theo?   Lou

SEPTEMBER 20

   Shelly Hansen

— 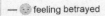 feeling betrayed

After undergoing a series of unexpected life challenges, it has become clear to me that my priorities need a serious face lift. Does anyone know anything about feng shui? I am looking to rearrange my house to promote spiritual growth, family, and youth, if that's an option. They say it's how Julia Roberts and Oprah found their chai.

17 👍, 5 😊

Lisa Van Williams: No fake flowers; lots of pink. 😊

Cathy Ryland: Tell me if it works! My office needs a pick-me-up!

Inez Lopez: If you're looking for chai, they make a great one at Starbucks.

1:55 P.M.

HELP. I'm living in an actual nightmare. Theo wants time apart to "think," Dad can hardly look me in the eye, he's so disappointed, and Mom is acting like a modern twist on a forlorn Tennessee Williams character. She was already in a bad place before, but I think I may have pushed her to the point of insanity. Early this morning, I woke up to discover random articles of discarded clothing haphazardly strewn about the hallway and a low groaning emanating from Mom's bedroom. I followed the suspicious trail of outfits/sounds to find her sitting cross-legged on the floor in her leopard-print robe, surrounded by piles of dresses and pants and shirts, tightly clutching a single Prada high heel to her chest. She was flanked by the two pugs, who suspiciously sniffed the land mine of expensive fabrics that Mom had clearly created in her mania.

"Mom? What's going on?" I asked, trying not to step on anything.

She swiveled her head toward me, narrowed her eyes, and dramatically cast her gaze to the side. "I'm giving away all of my possessions, since this family thinks I'm so shallow," she declared in a slight southern drawl.

I tilted my head, bewildered. "Mom, I never said you were shallow."

"You didn't have to. It's what you *didn't* say that matters, little lady."

"Okay, why are you speaking in a southern accent?"

"*Because*, Lulu, I'm from the South."

"You're from Miami."

"Oh, you think you're just so smart, don't you?" she snapped, banging the Prada shoe against the ground like a gavel. The pugs jumped in surprise. "*Oh*," she moaned, "how did I get here, Muffin? My oldest daughter resents me, my youngest is about to leave for college, my husband spends his whole life trying to financially support my spending . . . Honestly, it seems the best thing I could do is just run away! Or at least change everything about myself."

She lifted the Prada shoe up on her index finger, dangling it above Muffin's thick head. He crouched down and growled at the potential chew toy.

"Mother," I said, carefully, "please. Put the Prada down."

"Why? It's of no use to me now. My designer days are behind me," she professed. Baguette's and Muffin's curly tails started to wiggle as Mom lowered the shoe another inch. I could hear the theme from *Jaws* playing in my head as the pugs circled.

"Listen to me; you don't want to do this. You're not thinking clearly."

"Oh, I'm thinking clearly for the first time," she shot back, lowering the pump another inch.

"What's going on?" Val stepped into the room wearing her nightgown, a concerned expression on her beautiful face.

"Mom's having a nervous breakdown."

"I am doing what's best for my *family*."

"RRRRUFFF!" Muffin leapt into the air and grabbed the shoe by its heel, his fat rolls jiggling as he crashed back to the floor. Baguette pounced, sinking her teeth into the suede pointed toe and pulling with such force that the heel snapped off its base. The three of us gasped.

"NO!" Val screeched.

"You've got to be kidding me," I marveled.

"But Mom, those were your favorite shoes!" Val fretted.

Mom tossed her lob, which somehow still looked perfect from Friday night's blow-dry. "They were a symbol of my old life. It's better this way. Now everyone, OUT!" Mom gestured toward the door, the red paint on her nails starting to chip. "I need time to say goodbye to what was once my jewelry before I sell it all on eBay."

SEPTEMBER 21
8:13 P.M.

There's no way for me to confirm this, but I'm starting to worry that Mom may have been replaced by a robot. I do not recognize this person . . . This is the kind of woman who would wear mom jeans instead of Mother Denim. She spent most of her time today rearranging furniture with Rosa based on the different energy cycles of the house. Not once did she tell me to go to the gym or to put on a bra or pluck out my chin hairs. In fact, she only addressed me once the entire afternoon, and it was to ask me to help her set up an eBay account to sell her jewelry. I knew that this was a bad idea, so instead I just opened a Tumblr page, titled it "Shelly's eBay Account" and told her to post pictures on it. I doubt she'll ever notice.

But the most concerning part of the day came at around 6:00 P.M., after all our potted plants had been placed in the northeast corner of the house.

It's Monday, which can mean only one thing at the Hansens': Bachelor Night. This has been the rule of law since the dawn of the first *Bachelor* season, all the way back in the ancient time of 2002. I made my way into the living room, expecting to hear the usual squeals and giggles that accompany a Red Hot Party, but was instead met with the droning of a particularly stuffy, monotonic Englishman. Mom was curled up on the couch in one of Dad's old T-shirts, Muffin's chin snuggled on her shoulder, her expression resembling a five-year-old's after a shot of cough syrup. A large bowl of Skinny Pop popcorn rested on her lap, and a bottle of uncorked rosé was squeezed between the couch cushions to her right.

"Uh, Mom? What's going on?" I asked, taking in the room as though it were a crime scene. "Where are the ladies?"

"They're at Susan's tonight."

I quickly checked my phone to make sure that today was in fact Monday. Mom stuck her hand deep into the bowl and pulled out a handful of yellow puff balls, held it up to her shoulder for Muffin, and then finished the remaining snack in a large bite.

"But Bachelor Night has always been here . . ."

"I've decided that reality television is for silly, vapid people."

"What are you talking about? You love reality TV. You call it free Xanax!"

"That was the *old* Shelly. New Shelly cares about more serious things and takes *real* Xanax."

She reached over for the rosé and took a swig straight from the bottle, Muffin licking the edge of Mom's lips for a taste of sweet fermented grape. I turned toward the television screen just in time to see a man hold up two different-colored blobs of clay to the camera.

"So instead of *Bachelor in Paradise,* you're watching a special on . . . ceramic creation?"

"It's a documentary on the history of bricks."

"Bricks?"

"Yes. Did you know that the first bricks were sun-dried? Like the tomatoes? It's all painfully interesting."

Emphasis on the painful. This was the moment that I started to suspect the robot theory . . . Never in my wildest, most outlandish dreams did I imagine my mother missing a party to watch cement dry. Equally startling, and I can't believe I'm about to record this on paper . . . I sort of, kind of, maybe missed watching *The Bachelor*? I mean, don't get me wrong—I still think that reality television is an abomination sent to perpetuate the demise of art—but I really wished the Red Hots were here. I've gotten used to the cheers and chatters and the gluten-free kale dips . . .

Mostly I think I just missed the fun, even if I wasn't the one having it.

SEPTEMBER 22

Alyssa 👑

2:30 P.M.

> Lyss, I need advice. — Lou

> My whole life has fallen apart. — Lou

Al   What's going on, Squeeze?

> Theo's in a neck brace and won't talk to me, my mom is in the middle of a full-blown midlife crisis, Natasha is being held in India for refusing to seek medical attention for a parasite she never had, and I'm not even close to finding a suitable job for myself, much less a career path. — Lou

> Basically, I feel like a complete and total failure, and fully expect that I'll wind up serving chicken nuggets somewhere out of a drive-through window, lost and alone. **Lou**

Al Hold up . . . Natasha is being detained by a sovereign government against her will, and the United States hasn't come to her aid?

> Something like that, yes **Lou**

Al Wow.

Al Is she represented yet?

SEPTEMBER 23
4:35 P.M.

I think I'm coming down with something. Like pneumonia, or the plague. I don't think I've ever felt this terrible. Getting out of bed each morning makes me feel like a vampire emerging from centuries of sleep, only instead of searching for blood, I'm looking for motivation/a job/dignity of any kind.

I really miss Theo. He still hasn't texted or called me. I had to change his name in my contacts to DON'T YOU DARE LOU HANSEN just to keep from calling and telling him everything. But I couldn't do that without giving up Mother. There's no gentle way to explain that my mom has called him a dorky, weirdo serial killer with a flamboyant fashion sense without inevitably hurting his feelings. And I've already done enough damage to his neck.

That being said, it's been awful not talking to him. I feel like crying every time I so much as look at food, which hasn't stopped me from eating twice as much of it as usual.* One of his work friends tagged him in a picture on Facebook today, which I've examined at least fifteen times in the past three hours. The caption reads *PAREA Pals,* and features some of the chefs hanging out together on their lunch

---

*Some people lose their appetite when they're miserable. I like to think that these people are less suited for survival, and that my constant desire to snack is an indication that my instincts are strong.

break. It was definitely candid, since Theo is terrible at taking posed photos and he looks really, really cute in this one. His neck brace is off! And it looks like the black eye has started to turn yellow!! But in my excitement, I accidentally liked the picture, then freaked out about whether or not I should *unlike* it, but ultimately decided that he was going to see the notification anyway and that revoking the like would be much worse in the long run. *Ugh.* He doesn't look unhappy in this picture at all! I mean, not that I want him to be *unhappy* . . . but come on, our relationship is on the line here! Does he have to be smiling *so* wide??

Shit, I just heard a crash in Mom's room. Hoping she's not trying to dismantle her dresser to turn it into a doghouse again. I keep telling her that the dogs are practically in charge of our house already, and that they'd never settle for anything less than two thousand square feet. Going to check on her now. Wish me luck.

SEPTEMBER 24

Val

6:45 P.M.

Val — Babe, what did you do?

Val — You broke Mom.

I know. This is ridiculous. — Lou

I snuck in her room last night to check her Fitbit. She's only gotten, like, 3,000 steps for this whole week. — Lou

Val — Yeah, she's acting wack.

Val — I just watched her eat like half a pint of ice cream that Dad was hiding in the bottom of the freezer

Val — She didn't even use a spoon. She just chipped away at it with the back of a fork

My god. — Lou

Well, it's officially been a full week since the Worst Day of My Life, and things aren't looking any brighter in the Hansen house. Tonight is the beginning of Yom Kippur, which is normally Mom's favorite holiday, since she gets to fast for religious reasons. However, this year Mom is taking her atoning to a whole new, deranged level:

"Lisa and I are going on a minimalist hike through the desert," Mom announced this morning after gathering the family in the living room. "Tomorrow we leave at sunrise and won't be back until we break fast at dinner. No technology is allowed, so I'm leaving my cell phone here. I know this will be a relief to you all, since I won't be tracking your every movement, but please remember to feed the pugs in my absence."

Dad's frown emerged. Val and I exchanged concerned glances.

"But that's like . . . ten hours," Val said.

"It's supposed to push me, mind, body, and soul."

"Don't you have to train for those sorts of things?" I asked. "Build up endurance? Carb-load?"

"I've been urban hiking for weeks now. I'm sure I can handle it."

"Mom, you won't be eating or drinking anything tomorrow," I noted. "Don't you think this could be a bit dangerous?"

"If Jesus could do it, so can I."

"Mom, you're Jewish."

"And so was Jesus."

"Shelly," Dad said, "I understand that you've been going through a rough patch, but there's no way you're going on an all-day desert hike without any food or water or a cell phone. That's not realistic."

"Lisa is doing it!"

"Lisa isn't fasting," Val pointed out.

"Oh, please. Lisa is *always* fasting."

"Shell, this is a bad idea," Dad doubled down, his frown stretching further down his cheeks. "You're not going to strand yourself in the middle of nowhere on the one day you can't even hydrate. If you really want to go on some hippie desert trip, I'll buy you tickets to Coachella this year."

"Fine." Mom pouted, crossing her arms and sticking up her nose. "If you all won't support me, I'll just have to find my new purpose elsewhere."

"Your *new purpose*?" Val inquired.

"Yes, my *new purpose*, since I'm officially resigning from my old one." She explained theatrically, "I tried my best to be a good mother, but clearly I've failed miserably, since you all can't stand me."

"What are you talking about?" I asked. "*Can't stand you?* Are you nuts??"

"Don't lie to me!" she snapped. "You wish I were like one of those *normal* mothers, who let their hair dry naturally when it's humid outside, or bake gluten-filled cookies for bake sales and PTA meetings. One of those women who drive a minivan or shop at the Gap or let their daughters wear those tragic baggy uniform jerseys to soccer games without taking them to be altered first. Well, I'm sorry I was such a disappointment! I did my best without a handbook. But seeing as Val no longer needs me and you no longer trust me, I think it's time to turn in my badge."

She shot me a piercing look before stomping back to her room, reemerging a moment later wearing a plastic fanny pack.

"I'm meeting Lisa at Lululemon to help her find the perfect spiritual awakening outfit. Don't worry, Charlie—since I'm not going on the journey tomorrow, I left my credit cards in the trash can where they belong . . . which is now hidden from view in the southwest corner of our bathroom."

And with that, she exited stage left, tossing her lob as a flourish before marching through the foyer and out the front door.

I don't know what to do. The situation has gone from bad to worse to positively unbearable and shows zero signs of letting up. Who is this joyless, senseless, mascaraless monster that I've unleashed upon the world? And where on earth did she get a fanny pack??

But even more important: Does Mom *really* think that I can't stand her? Was that monologue all just irrational martyr blabber meant to guilt Val and me into eternal indentured servitude . . . or does she honestly believe I wish she were someone else? That can't be true. That's ridiculous! I don't want Mom to suddenly stop being *Mom*; I just don't want her to judge me for being *me*.

Oh god. I know what I have to do. But it's not going to be fun. In fact, it's going to involve one of the most excruciating moments of my entire life so far, and that includes watching Theo get his face crammed into a plate of sriracha yolk.

Megan Bitchell 💡

2:10 P.M.

> Hey, Megan, I need your help. — Lou

> Text me when you're on your break. — Lou

2:45 P.M.

MB BAAAAAAAABE! What's up? Do you want me to help you finally get rid of that stache? Cuz I have the BEST electrolysis person ever, she's like, a queen.

> No, my stache is doing just fine, thanks. I actually have a question for my mom. — Lou

> How long does it normally take to make one of those name necklaces you have? — Lou

> I want to buy her one, and I need it ASAP. — Lou

MB OMG. I'm DED.

MB My friend who makes them is at work today. I can ask her right now!

> Thank you. Also, this is a secret, so you REALLY can't tell Mom or Stacey. I mean it. — Lou

MB LOL, obvi! My gosh, what kind of bitch do you think I am??

MB Hahaha jk. 😜

MB   Anywho, she says it normally takes, like, 5 - 7 days tops.

MB   She just needs the name spelled out EXACTLY how you want it. So, like, tell me if it's SHELLY or Shelly or Sexy Shelly or whatevs.

Actually, I have something else in mind.   Lou

SEPTEMBER 26

2:14 P.M.

Ugh. Today is Yom Kippur—the Jewish holiday of atonement—and though I am genuinely remorseful for the multitude of sins I've committed in the last six months, I am also deeply grumpy from the lack of sustenance I've had in the last twelve hours. I've been stress-eating so much as of late, I'm pretty sure my body has adapted from the constant intake to need food every twenty minutes or so. Either that, or I grew an extra three stomachs. I can't be sure which.

I'm not the only cranky member of the Hansen family. Dad fasts every year out of solidarity with Mom,* and every year I fear for my life because of it. For him, things always take a turn for the worse around noon, when the first wave of "fuck this" hits, which is why I locked myself in the bathroom for that whole hour pretending to "feel queasy." In reality, I was sending this Facebook message out to the Red Hot Ladies:

Hi, everyone! I just wanted to let you know that Bachelor Night is back on at our house for this Monday. Technically, Mom doesn't know this yet, but don't worry! She will by six o'clock on Monday!

Speaking of Mom: She has set up a "meditation tent" in the backyard among the rose bushes as an alternative to her minimalist hike, which is basically a fort made from her duvet cover, two beach chairs, and a bunch of faux-fur pillows. Apparently she's trying to become

---

*She forces him.

"one with nature"—at least until 3:00 P.M., when the sprinklers are set to turn on. We haven't spoken much since her outburst . . . By the time she got home from "assistant shopping" last night, Yom Kippur had already begun, and the last thing I wanted was to make matters worse with a hangry encounter. Nope, until I've consumed at least five hundred calories, I will keep my human contact minimal, for the sake of my family and myself.

While I'm completely isolated, I should take the time to write down a new list of goals, seeing as most of my Roshalutions have been rendered irrelevant. Somehow I've managed to make everyone I love think I'm ashamed of them, which my old psychology teacher might say is a symptom of "projecting," but I'm way too hungry to diagnose myself right now.

YOM KIPPUR GOALS

- Make up with Mom.
- Make up with Theo.
- Make up with Dad.
- Make up with Natasha.
- Express genuine appreciation to ~~Bitchell~~ Megan.
- Get a job _interview_. (You don't even have to get the job; just an interview.)

DON'T YOU DARE LOU HANSEN

1:05 A.M.

So I was thinking about you a lot today, because I wasn't sure if you had to work on Yom Kippur while you were fasting. Did you? Frankly, that seems like an exceptionally cruel fate for a chef, if you ask me.

1:07 A.M.

I am the biggest loser idiot in the entire world and I don't deserve you or your kindness or your mini pork sliders, but you're my favorite person in the whole wide world and if you could just give me another chance to prove myself . . . ugh, no.

1:10 A.M.

> I know you probably don't want to talk to me, and I'm not even sure if we're dating anymore, but I just want to tell you that I miss you, and that I screwed up, and that I'm sorry. Call me when you can.

Lou

delivered

SEPTEMBER 27

9:15 A.M.

Just heard back from Theo, and I think I'm going to be sick.

Hey, I've thought it over, and I really want to talk . . . but I would rather do it in person. Let me know when you're free this week, and we'll pick a time to meet.

Oh god. It's over. It's so obviously over. No one asks to "talk in person" unless it's 100 percent, definitely over. AHHHHHH, what am I going to do? Do I call him?? No, I can't call him . . . *He* somehow has managed to maintain enough cool to refrain from calling *me*, so why should I degrade myself by calling him first? As it is, I texted him first, and at one o'clock in the morning, like a fool. No form of virtual communication is ever honorable after eleven at night unless it's an emergency, and even then, holding off until the morning will always win you brownie points.

Oh, who was I kidding? Of course he wants to end it! After the humiliation I caused him at work? And the lying/compulsive ring-fiddling? Let's be honest. It was only a matter of time. Theo already has his life put together—his own apartment, a successful job, naturally angular features. I, on the other hand, have been an egotistical, entitled little brat with no sense of how lucky I've been. This whole year I've had a boyfriend, a home, endless options and opportunities, and all I've done is compare and complain. I mean, I've only applied to one job! What is wrong with me? Why did I think the world would just open up for me with the mention of some clubs and a Columbia degree?? Officially adding, "stop whining and start working" to my list of Yom Kippur goals.

Hold on, I'm getting a text.

Megan Mitchell

10:46 A.M.

MM Ay bay bay!! Are you free at all today?

Probably freer than I'd like to be. Why? **Lou**

MM Welllllll, I told my work friend that this necklace was, like, SUPES important and for someone SUPES special . . .

MM So after working a bit of that Mitchell Magic, she decided to put a rush order on your necklace!

Are you serious?? **Lou**

MM YAS! We talked about it yesterday after kick boxing. She said it should be ready by the end of the day!

Oh my god! That's fantastic!! **Lou**

MM I know, right?

MM I can totes drop it by your house later if you want. You're, like, five minutes away from my favorite juice bar in LA, and I've been DYING to try their new mushroom powder.

5:25 P.M.

Startling. A positively startling series of events.

I heard Megan's car before I saw it—the high-pitched screech of her poor, innocent tires scraping against the pavement of my residential street as her black BMW convertible violently rounded the corner. She honked twice before skidding into my driveway, her hair perfectly tussled from the 101 freeway, one of her arms dangling out the side of the car with a tiny white gift bag in hand.

"Special delivery for Auntie Shells!" she cheered, pushing her pink cat-eye sunglasses onto her head. I quickly trotted over to the car and grabbed the bag from her, curiously peering inside.

"Have you seen it yet?" I asked her, noticing a little black box.

"I took a little *sneaky peek*. Lulu, it's so, so, SO gorge. Your mom's going to *die*. Like, literally die."

"If by literally, you mean figuratively, then great."

I reached into my back pocket and pulled out my checkbook. "How much do I owe you?" I asked, checking over my shoulder to make sure Mom wasn't watching. "And should I make it out to your name or your friend's?"

"Oh my gosh, babe, do NOT worry," she said, putting a hand up in protest. I blinked at her, not understanding.

"What, do you only use Venmo? Val keeps trying to get me to download Venmo, but I'm nervous it's going to get hacked . . ."

"No, I mean, I got this!" she said, flicking her wrist at me, shooing my checkbook away.

I stared at her suspiciously, certain she was about to pull a prank. "I'm sorry, but . . . are you offering to pay?"

She rolled her eyes and scoffed. "OMG, for the like, zillionth time, *yes*! It's really no biggie. My girl gave me a supes juicy discount, and I told your mom I'd get her one, anywho."

For a moment, I genuinely considered that I had stumbled into a black hole. Between Mom's serious demeanor and now Megan's generosity, I wasn't sure what I could believe in anymore.

"Megan, don't be ridiculous. I asked for this necklace, and I want to pay for it."

"Oh, what's that? I can't hear you over the sound of my not listening."

She reached a hand to the dial of her car radio and turned up the pop music, cupping the other hand up to her ear, like the world's richest mime.

"Okay, okay! Turn it down, I don't want Mom to hear you," I said, sneaking a quick look back at the house. "Wow, Megan, that's . . . this is really thoughtful. Thank you."

"Of course! Anything for your mama. She's like, my idol."

"She is?"

"Um, obvi!" she said, running a hand through the ends of her tangled hair. "She's taken care of me every summer since I was, like, five. And I *wish* I could talk to my mom about clothes and boys and friends and stuff . . ."

For a split second, I felt something way, way, *way* deep down inside my heart . . . something that if you squinted and leaned in closely would almost, sort of, maybe resemble affection. We smiled at each other briefly before Megan's lips puckered into a curt smile.

". . . Anywho, I'm the one with the job. It's the least I can do for the funemployed."

Andddddd she's back.

"Well, thank you for your contribution," I said, putting my checkbook back into my pocket. She flipped her sunglasses back onto her nose and put her car into reverse.

"Always, babe. Just here to help!" She waved at me with three fingers as she backed out of the driveway. "See ya later, be-yotch!" she yelled, before zooming off to snort some powdered mushrooms.

SEPTEMBER 28
11:05 A.M.

All right. The Red Hots are coming over at six for Bachelor Night, and Mom still doesn't know that it's happening. While she's out "running errands" for the next few hours,* Rosa and I will be tidying up the

---

*I put this in quotes because quite frankly, running errands just feels too dreadfully dull for my mother. She doesn't really "run errands" so much as "go on practical outings."

house, hiding all traces of the mid- and quarter-life crises that have been simultaneously taking place in it. I'm thrilled to report that all the ladies will be present at tonight's gathering! Lisa's now dating her minimalist hike guide, so I guess it's fair to say that hers was a transcendent experience. But apparently, when this guy is not leading people through the wilderness for ten hours at a time, he's a florist, so we were able to score two dozen free roses for the evening festivities.

I told Val about my master plan. She's completely on board and is even picking up Shell-tini ingredients on her way home from school.

"Do you need me to go buy the gin?" I asked her.

"No, don't worry. I've got a fake," she said.

"When did you get a fake?"

"Like, two months ago. Mom got it for me in case of emergencies so I could go pick up rosé."

7:40 P.M.

Mom came home at around five thirty with two armfuls of dog food. She took one look at the roses and froze, panic flashing across her face.

"What's going on? Is it my birthday? Please don't tell me it's my birthday . . ."

"No, it's not your birthday," I assured her. "Don't worry, you're still fift—"

"HUSH! Don't say that number," Mom demanded.

"Okay," I agreed, proceeding with caution. "It's for Bachelor Night. The Red Hot Ladies are coming over. That's why there are roses."

Mom turned her nose up at me over the bags of gourmet kibble. "Why are they coming *here*? I told them to go to Stacey's."

"Well, I told them I wanted them to come here instead," I explained. "I'm interested in tonight's . . . er . . . episode."

I swear, this is the last lie I will ever tell. Mom made her way past the flowers and into the kitchen, setting the dog food down on the table before slowly walking back to where I was standing, eyeing the setup distrustfully.

"You were planning on watching *Bachelor in Paradise* with my best friends without me?"

"Well, actually, that's the thing . . ." I said, swiftly pulling the tiny black box out from behind a couch cushion and hiding it behind my back. "You're going to be watching it with us."

She put her hands on her hips, equal parts frustrated and confused. "I already told you. I've given up reality TV."

"No, Mom, I think you've given up reality," I said, squeezing the box a little tighter. "You love *The Bachelor*. You love your wardrobe. You love getting your nails done just because it's a Tuesday."

"And you've all made it clear that you don't. You think it's all silly, shallow . . ." She craned her neck to the side, trying to look behind my back. "And what is it that you're hiding back there??"

I rolled my eyes and handed her the box, disappointed that I wasn't being as sly as I thought.

She stared down at the gift like she'd never seen one before. "What—what's this? Are you sure it isn't my birthday?"

"Just open it. You'll understand," I said cryptically. She shot me a suspicious look before gingerly lifting the lid, and gasped as she pulled out a gold chain with tiny golden letters spelling out: *Mama Shell.*

"*How did you— I don't— What is—*"

"I know you said you wanted to turn in your Mom badge," I explained, my hands clasped nervously in front of my stomach. "But I'm sorry; I can't let you do that. It's kind of a lifelong position."*

Mom tightly wrapped her fingers around the necklace, clutching her other hand to her heart as tears formed in her makeupless eyes. "Oh, *Lulu!*" she cried. "It's *perfect!*"

---

*For the record: I don't think I've ever been so smooth in my entire life. In fact, I don't know if I will ever get the chance to be this smooth again.

She threw her arms around me and wept, letting all one hundred and ten pounds of her collapse onto my body. Once she started crying, I started crying, and the two of us blubbered all over each other for five whole minutes before I finally managed to speak.

"I'm so, so sorry I lied to you," I said, pulling back to wipe my tears. "I never want to lie to you! I'm a terrible liar! I was just scared you wouldn't approve of Theo."

"But *why*?" Mom asked, pushing back her own tears with her shirt. "What made you think I wouldn't approve of your boyfriend?"

"Well, for one thing, you *literally* have been calling him a serial killer," I bluntly noted.

Mom shook her head, unconvinced. "I know, and that was wretched, but to be fair, he does come off rather brooding." I nodded, since she made a fair point. "But Lulu, you were dating this boy for months before I started calling him that, um . . . *name*. You must have had other reasons to hide him from me."

The question took me by surprise, but she was right. I considered for a moment, reflecting on all the lies I'd told in the past year.

"In all honesty," I started, unsure of how to articulate my next thought, "I think it's . . . well, it's because you're like my mirror."

Mom raised a perplexed brow. "Your mirror?"

I nodded, suddenly confident in the idea. "Yeah, my mirror," I went on. "You reflect me, for better and for worse." Mom still looked confused, so I tried to break it down a different way. "Okay, so, when you look in a mirror, you see the truth of what is there, right? Not what you wish you were or what you're trying to be—it's just you: plain and simple. And once you take a look in that mirror, you can't unsee it, no matter how badly you want to."

I took a deep breath, trying to bring this metaphor to a close.

"So if you met Theo, and you thought that he was weird or creepy, or not the exact man you had envisioned for me . . ."

"Hold on." Mom cut me off, holding a finger up to my face. "I have to stop you. Exactly what kind of person do you think I *envision* for you?"

I crossed my arms, starting to feel defensive. "Well, you've always talked about these big strong handsome manly men . . ."

"Oh, honey." Mom sighed, the chain of her necklace still dangling through her fingers. "Do you really think I care if you date an athlete? Please! I married your real estate agent father!"

"But you told me to find a guy who was 'all packaged up and ready to go,'" I argued.

"Because I don't want you to settle for anything or anyone who isn't worthy of you." She tucked a strand of my frizzy hair behind one of my ears. "Listen to me, Lulu Laurent: your happiness is the only thing I envision for you. I know what makes *me* happy—shallow and silly as you may think I am—but if you want to move to the Arctic and become a dogsled driver, so be it! I'll buy a Moncler down coat and decorate the hell out of my igloo."

I snorted, envisioning Muffin's tongue stuck to the side of Mom's imaginary ice hut. "I'm sorry, Mom."

"Shhh." She pulled me in for another hug and we stayed there for a long time, until finally a jealous Baguette started pawing at my leg. Mom bent over and picked up the pug in her arms, cradling her as only a mom could.

"All right. So." She composed herself, standing up straight as Baguette licked her salty cheeks. "When do I finally get to meet this boyfriend?"

I looked down at my feet, my stomach twisting in knots again. "Honestly, I'm not sure he's going to be my boyfriend for much longer."

Mom nodded slowly, the memory of Theo's takedown by Dad probably playing over in her mind's eye.

"Hmmm. Well then, we have a lot of catching up to do. What time is it? Oh, perfect! We still have another twenty minutes until the Red Hots arrive. Sit down on the couch, and we'll talk this whole thing out. Do we have any more rosé, or did I drink it all in my frenzy? Oh, Val's getting Shell-tinis?? Thank goodness! I told Charlie that fake ID would come in handy!"

I guess it's true what they say: you can never change the spots on a leopard-print robe.

SEPTEMBER 30

📶 AT&T 📶   🔋 ⚡ 80% 🔋

‹ Home   **Natasha McPatterson**   📞   📹

1:10 P.M.

Hey, Tash, I know I haven't exactly been the best friend as of late, and I know that I can sometimes come off a little uptight and judgmental about some of your more creative ideas . . . but I just wanted to let you know how much I value your friendship.

If you want to break international law, I can't exactly support you legally, but I support you emotionally, and that's what matters.

I miss you, and as soon as you're allowed back on American soil, I want to come visit.

1:45 P.M.

Dearest Lou-isiana Purchase, thank you so much for the thoughtful message, and for setting me on the path toward becoming my truest self. I owe so much to you, and can only hope to one day return the favor. Unfortunately, it might take some time before I'm allowed back in the United States, considering the BBC story that just broke. But fret not: I'm hiring Alyssa as my lawyer, and though she's only in her first year of law school, I sense that she is wise beyond her years.

However, if you really would like to visit, would you consider coming to India? Last I heard, you were still looking for a job, which would certainly give you time enough for the journey! Let me know, and I'll have a bowl of vegan curry waiting.

Love always, Me.

BBC NEWS REPORT

AMERICAN CITIZEN DETAINED IN INDIA LAUNCHES ONLINE CAMPAIGN AGAINST THE U.S. CENTERS FOR DISEASE CONTROL AND PREVENTION

In late May, Arizona native Natasha McPatterson contracted parasites on her academic trip abroad. After she had suffered from extreme symptoms for a month and a half, McPatterson's illness caught the attention of the Centers for Disease Control and Prevention. Now, McPatterson has started an online campaign against the CDC, asking for the U.S. government to interfere.

"After undergoing multiple Reiki and sound bath treatments, I was declared healthy by three different healers. However, the Centers for Disease Control refuse to acknowledge this as a proper diagnosis, and insists that I see a Western doctor before returning to my home in the United States. This is clear discrimination, and furthers the imperialist narrative that Western medicine is the only legitimate form of medicine. I call upon the U.S. government to release a statement in support of these ancient practices, and for the CDC to release a formal apology. Until that time, I will remain in India, parasite-free, separated from my friends and family. Please show your support by sharing my story."

Thousands of people have been chiming in on Twitter:

@Vegan4lyfe
Natasha being denied entry into the U.S. is a slap in the face to all marginalized groups. Disgusted. #PrayForNatasha

@IsabellHix3
My yoga teacher does Reiki and swears by it. Haters gonna hate! Fight the good fight, my girl! #PrayForNatasha

Despite the flood of support, there has been equal backlash against Natasha and her campaign, many questioning whether Ms. McPatterson would pose a threat to national security:

@terryjohnson19
People are upset b/c she's being asked to see a doctor? What if she's contagious? Idk, just seems practical. #prayfornatasha

@WORLD_IS_ENDING
Another liberal crybaby pushing the gay agenda. I hope the parasites eat her ugly snowflake guts out. #dont #prayfornatasha

Month Six

Falling Back

Mama Shell

1:05 P.M.

MS What are you thinking about for your Halloween costume?

It's October first . . . Lou

MS So? It's never too early to start outfit planning.

MS The Red Hots are going as Tiffany Swan's Squad. We're going to have Val tag her on Twitter!

Hmm, I'm not sure what I should be. Lou

Maybe I'll go classic and be Princess Leia. Lou

MS You're going to wear a long baggy dress? And a wig??

MS Why can't you be a normal twentysomething and go as a slutty cat?

OCTOBER 2

2:15 P.M.

After what was virtually a master class in absurdity, I'm happy to report that my mother is back to her old crazy self—and with a vengeance. She's decided, now that Val is going to college, that it's time to embrace her newfound freedom as a "renaissance of adolescence."

"Fifty really is the new thirty," she said, double-fisting a shot of algae and cayenne water. "And by thirty, I mean twenty-five."

We spent most of yesterday refilling and reorganizing her closet, which was still a total shambles from her southern belle breakdown. The process was oddly therapeutic, and a wonderful distraction from my seemingly imminent breakup. I'm meeting Theo after work at PAREA today, per his request to talk in person. Mom and I decided on my game plan over Shell-tinis before *The Bachelor,* but what if Theo doesn't want to listen? What if he's already decided that he's done with me? What if I pour my heart out and he rejects it, like Tyler Jacoby or Megan or the popular girls from my high school did??

Ugh, I simply can't think about it, lest I get caught in a whirlpool of anxiety and nausea. I'd much rather focus on helping Val with her USC application, answering trivial, lighthearted theoreticals like "What would you do with a billion dollars?" or "If you could have dinner with one person, living or dead, who would it be?"

OCTOBER 3
1:15 P.M.

Well, if the events of last night prove anything, it's that expectations are the poorly placed magnets under life's compass.

I showed up to PAREA half an hour before closing, waiting in the car as super-hip patrons in bowler hats and suspenders lazily made their way out of the restaurant. Occasionally, I'd recognize one of them from the opening party—another chef or waiter Theo had introduced me to—and quickly duck under the steering wheel until they were out of sight to avoid reliving the humiliation. At five past eleven, I finally got out of my car and strode over to the double doors of the restaurant, opening one slightly and peeking inside at the remaining stragglers. It was mostly deserted, with the wooden chairs flipped upside down onto the communal tabletops. I heard Theo's laugh before I saw him: he was chatting with a coworker in the kitchen, buck teeth on full display. My throat dropped into my stomach as I stared at him for a while, like a stalker, watching as his eyes crinkled at the corners when he smiled. He must have felt the heat of my gaze, though, because without any warning, he turned his head to face me— his neck clearly back to its full capability. His ears turned pink against his dark hair net as he mumbled, "See you later," to his coworker, who swiftly left through the back exit.

"Hi there," I called out, timidly stepping into the dining room.

"Oh. Hi," he answered, a bit nervously. We stood in silence for a few seconds, unsure of how to proceed.

I cleared my throat. "How was work?" I decided on, not wanting to jump right into the fate of our relationship.

He nodded lightly, happy to indulge the casual topic. "It was solid. We're starting to get into a rhythm here."

"That's great!" I replied, a bit too loudly. Theo made his way into the dining room, and I could feel my own cheeks burning red. "That's really good; I'm glad to hear it."

More silence. I could feel my heart thumping in my throat as I gazed down at Theo's bright yellow shoelaces.

After what felt like an eternity, he opened his mouth to speak, but I quickly cut him off: "No, wait. I'm going to say something. And if you don't want anything to do with me by the end of it, then there's nothing I can do, but at least I'll know that I said everything I could."

His brows knit together skeptically, but he nodded. "All right. Go ahead."

I swallowed hard, trying to push my pulse back into my chest. "Okay, here's the truth: I didn't tell my mom about you."

"I gathered that."

"It was awful, and I wish I could say it had nothing to do with you, but that wouldn't be the truth, which is what I promised." I could feel my hands slightly shaking. I took a deep breath, purposefully keeping them by my sides as I spoke. "Mom's always been highly critical of the people I've dated—few as they have been—and in both of those cases, she was part of the reason things ended . . ."

Theo crossed his arms, unconvinced. I pushed on, despite my mounting anxiety. "But you weren't someone I was willing to take that risk with, because honestly, you are the most special person who's ever come into my life. So, yeah, it had everything to do with you, but not because I was embarrassed. It was because you were important—and you still are." Another thought suddenly occurred to me: "Also,

Natasha never had parasites, and she may very well be facing exile from America . . ."

"Yeah, I saw that article online."

"It's deeply distressing." I zoned out for a quick moment, envisioning Natasha reading the palms of fellow inmates at an Indian prison. I shook my head to rid myself of the image. "But that's not the point. The point is, I'm being one hundred percent honest with you from here on out. Not just with you—with Natasha, with my family, especially with myself . . ."

One of his brows raised. My fingers were itching to fiddle with something, but I forced them to stay still.

". . . so I understand if I've screwed things up for good, but I really, *really* hope that I haven't, because I love you. And I'm lucky to call you my boyfriend. And I want you to be a part of my family, which of course means meeting my parents."

By the time I finished talking, I was dizzy from all the oxygen I'd failed to get. I inhaled sharply through my nose and watched as Theo's lips tightened into a thin, thoughtful line.

"Is that all?" he asked bluntly. I blinked at him.

"Yes," I replied, unsure of what else to say.

He nodded, his brows practically touching, they were so furrowed. Another eternity passed before he finally spoke. "I'm still mad at you."

I let my head fall to my chest, hanging it in shame. "I understand."

"You almost got me fired from my job."

"I'm *so* sorry."

"You kept secrets from me and your family for months . . ."

"I know."

". . . And you still haven't tried these damn eggs."

"I—huh?"

I lifted my head, startled by the random food comment. Theo took a few long strides over to where the dining room of PAREA met the kitchen, reached an arm over the counter that divided it, and pulled out a plate of freshly cooked sriracha deviled eggs.

"Your dad ruined these before you had the chance to try them," he said, slowly walking back over to me with the tray in hand, "and I just couldn't get over it. No matter what I did. I'd think about the way you lied, and how your dad pretty much beat me up in front of my entire team, and how you may very well have caused an international crisis over Natasha . . . and despite all of that—no matter how angry or hurt I got—the one thing I kept coming back to this whole week was that you never got to try these stupid eggs, and how I *know* they'd be your favorite."

He reached where I was standing and put the eggs down on a table next to me. "So here's your first truth test, Louie. What do you think of these? I want your *honest* opinion."

I stared at the plate and then up at him, dumbfounded. "You—you're not breaking up with me?"

He shrugged, the faintest hint of a smile lifting the corner of his mouth. "Not unless you tell me those *aren't* the best eggs you've ever tasted."

I lunged toward him, throwing my arms around his neck and squeezing him as tightly as I could. He wrapped his arms around my waist, hugging me back, and for the first time in weeks, I felt the glorious and overwhelming sensation of relief. We stayed there for who knows how long, reveling in our not-broken-up-ness, until suddenly my dad's voice came booming from the front of the restaurant: "This time I'll really break your neck."

Theo leapt away from me so quickly, I almost lost my balance and landed in the eggs. He instinctually threw both hands over his head in submission as Dad laughed, clearly pleased to have instilled a healthy dose of fear in my boyfriend. Next to Dad stood Mama Shell: hair blown out, mascara on, two shopping bags dangling from her left forearm, gold necklace glimmering on her neck.

"Sorry we're late, Lulu," she said, tossing her hair behind one shoulder. "But I just *had* to pick a few things up at Williams-Sonoma before they closed, and I got a bit sidetracked at the mall. Anyway, they have the most wonderful wheat-free cookbook that I wanted to pick up for you, Theo. Not that you need to lose any weight, of course, but if you're going to be a part of this family, you're going to have to learn to curb the carbs."

Poor Theo swiveled his head back and forth between the three of us Hansens, trying to piece together what on earth was going on. "What, how is . . ."

"Theo," I started, not wanting to prolong his confusion, "these are my parents. Mom, Dad: this is Theo."

"Well, it's about damn time!" Mom swiftly made her way into the restaurant with outstretched arms. "Oh, Theo, sweetie, we've all heard *so* much about you. Really, we have this time . . . I promise!"

Epilogue

Month Twelve

Commencement

TIME 100

NATASHA MCPATTERSON
by Grace Franke

When I first heard of Natasha McPatterson, it was in the context of a raging online debate regarding her detention in New Delhi. Little did I know that within a matter of months, this twenty-four-year-old's influential yet controversial message would send a shock wave down the spines of journalists and artists across the world.

After launching her online campaign against the CDC, McPatterson became the face of an international hot-topic discussion surrounding race, cultural appropriation, globalization, and mental health. The world held its collective breath as she livestreamed herself for seventy-two hours straight—including meals, sleep, and restroom visits—all to prove her physical well-being. When she infamously stepped off the plane and onto U.S. soil, brazenly displaying the word *LIAR* painted in red across her bare chest, the Internet caught fire. Since confessing that it was all a charade, she has endured death threats and more, yet Ms. McPatterson has held true to her expressed ideals.

Her powerful statement about the authenticity of modern-day reporting pushed the boundaries of performance so far, it has caused many to question the definition of art itself. Duchamp, Warhol, Pollock, Abramović, and now McPatterson . . . Whether you love her or hate her, it's impossible to ignore the impact this young woman has had on the global conversation about honest reporting, the spread of false information, and performance art, making her a natural selection for this list.

Now regarded as one of the most controversial performance artists of the last decade, Natasha resides in an artists' collective somewhere in San Francisco, where she's developing her latest highly anticipated happening.

📎 **Email**
> **To:** **Lou Hansen**
> **From:** **Tyler Brian Jacoby**
> **Subject:** **Culturevate Opportunity**

Howdy there, stranger!

Well, I told you if the right job presented itself, I would call you first . . . and I lied.

I'm *emailing* you first.

Ha-ha-ha! I tease, I tease. Just pulling your leg there, hun. ;)

So, how much do you know about the Arts and Culture blog Culturevate? I'm sure you've heard of it, but just in case you're living under a rock, allow me to change your life. It's a lifestyle website that features all the hottest trends in town . . . what to do, where to go, who to be seen with, etc., etc. They are big, BIG fans of us here at Holistic—our line of sugar-free fruit is *constantly* being featured in their "Culture-eats" section—so I've developed a pretty stellar rapport with their editor in chief, Linda.

Time to talk shop: she's looking for a new editorial assistant and asked if I had any referrals. They want someone sharp, good with deadlines, and well versed in visual art/theater/food. Naturally, I thought of you, Ms. Geek Chic. So, surprise! I recommended you for the position.

I took the liberty of sending your Holistic application her way as a writing sample. It was a perfect fit: well-written, witty, full of nerdy references. If you're still shopping the job market and are interested in working for Culturevate (which you should be), Linda would *love* to take an interview.

Let me know your thoughts, hun. Hope to be hearing from you soon.

Ciao,
Tyler B. Jacoby

Associate at Holistic Public, PR
Health—Happiness—Holistic

Mama Shell

2:15 P.M.

MS   Lulu, I just found the most adorable chandelier that you HAVE to put in your new bedroom.

MS   Also, I bought you these amazing jersey sheets that were recently featured in Vogue . . . SO cozy, you'll never want to get out of bed.

MS   But you really should get out of bed; it's best if you work out in the morning.

MS   Have you gotten your parking spot yet? I really want to make sure your spot is in the parking garage before move in. I don't want you walking back to your apartment alone at night.

MS   What floor is the apartment on?

MS   It's not the first floor, right? Burglaries are more common on the first floor.

MS   But also not above 100 feet. Firefighters' ladders don't go higher than 100 feet.

MS   Susan wants to know what day she can decorate. I know you said no poufs, but she has the cutest Pinterest board full of ideas for you.

MS   Megan also has one that I'm OBSESSED with, it's called "Pretty Pink Palace." You should follow it!

MS   Call me.

MAY 25

6:15 P.M.

Hey! I thought I'd lost this old thing!!

Rosa found it under a pile of old *People* magazines while helping lug my packed boxes into the garage. Thank god, she found it before the movers come tomorrow morning . . . If Mom ever came across this diary, I would finally get my *60 Minutes* special for being the first human to die of sheer mortification.

Val's high school graduation was today, which officially makes me a fossil. How has it already been *five years* since my own high school graduation?? That's half a decade! Ugh. It makes me feel very, very old . . . not that I'd ever say this aloud. Mom thinks anyone who calls themselves old before the age of thirty-five needs to "seriously check their privilege."

But while most people look frumpy in their caps and gowns (I don't have to remind you of the belt incident), Val managed to look like a real-life angel with a square halo walking across the stage. Mom set off streamers and a bell horn as Val—who somehow managed to whip out her phone and take a selfie with the school's notoriously strict headmaster—received her high school diploma. And though she wasn't valedictorian or even salutatorian, she *did* win the senior superlative for best hair, which will probably prove more useful.

Mom dressed me for the occasion in a loose-fitting summer dress that made me feel like a giant raspberry. She also helped dress Theo, who's made a habit of bringing at least three different outfit options whenever he visits my house. There's even an emergency plain white T-shirt in the trunk of his car for when Mom rejects his more "eccentric" clothing choices altogether. But in exchange for the fashion advice, Theo's been teaching Mom how to cook . . . or at least trying to. Miraculously, he was able to convince her to start using olive oil by claiming it reduces wrinkles. I imagine this is what eventually won Dad over, since our home-cooked meals have been improving exponentially over the past six months. Also, we've had fewer visits from the fire department, which is always a pleasant plus.

Speaking of pleasant plusses: I HAVE A JOB!!! An honest-to-goodness, office-visiting, paid-with-money job! I have assignments and a set schedule and a desk with a little succulent in the corner . . .

though Mom is concerned I don't get enough steps per day. She keeps sending me links to buy one of those treadmill desks, and I recently found a mysterious Fitbit in the pocket of my favorite work pants. Suspecting foul play, I secretly attached it to the inside of Muffin's collar as an experiment.

"You look good, sweetie," Mom said casually yesterday. "You look like you've been very active . . . Tell me, have you been walking a lot at work?"

Fitbit suspicions confirmed.

Regardless, I'm really enjoying my job, even if I am just editing other people's pieces. I basically look out for typos and insert witty quips whenever possible. Would I call it my life's passion? No, probably not. I can't say I'm changing the world one punny blog editorial at a time. But it's a definite start! And I *do* get the inside scoop on the city's best gallery openings . . . And if I'm promoted, I'll be writing my own segments, which means I'll basically be getting paid to review different restaurants and plays and concerts.

. . . huh. Maybe this *will* be my life's passion.

All right, I have to go finish packing. Tomorrow's the big move, and I still have to pack my toiletries. Here we go! In T-minus fourteen hours, I take my first step into the world as a financially and emotionally independent woman. Let real-life adulthood begin!

·   ·   ·

MOVE OUT / NEW APARTMENT GOALS
Short Term

- Establish new apartment rules/expectations with parents/Theo.
- Make bed in the morning before work.
- Email Tyler Jacoby about new veggie pasta brand.
- Work out 3-4 times a week.
- Limit visit to office snack room to _twice a day_.

Medium Term
- *Get promoted to editorial writer.*
- *Learn how to cook three impressive meals (for apartment parties, pot lucks, etc.).*
- *Lose 5-7 pounds.*
- *Teach Mom how to turn on the television (so she won't constantly call me about it).*

Long Term
- <u>*Forbes*</u> *30 Under 30 article (still have time!).*
- *Run a half marathon.*
- *Buy a house, have some kids.*
- *Rise to the top of my career path (be it at Culturvate or elsewhere).*
- *...????*

MAY 30

Mama Shell

3:15 P.M.

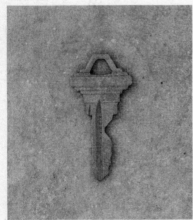

MS Finally got my duplicate! Now I just need to buy a cute key chain.

MS Are you at home? Can I come over?

MS I'm coming over!

Acknowledgments

To my family—Mom, Dad, and Odessa—for your unwavering support, your limitless love, and for absolutely refusing to be normal. You are everything (except, as I mentioned, normal).

Erin Malone, my gratitude is boundless. Thank you for pointing me down this yellow brick road, and for seeing something in me that I didn't even see in myself. Your mentorship has changed my life, and for that I am forever indebted.

To Jaime Coyne, for your invaluable guidance throughout what has undoubtedly been the most challenging and exhilarating year of my life. Thank you for being my lighthouse—you've kept this rookie captain afloat.

To Evelyn O'Neil, for opening each and every door until I found myself in the room where it happens. Thank you for your ferocity, for getting behind this project, and for loving Mama Shell as much as I do.

Dor Gvirtsman—if I've managed to stay this course, it's been because you've held me steady. Thank you for your patience, your laughter, your miraculous belief in me, and your love. Also, your kimchi tacos.

To everyone at St. Martin's Press and Wednesday Books for literally making my dreams come true. Thank you for taking a chance on a baby postgrad writer, and for subsequently keeping me from turning into Lou. Thank you, Kathryn Parise and Patrice Sheridan, for taking my vision and making it better, and to Jonathan Bush, for your pitch-perfect cover art.

To Karen Ray—who has read every word of every chapter—for your inspiration and overwhelming encouragement. To Neil Meyer, for your time and tremendous thoughtfulness; to Maria and Keven, whose generosity never ceases to amaze me; and to Liz York, for insisting that I put fingers to keys and write. And of course, to Eduardo, for being an actual super human.

In the most loving memory of my Pop Steve Epstein, for starting the madness, and John Cygan, who always made us laugh.

About the Author

AUTUMN CHIKLIS is a recent graduate of the University of Southern California, where she studied theater and screenwriting. She's an actor, stand-up comedian, and contributor to *The Huffington Post*. She currently resides in Los Angeles, California.